The second body was found by a tiny redheaded Cookie Monster. He told his mother about it immediately, of course. She had been patiently waiting for him back at the curb, munching on peanut butter cups snitched from his plastic pumpkin. At first she was inclined to ignore the child. It was, after all, a day when scary things were supposed to happen, and excited seven-year-olds aren't reliable reporters even in ordinary circumstances. But then she saw blood on his hands. It wasn't immediately identifiable, being mixed with a melted Mars bar, but this woman had been a nurse, and she recognized blood when she saw it. And as a devoted viewer of early morning television, she had no trouble recognizing Jason Armstrong, the handsome anchorman on "This Morning, Every Morning." Even though he didn't usually have a butcher knife sticking out of his neck.

Also by Valerie Wolzien
Published by Fawcett Books:

MURDER AT THE PTA LUNCHEON
THE FORTIETH BIRTHDAY BODY
WE WISH YOU A MERRY MURDER
AN OLD FAITHFUL MURDER

ALL HALLOWS' EVIL

VALERIE WOLZIEN

FAWCETT GOLD MEDAL • NEW YORK

A Fawcett Gold Medal Book
Published by Ballantine Books
Copyright © 1992 by Valerie Wolzien

Library of Congress Catalog Card Number: 92-90608

ISBN 0-449-14745-2

Manufactured in the United States of America

First Edition: October 1992

This book is dedicated to my grandmother,
Lena Lisanby

ONE

A̲N̲ ̲A̲N̲G̲E̲L̲ ̲W̲A̲S̲ ̲C̲H̲E̲C̲K̲I̲N̲G̲ ̲O̲U̲T̲ ̲B̲O̲O̲K̲S̲ ̲A̲T̲ ̲T̲H̲E̲ ̲C̲I̲R̲C̲U̲L̲A̲-̲ tion desk, a mermaid was sprawled on the floor in the magazine section, and a tall gray-haired witch was helping a four-foot werewolf search for a 1976 almanac. So Susan Henshaw wasn't terribly surprised when she almost stepped on a man in a business suit with a knife in his chest. At first she thought he was a dummy. Then, when his eyes opened and he gasped for breath, she decided he was a teenager in the middle of some gruesome prank. But when he died, she knew he was the victim of murder.

Middle-aged housewives rarely scream in libraries, so it's definitely an attention getter. In moments she was surrounded by most of the staff as well as curious patrons.

"What the . . . ?"

"Someone call the police!" The order came from the tall caterpillar, who yanked off a mask. It was Charles Grace, the head librarian, a man in his early thirties, who, Susan had heard it said, looked like a librarian. An elderly gypsy scooted off toward the phone, strings of beads flopping around her shoulders as she went. A kind witch yanked her black robe over her head and placed it gingerly on the body. Although the knife piercing the man's chest stuck up in a macabre way, it was a relief when he was out of sight.

"Who found him?" Charles Grace peered around the gathering through tortoiseshell glasses.

"I did," Susan answered quietly. "I found him," she said more loudly.

"Then you'll have to wait for the police to arrive," Mr. Grace continued, taking charge. "Everyone else should leave the area." He looked around. "If one or two of you women could make sure the children stay away from this part of the library," he suggested to a group standing around with their mouths open, "then our other patrons could congregate in the reading area near the checkout desk. I'm sure the police are going to want a complete record of where everybody was and exactly what everyone was doing when . . . when this happened. Perhaps, Miss Marshall, you could go over there and make sure no one touches anything."

"And you, Mrs . . . ?" He looked at Susan, eyebrows raised in inquiry.

Susan introduced herself.

"Mrs. Henshaw." He chose to ignore the familiarity of her given name. "You had better stay close to me. We'll just sit over there." He indicated a tiny seating area where they would be able to continue their viewing of the body. "And we'll wait for the police, won't we?"

Susan, who did not appreciate being treated as a child, didn't bother to answer, though she did as he suggested. She picked a chair where she could turn her back on the body, and sat. Her hands were shaking, and her knees weren't much more stable. Fortunately Hancock, Connecticut, was a small suburb, and the police station was only a few miles from the library; help would be here soon.

The police would undoubtedly want information from her, but, although she was apparently first on the scene, she really didn't have anything to say about it. She wasn't even sure exactly when she had discovered the body, she thought, looking guiltily at her watch. It was 11:32. She concentrated on her day. She had left the house early, rushing to get errands done so she'd be home when the first trick or treaters appeared. Generally the preschool children started knocking on the door immediately after lunch. They were her favorites, reminding Susan of when her son and daughter had gone out for the first time in handmade clown costumes, bouncing down the sidewalk with their ruffs flopping in the breeze, thrilled and surprised to discover that all they had to do was hold out a bag and an adult would drop candy bars into it.

They had been so sweet. Susan smiled nostalgically, wondering what those same children were planning to wear when they went out tonight. Both had insisted that this year their costumes were to be a surprise to their family, although each teen had spent untold hours on the phone with their friends planning the evening.

Susan brushed her honey brown hair off her forehead and sighed. At forty-three, she was beginning to forget the hassles of raising children and yearn for the "good old days"— back before she had teenagers in the house and bodies in the town library. She sighed again and unbuckled the flap on her purse. She hadn't had any breakfast or lunch; maybe there was some gum or something . . .

"Exactly what are you doing?"

Susan, startled, looked into the outraged face of Charles Grace. "I was looking for something to eat."

"I would feel more comfortable if you would just leave everything where it is. And I'm sure the police will agree with me."

Susan looked down at the Mark Cross bag, a present from her mother-in-law on her last birthday. Did this meek-looking man think she was going to pull a knife from its smooth interior and stab him? Or anyone else? "This is my purse. I had it with me when I came into the library. It has nothing to do with this . . . this death," she insisted.

"We'll see what the police say, won't we?" he answered rather priggishly.

"We certainly will," Susan agreed emphatically, thinking of her relationship with the town's police. She had helped them solve more than one crime already. And she was ready to do it again whether they wanted her assistance or not. Because, in truth, her children didn't need her very much anymore, her husband was busier than ever at work, and she was getting just a bit bored at home.

"They're here." The head librarian announced the police officers' arrival.

From the tone of his voice, Susan wondered if he was planning to have her hanged or just arrested. She turned around and smiled at·the uniformed officers' approach.

"Mrs. Henshaw." The taller of the two young men smiled at her as he spoke. "Why do we always find you around dead bodies?"

Charles Grace looked from the policeman to the woman who sat across from him, and smirked, apparently thinking he had single-handedly apprehended a serial killer. Susan got up and shook hands with the two officers.

"The body is right over there." She pointed. "I don't know who he is," she continued, as the two officers walked over to the man on the floor. "But this is Charles Grace." She nodded to the librarian.

Apparently Charles Grace didn't think her introduction was adequate; he pushed ahead of her and spoke hurriedly to the men. "I am the head librarian. I'm in charge of everything that goes on in this library. Everything," he repeated, when no one even bothered looking at him.

One of the policemen bent down and gazed under the black drape. Nothing was said for a moment as they looked from the body to each other.

"This is murder, Mr. Grace. And when it comes to murder, we're in charge, whether it happens in your library or anyplace else in town," one of the officers said, standing up.

The other man turned away and spoke quietly into the walkie-talkie he pulled from his hip. Charles Grace seemed slightly nonplussed, glancing around as if hoping to find compensation by nagging someone. Unfortunately Susan was nearby.

"Perhaps, Mrs. Henshaw, you might be so good as to . . ." he began in an obnoxious voice.

"We will need Mrs. Henshaw here," one of the policemen announced. "But you could do something for us Mr. Grace."

"Naturally, anything. We are all employees of Hancock, after all," the librarian agreed, trying to ingratiate himself with the men. "We should do everything possible to help each other, shouldn't we?"

"I wonder if we could use your office? You do have a private office, don't you?"

"Yes. The other librarians use the large room behind the checkout desk, but my work area is considerably more private. Do you want to go there now?"

"Yes. My partner can stay with the body until the county medical officer arrives, but I'd like to talk to Mrs. Henshaw someplace where we can't be overheard, if . . ."

"You'll have no problem in my office. I had an excellent acoustic firm come out from the city to soundproof my office—at my own expense. Most people don't realize how much confidential information comes to a librarian. I can assure you that no one will overhear us there. Just follow me." And he spun on his heels and headed out of the stacks toward the open area of the room.

Hancock was proud of its library, and color pictures of it appeared on all literature distributed by the chamber of commerce. People who didn't know the building's history were sometimes surprised that the town had chosen to display a church on its official masthead. They didn't know the effort that had gone into turning the dilapidated old Presbyterian church, long ago abandoned by a congregation that preferred light and space to termite-ridden charm, into a modern suburban library.

The basic design had changed during a year of committee meetings, the original wing metastasizing into three. The interior of the old building had been gutted and joined with the new structures, providing wonderful internal space with a unique and charming exterior. And civic-minded Hancock had been so successful in passing a bond issue in the middle of a recession that it had received a full-page accolade in a recent issue of the *Library Journal*.

"Do you know where he's taking us?" the officer whispered to Susan, as they walked between the stacks and by a series of low shelves housing an extensive collection of videocassettes.

"His office is in the belfry—the old church's bell tower." Even in these circumstances, she smiled slightly. She had been wanting to see this room ever since she first heard about its existence. She hurried along between the two men, ignoring the stares of library patrons awaiting police questioning. So what if they thought she was the murderer? She noticed a woman pull her tiny son, dressed as a computer, out of her sight. She also noticed a reporter from the local paper; if she spoke to him later, possibly his story would clear her name. But, at present, she was too busy to worry about her reputation.

The trio hurried around the large circulation desk, through a door to the right of the building's main entrance, and up a circular oak staircase. Susan had just time enough to note how beautifully the wood had been refinished when they reached the top and Charles Grace's office.

Wow. She was so impressed that she almost said it aloud. The room was a hexagon. Built-in worktables, desks, and shelves lined the walls, and eight tall, pointed windows looked out over the town, the pond, and a distant mall on the highway. The ceiling peaked high in the center, and it wasn't hard to imagine the bell that must have hung there. Unfortunately there wasn't time to think about such things. They weren't alone. A woman was sitting at Charles Grace's desk. And, with her head down in her arms, it appeared that she was crying.

"Who . . . ?"

"I thought you were going to stay with our patrons, Marion." Charles Grace didn't let the policeman finish his statement.

"I couldn't. I just couldn't." The middle-aged woman

raised her head and looked earnestly at the intruders through clear blue eyes. She paused to smooth her short blond hair with a well-groomed hand. Not that it needed it. For a woman professing acute distress, she seemed in remarkable control. Her curls were in place, her conservative clothing uncrumpled, her discreet makeup not smeared. And Susan noticed that there weren't any tears in her eyes. "I know you asked me to help out, but I just could not bring myself to stay in the same room with that body. I'm very sensitive about this type of thing. I always have been."

Susan wondered where she had gotten this experience with dead bodies. Charles Grace, apparently annoyed that one of his employees had chosen to ignore his direct order, scowled at the woman. Susan and the policeman exchanged looks.

"I would like to talk with Mrs. Henshaw in private," the policeman reminded the other man.

Marion Marshall had no trouble taking the hint. "I'll be fine," she assured the group, getting up quickly. "I'll just get out of your way." She looked around. "I do need to find my purse."

"Right here." Charles Grace removed the well-polished taupe bag from the top of a file cabinet and handed it to her. "If you don't need me," he began to the policeman, "we can go downstairs and see how everyone else is getting along."

"Excellent idea. But you'll both stay around until we've finished questioning everybody."

"Naturally. I, myself, won't leave the building until this is all cleared up." He motioned his employee to precede him down the stairs. "You will call me when I can be of service, of course."

"Of course." This last was said to the balding top of his head. "We will call you both as soon as possible." The policeman didn't say anything more until he had heard the door at the bottom of the stairs shut tight; then he turned to Susan.

"So what do you know about these people?"

"I . . . I don't even know who the dead man is," she stammered, surprised by the question.

"We'll get an ID on him soon enough, but what I could use is some information about this place and the people who work here."

"You're thinking that there must be a reason why he was killed here instead of someplace else," Susan said slowly.

"I haven't the foggiest. But I do know we're going to be spending a lot of time questioning the people here, and I was wondering who you would consider the most reliable—if you have any opinions at all. I . . ." He was interrupted by strange cheeping sounds coming from his belt. He checked his beeper and quickly reached for the phone. "That's headquarters. I'd better call in."

"Do you want me to leave?" She started for the stairs.

"Just hang around a moment, will you?" he asked, dialing. "Oh, hi."

Susan decided to take the call as an opportunity to snoop around the office a little. She peered at a long strip of cork that wound around three walls of the room and functioned as a bulletin board. Just what would a head librarian hang up to inspire him at his work? Quotations from famous books? Author's thoughts on great literature? Reading lists? She leaned forward, squinting slightly. It took her only a few minutes to read her way around the walls, and when she was done, she was more than a little disappointed. Notices of meetings and business conventions, more than a few copies of preliminary budgets for the library's next fiscal year, personnel schedules for the next three months . . . Except for a sheet listing some Dewey decimal notations, nothing that wouldn't be found in almost any business office. So much for literary ambience. In fact, she thought, looking around the entire room, there were possibly fewer books here than in most offices. There was, however, one sign that this was a librarian's office: on the floor she saw one of those tiny purple slips of paper that were stuck in the back of books to indicate the due date. Susan bent down and picked it up. She smiled, wondering if Charles Grace used them to mark his spot in books he was reading—and if they were forever falling out so he, like many of his patrons, couldn't remember the book's due date.

"Find something interesting?"

Susan looked around for a wastepaper basket and, not seeing one, put the scrap in her pocket and shook her head. "No. Are you done?"

"Yes, but we're not going to have time to talk. The chief is here. I'd better get back downstairs. It looks as if this investigation is going to proceed in an orderly fashion."

Susan looked at him curiously.

"We have a new police chief," he explained. "You didn't know? I thought there had been a lot written about it in the paper."

"I frequently don't get time to read it all that thoroughly," she explained, thinking about the local paper that was tossed on her lawn each week. She usually checked out the specials at the grocery store and then dumped the paper in the recycle bag beside the week's *New York Times*.

"Well, he's tough—believes in following the rules exactly, traveling in a straight line. Probably trying to make a reputation for himself . . ." He stopped talking. "Well, you'll see when you meet him. But he might think it a little irregular that I'm talking to you first." He stopped and smiled. "I'd better get going."

"I'll come down, too," Susan offered. There wasn't anything to keep her up here.

The police chief had indeed arrived, and Susan discovered that there were many more people around than when they had gone up into the belfry. The number of people in uniform had tripled, and most of them were standing around a tall man with his back to her. Her heart stopped for a moment when he turned. Brett Fortesque. The detective who had investigated the first murder in which she'd been involved. And he was as good-looking as he had been those many years ago. Would he remember . . . ?

He did. He was coming over with both his hands stretched out. ''Susan.'' He smiled. ''It's good to see you again.''

Well, maybe she hadn't aged all that badly in the past few years.

''I've been looking forward to running into you ever since I took this job.'' They joined hands.

Of course, it wasn't as if he was running into her on the street in New York City. Hancock was a small town, and of course he would be on the lookout for her. How vain she was getting in her old age. She smiled back at him, glad he couldn't read her thoughts. ''It's good to see you, too. I didn't know you were the new police chief. In fact, I didn't know there was a new police chief. You see, I don't always read the local papers, and we were up on Deer Isle most of last summer. . . .'' She heard herself starting to babble. Why did she always act this way around him?

''But you're around to help me with another murder.''

''Yes. Yes, of course. Anything I can do . . .'' She bit her lip. There must be some way to stop talking.

''Mrs. Henshaw found the body,'' Charles Grace announced.

''Mrs. Henshaw always finds the body,'' Brett replied with a knowing smile at her. ''And now I had better start this investigation. If you'll just wait in that area near the magazines with everyone else.''

''Of course.'' Susan hurried off. So much for special treatment. Well, maybe she'd find someone she knew there, someone to talk to. And something to munch on. She was starving.

And she wasn't the only one. There had been a costume party in the children's book section earlier in the morning, and someone had gathered together leftover refreshments, adding the few bags of goodies that the library was planning to hand out to trick or treaters. Everything was being devoured by a half-dozen mothers and four times as many kids. Susan grabbed, beating out two monsters for an M&M cookie and a paper cup of apple juice; their stained costumes belied their protests that they hadn't had any yet.

"Hungry?"

Susan turned and looked into the smiling face that millions of Americans depended on to wake them up in the morning.

"I'm starving, too." Rebecca Armstrong reached for another cookie, and even the children, possibly awed by her celebrity status, remembered their manners and stopped grabbing for a moment.

"This must be almost dinnertime for you." Susan smiled back, unsure of exactly how people who appeared on television, while most everyone else was in bed, arranged their days.

"Well, hardly that. More like afternoon tea. But being nervous makes me hungry; how about you?"

"Nervous?" When Susan was nervous, she tended to keep quiet about it.

"We're all suspects in a murder." Rebecca opened her beautiful dark eyes their widest. "But someone told me you've had experience with this type of thing before, haven't you?"

They were approached by an ebullient witch before Susan could decide how to answer. "You're Rebecca Armstrong, aren't you? The anchorwoman on 'This Morning, Every Morning,' " she added, apparently thinking the other woman might need reminding of her profession. "My husband turns you on before he even gets out of bed!" She giggled loudly. "That's not quite what I meant. What I meant . . ." She giggled even more.

"That's okay. I know what you mean—and I'm always glad to hear from people who watch the show." Rebecca Armstrong smiled warmly. "We depend on our viewers, after all. Do you watch, too?"

Susan moved out of the conversation, impressed with how easily Rebecca Amstrong conveyed warmth and interest to strangers. Imagine knowing that Susan had a small reputation as an amateur detective! Of course, Rebecca must be used to charming newcomers. She had been on the popular network show for almost ten years now, and her extraordinary good looks—pale skin, gigantic dark eyes, and thick mane of auburn hair—were pretty sure to be noticed in a crowd. Even without reading the paper, she had heard that Rebecca and her new husband, the handsome young cohost of the show, had moved to town recently. Susan noticed that Rebecca was being watched by the others awaiting the police's return. Well, celebrity watching gave them all something to do. She sat down on a comfortable couch and picked up a magazine.

"Do computers interest you?"

Susan looked up at a tall man dressed in shabby clothes. She considered the possibility that he was a gardener until her nose told her that he was probably homeless, a man without access to a shower, unable to live up to normal standards of cleanliness.

"The magazine," he continued his cryptic comments.

She looked down and saw that she was holding a highly technical computer magazine. "I . . ." She didn't know how to finish. "I guess I didn't know exactly what I was doing. What magazine, I mean."

"We're all a little upset by this," he surprised her by saying. "It's not like there's some sort of etiquette in place to cover this situation, is there?" He smiled a wry smile.

"No," she answered, a little startled by his perception. "I guess there isn't."

"Of course," he continued, without acknowledging her comment, "it's going to be easier for you than for me. They're going to blame me for this, you know."

She was startled. "You? Why you?"

"Who else is there?" There was that smile again. Did it appear a little sinister this time? He started to walk away, as though anything she might say was of no interest to him. "There's only me. Everyone else belongs here." He threw the comment back over his shoulder and turned the corner of a shelf of magazines.

"My next-door neighbor is a lawyer, and he says we have to let them in here—something to do with accepting federal or state funds or freedom of information."

"There's always a way around that type of thing. Someone ought to do something. It's not safe having people like that in the library."

"It's not sanitary having people like that in the library!" Both voices dissolved into giggles.

Susan looked around at two women she recognized from PTA and Board of Education meetings. It had occurred to her before that their main enjoyment in life came from laughing at other people. Personally she found them stupid. She refused to have eye contact with either of them, returning to the magazine she still held. Even floppy disks, modems, and emulators were more interesting than habitual bitchiness. She might actually have been forced to be polite if Brett Fortesque hadn't asked that she be questioned first.

He had chosen the main office as his temporary headquarters, and Susan was called into the large room where each librarian had her own desk, one of a dozen arranged around the outside walls. Brett and two other officers were seated at the large worktable in the middle of the room. He glanced up and smiled warmly at her as she entered.

"Susan, I can't tell you how glad I am that you're here. Some of my men have been telling me stories about the murders you've helped solve in the last few years—you've probably had more experience than a lot of policemen."

Susan blushed, smiled, and sat down on the hard chair that was pulled out for her.

"You know the routine, so we may as well get started. Can you tell me everything that happened after you walked in the front door of the library? I'll just interrupt with questions as we go along, okay?"

"Sure. Well, I guess I got here about eleven this morning. I only planned on dropping off a pile of books. Both Chad and Chrissy had reports due in school last week, and I knew we were going to pay a fortune in fines unless I got over today. So I dumped everything at the circulation desk and then decided to take the time to browse around. There's this new mystery novelist who writes great books about San Francisco that I just discovered, and we're thinking of adding a poolroom in the basement, and I thought there might be something about remodeling that I could use . . . anyway.'' She realized that what she was saying had no bearing on the murder and changed direction. ''I looked around the mystery section for a few minutes and spent about five minutes more searching for a book on basement renovations, and then I remembered that we're having a few friends in for drinks on Sunday, and I wanted to find a book on sugarless cooking— one of the men coming is diabetic. So I went over to the section of cookbooks . . .''

''Which is where in relation to where you'd been?''

''Excuse me?''

''Could you use this map and show us exactly where you were in the building to find all the different books you were looking for?''

''Of course,'' Susan agreed, taking from him the diagram of the building that was given to all new residents of the town and spreading it out in the middle of the table. ''This is the circulation desk.'' She pointed to the horseshoe-shaped object almost directly under the bell tower. ''Now, the mystery novels are behind the fiction shelves—way back here in the farthest wing from the entrance.'' She pointed. ''And then I looked at the section of decorating books—they're in the other long wing. About here.'' She pointed again. ''And the cookbooks are close by . . .''

''And that's where you stumbled on the body?''

''Yes. I turned the corner at the back of the stacks . . .''

''That's the wall farthest away from the circulation desk and the main part of the library.'' Brett checked out the location.

''Exactly. And there he was. Almost leaning against the wall, in fact. There are chairs against that back wall—it's a wonderful place to sit and read with those long windows looking out over the duck pond—and the body was right there.''

''Did you touch him?''

''No, I thought at first that he was a dummy. You know, some sort of Halloween joke or decoration, but when I looked closer, it was obvious that he . . . he wasn't.''

''And he was dead when you found him.'' It was a statement.

''No. He wasn't.''

All three men looked at her, surprised.

''He wasn't. He groaned . . . moaned. I don't know what to call it. It sounded weird and grating, almost artificial. I thought for a second that he was playing a joke on me . . .''

''And then?'' Brett asked gently.

''Then he looked at me and died.''

''And you knew he was dead?''

''I saw the knife and all the blood. I don't really know why, but I knew that he was dead.'' She was silent, reliving the moment. ''And then I probably screamed.''

''And who came to help you first?''

Susan thought for a moment. ''I think it was Charles Grace.''

''But you're not sure.''

''It's possible that he just spoke first. I was surrounded by people in minutes. Mainly staff, I think.''

''We'll get back to that later.'' He shuffled through some notes he had been taking and then looked again at the diagram of the building. ''There are long, straight aisles through the stacks. If I said that the body must have been there for a very short time, otherwise it would have been seen, would I be right?''

''You're asking if it was lying in a position where anyone could look straight down an aisle and see it?'' Susan asked slowly.

''Yes.''

''No, it isn't as clear-cut as that. You see, the diagram shows everything that is permanent—the shelves and the chairs and desks—but there are always things that aren't permanent. Like those little stools that roll around so that patrons can climb up and reach books on the highest shelves. And . . ." she paused and thought carefully, "and I'm sure there was more than one of those rolling carts that are used to carry books around when the librarians are shelving them. I know I had to move one out of my way when I was looking at remodeling books, and I think there was probably one in the aisle behind that. So at least two aisles were . . . well, not filled, but they weren't cleared enough for anyone to look straight down and see anything—or anyone—lying on the floor."

"Now, think back carefully, Susan. Did these moving shelves look like they had been put in place to hide the body?"

She followed his directions, but she couldn't come up with an answer, and she told him so. "But, you know, if you found out that the librarians didn't shelve books in the middle of the day, or something similar that made those two shelves unusual, then you would probably think that they were placed there for a reason. . . . I don't mean to be telling you your job . . ."

"Don't worry about that. I'll take any and all suggestions at this point. And you're right. I need to know as much about regular library routine as I can find out." He made himself a note in the margin of his paper.

"This wasn't a routine day at the library," Susan said, and explained about the annual children's Halloween party.

"The children's room is downstairs, though, isn't it?"

"Yes, but by the time I got there, the party had ended and they were all over the place. And you know how excited kids get at Halloween; they were noisy and keyed up." She remembered a tiny blond elf that had been crawling around under the computerized card catalog. "I think the librarians were busier than usual—or at least more distracted. The woman at the desk when I came in looked terribly harried, and the place had been open for only a few hours."

"What is your impression of the people who work here?"

Susan exchanged glances with the officer who had asked her the same question earlier. "I don't know many of them very well." But she knew he was going to insist on a more complete answer than that. "Charles Grace is, well, a little dull, I've always thought. Something of a boring man, to be honest. I've heard it said that he is exactly what you would expect a librarian to be—mild, unassuming, quiet."

"Exactly what you first said, a little dull," Brett suggested.

"Yes, but not, well, not literary. I would have thought that most librarians loved books, but I don't get that impression from him." She remembered her disappointment at his office. "I do think he loves running the library. I have also heard people say that the place has never been so well organized. He's got a growing group of volunteers who run annual book sales to raise money. There are monthly programs for adults and weekly programs for children. There's even a nightly study hall organized for students who need access to research materials and a quiet place to work."

"Sounds very impressive. But you don't like him, do you? I remember that you always worked very hard to say good things about people you didn't particularly care for," he added, seeing the puzzled look on her face.

"I don't know why I don't. I don't know anything against him," Susan protested.

"We'll just leave it that you're not crazy about the man and move on from there. How about the rest of the staff?"

"I don't know them very well. I've done some bits and pieces of research here, and the research woman is wonderful. I've heard a lot of good about the children's librarian, too. To tell you the truth, I don't even know if the other women have different titles or if they all do the same work."

"But they are all women? All the other librarians are females?"

"You know, they are. I've never realized that before."

"What?"

"Oh, it has nothing to do with the murder. It's just that I hadn't realized that the only male here is the boss." Susan, her consciousness raised in the sixties, had only one opinion about that, but Brett was changing the subject.

"I understand that you don't know who the dead man is," he stated.

"Apparently no one does. He doesn't look at all familiar to me. I did recognize the knife, though." She smiled brightly.

"You did?"

"Sure. It's a Slim Sharpie."

"It looked to me like an ordinary boning knife," Brett answered. "But if you're sure it is something else . . ."

"You don't understand; Slim Sharpie is a brand name. They're very expensive knives made in some tiny town in the Midwest."

"That's good." Brett was enthusiastic. "Then they're probably not very popular, and we just might be able to track down the owner of this one. . . ."

"Not a chance," Susan corrected him. "They were sold by every kid in the high school orchestra last spring. I'll bet there isn't a house in town that doesn't have at least one Slim Sharpie. And if the murder weapon was the boning knife, you'll never pin it down. That knife was one of six in the master chef's set; it was very expensive and completely impractical. But most parents felt obliged to buy it—to support such a good cause," she explained.

"Well, that's fine." Brett's tone was sarcastic. "The murder weapon is a symbol of parental devotion. Sounds like our murderer is pretty clever. Damn it."

TWO

THE SECOND BODY WAS FOUND BY A TINY REDHEADED
Cookie Monster. He told his mother about it immediately,
of course. She had been patiently waiting for him back at the
curb, munching on peanut butter cups snitched from his plastic pumpkin. At first she was inclined to ignore the child. It
was, after all, a day when scary things are supposed to happen, and excited seven-year-olds aren't reliable reporters even
in ordinary circumstances. But then she saw blood on his
hands. It wasn't immediately identifiable, being mixed with
a melted Mars bar, but this woman had been a nurse and she
recognized blood when she saw it. And as a devoted viewer
of early-morning television, she had no trouble recognizing
Jason Armstrong, the handsome anchorman on "This Morning, Every Morning." Even though he didn't usually have a
butcher knife sticking out of his neck.

The Armstrongs had recently bought a large Victorian on
one of the most expensive streets in town. Their decorator
was one of the best in New York City. Enticed to the suburbs
by the potential publicity emanating from working for the
famous, he had just completed furnishing the entire house
with period antiques. So Jason Armstrong had bled to death
on a genuine cast-iron Gothic settee made by the Berlin Iron
Company in 1856. It was possibly the most uncomfortable
piece of furniture ever made, but, of course, that didn't matter to Jason Armstrong now.

No one screamed when they saw Jason Armstrong dead.

The children thought it was a grand joke, and their mothers knew better than to disillusion them. The first lady on the scene was quickly joined by others, a half-dozen women herding their children door-to-door were the next group to arrive. They quickly organized themselves, collecting their little trick or treaters and urging them on down the street, knowing that the promise of more candy would offer plenty of distraction. The front door was discovered to be unlocked, and two women volunteered to enter and call the police. One of them grabbed a silk shawl that was in the hallway, artistically thrown across an Empire mahogany pedestal table, and carried it outside to cover the body. The other resisted a natural urge to look around and joined her on the porch. When Brett Fortesque arrived, he found six women, one little boy (who had taken off his mask and was stuffing himself with candy), and a second body draped in black.

"And that's more than enough for one day, thank you," he said, looking at himself in the rearview mirror of the police car he was driving. He looked back with a wry expression. "And to think I accepted this job to find a little peace and quiet. Wrong again." He caught sight of a gigantic fluffy pink tube out of the corner of his eye and slowed the car to see just what it was supposed to represent. The tall person carrying this strange object had scraggly hair pouring over his shoulders, shredded jeans, and, surprisingly, a short white jacket and a white top hat just like the ones worn by dancers in movies of the thirties. There were black diamonds drawn around his eyes. (Brett knew it was a boy; apparently the costume was complete without a shirt.) Upon closer look, he saw that the pink thing was a stuffed snake. He had opened his mouth to speak when he realized that he knew this particular child.

And from the shy smile on the boy's face, he suspected the recognition was mutual. But was it possible that Chad Henshaw had grown so much in four years? Brett, unmarried, had limited experience with which to judge children. Chad had been a perky ten-year-old when he last saw him

. . . and it looked like now he had become a teenager, complete with long black hair and torn jeans. Unless . . . He pulled over to the curb and stopped the car.

"Hi Remember me?" The boy pulled his bangs up and off his face, revealing stray wisps of a lighter-color hair underneath. "It's a wig."

"Hop in." Brett leaned over and opened the door. "I'll give you a ride home. You are going home, aren't you? I seem to remember this as being the way to your house."

Chad looked a bit hesitant.

"It's okay," Brett assured him, realizing that the teen might feel less than comfortable if seen riding home from school in a police car. "In that getup no one will recognize you.

"Just what . . . who are you supposed to be?" he asked as the car door slammed.

"Alice Cooper. Don't you recognize me? Everyone in school recognized me right away."

Brett chuckled. "I see the resemblance now, but, to be honest, I always thought of Alice Cooper with a guillotine, not a pink snake."

"Yeah, it's pretty dumb, isn't it?" The boy kicked at the pink fluff that he had dumped by his feet. "One of Chrissy's boyfriends won it for her on the boardwalk at Coney Island last summer. I was going to have a real snake. One of the kids in my class has a boa constrictor for a pet—it's really neat, but a teacher got wind of the whole thing and stopped it. We're not allowed to have pets in school was what the principal said."

"You don't think that's fair?" Brett was amused at the vehemence of the statement.

"We have a biology lab full of animals: gerbils, mice, rats, garter snakes, and I don't know what else. I don't see what harm it would have been for me to have a snake for a day. And, besides . . ."

"Besides?" Brett urged him to continue.

"Well, it's just that I told Tiffany Parker that I was going to have a real boa constrictor at Halloween. She's never going to believe anything I say again.'' He kicked the fake in despair.

''Can't you trick-or-treat with the real thing over at her house tonight?''

''Only if it isn't too cold. Snakes don't like the cold, so I promised my friend that I wouldn't take Julius out if it got chilly.''

''Julius?''

''Julius Squeezer. The snake's name. Dumb, isn't it?''

''A little precious,'' the policeman conceded.

''Why are you here?'' Chad asked after a short silence.

''I'm the new police chief.'' Didn't anyone in this town know—or care—who its officials were?

''You are? Hey, that's neat!''

Brett smiled at the approval. This is the way he had envisioned working in a small suburb: getting to know the population, being there for them when they were in need, developing relationships with the children and teens. . . . His smile turned to a frown as he remembered that reality included two murders in one day.

''What's wrong?''

Brett gave him a brief rundown of events.

''And my mother was on the scene as usual'' was the boy's only comment.

''True.'' Brett glanced at him. ''She's a wonderful witness, you know.''

''She thinks she's a detective,'' the boy said sullenly. ''It's embarrassing. She and Mrs. Gordon are always getting together and solving these crimes. . . .'' He seemed to be getting more depressed the more he thought about it, until . . . ''You would think that Mrs. Gordon would be too busy to help now that she's a mother, but the two of them will just ignore their families and pretend they're Cagney and Lacey.''

''Mrs. Gordon?''

''Sure. Kathleen Gordon. She used to be a detective with you, didn't she? Back when you came to town years ago?

She's married now. And she had a baby last year. A little boy with big eyes and almost black hair—he laughs every time he sees me. He's my first fan. I'm going to be a rock singer when I grow up, you know.''

''No, I didn't,'' Brett replied absently. He remembered back when he had worked with Kathleen. Dedicated, hard-working, beautiful with long legs and long hair . . . And now a housewife with a baby, he reminded himself. She had probably cut her hair into a style ''easier'' to manage and gained weight, and, anyway, she was married.

''Hey, this is my house, remember?''

Brett looked up at the brick drive leading to the large colonial that he did, in fact, remember. ''Think your mother would have a cup of coffee handy?''

''My mother? We call her the caffeine fiend. There's always a pot ready. Come on.'' And he got out of the car and led the way to the front door.

Brett followed him into the hall, where the pink snake clashed with a large glazed basket of treats, dumping it onto the thick carpeting.

''Oh, damn!'' Chad threw the fake animal ahead of him into the living room and stopped to pick up the mess.

''Let me help,'' Brett offered, being careful not to step on any of the miniature candy bars as he stooped down. ''Lucky your mother likes candy that's well wrapped,'' he commented, tossing six Nestlé Crunch bars into the basket and one into his mouth. ''When I was a kid, we used to give out little bags of home-popped corn. That stuff really made a mess.''

''Yeah. But with all the stories in the papers and on TV about people sticking pins and poison into candy bars that they pass out, no one gives away that stuff anymore.''

Of course not, Brett thought to himself. Some police chief I am. I've spent so much time worrying about drug traffic and felonies that I've lost touch with the average citizen's concerns. ''Stupid of me,'' he admitted to Chad.

''You better not be eating all of that. You know Mother

will be furious if there isn't enough for the trick or treaters tonight.'' A voice appeared in the air above them. ''And you should tell your friend, Chad, that it is illegal to impersonate a police officer.''

Brett looked up the elegant staircase at a lovely, blond teenage girl. A very embarrassed teenage girl, as she recognized that her brother's companion was an adult. ''Is something wrong, Officer?'' She gathered together her wits and managed to ask the question with admirable aplomb. ''I . . . I didn't know . . . I thought you were a trick or treater . . .''

''That's a perfectly normal assumption to make. After all, it is Halloween, Chrissy.'' He smiled. ''You don't remember me?''

''You're the policeman . . . I mean the detective who was here when all those PTA mothers were killed, aren't you?'' She was scarlet, but she walked down the stairs to shake hands.

''Got it in one,'' he agreed. ''It is good to see you again.'' She had become a beautiful young lady, but Brett knew better than to embarrass her by mentioning it. He shook her hand. ''Your brother promised me a cup of coffee. . . .''

''He's the new police chief, Chrissy.''

That didn't explain why he was standing in their hall, but the girl took it in stride. ''Then why don't you both go into the living room, and I'll get it.''

''Okay. Get me a grape soda while you're at it,'' Chad ordered, pulling off his wig and throwing it down on the small table that held the basket of candy. ''We'll wait.'' He led the way to the living room, oblivious of his sister's glare.

As Chrissy headed to the back of the house, presumably to get the required drinks, a phone rang in the distance.

''That's my line.'' Chad leapt to his feet. ''I'll . . .'' He stopped and looked at the policeman.

''Go ahead and answer your phone.''

Chad responded to the suggestion by getting to the doorway before the ringing stopped. Brett stood up and wandered around the attractive room. A handmade basket was sitting in front of the fireplace with a strip of elaborately patterned knitting in a striking silk yarn hanging over the side. He flopped down in a comfortable lawson chair, hitting something propped by its side with his arm. He bent over and picked up a flat loom with what appeared to be a spider woven into the middle of it. Or was it a sea urchin?

"That's my latest project. I'm taking a class in tapestry weaving at an art school nearby."

Brett stood up as Susan entered the room. "I gave Chad a ride home from school. And he offered me some coffee." He felt it necessary to explain. Why was he here anyway? There was a murderer loose somewhere. He should be out leading the investigation, and here he was, waiting for coffee like some cop on a bad TV show. "There's been another murder," he went on, as though that were an explanation for his presence.

"Who . . . ?"

"Jason Armstrong—you know, the host of that morning show . . ."

"Jason . . ." Susan sat down on the couch. "That's really strange, you know. His wife was at the library this morning. I talked to her."

"His wife . . ."

"Rebecca Armstrong. The cohost of the show. The same show her husband is on," Susan explained. "You don't know who I'm talking about, do you?"

"I don't watch TV in the morning," he admitted. "And I don't think I interviewed her. There were three groups doing interviews. I just spoke with the people most likely to be directly involved."

"You would remember her. She's a beautiful redhead."

He thought back through those he had seen. "I don't remember any beautiful redheads." He paused. "I better skip that coffee and get back to my car and call in. Rebecca Armstrong probably knows that her husband is dead by this time. I think I'm going to be meeting her."

Susan walked him to the door. "If there's anything I can

do . . ." she offered, not really knowing what she could do but feeling that she should say something.

He was already thinking of other things. "No, but thanks. I'll call," he promised vaguely as he left.

But Susan didn't know what he would call about. She wandered back to the living room and picked up the loom that he had again dislodged when he stood. It wasn't a spider or a sea urchin; it was a misshapen pine tree blowing in the wind, or it would be if she had any talent at all. She tucked it out of sight. Maybe she'd take a different class after Christmas; tapestry weaving didn't seem to be her thing.

She was thinking about the dead man when her daughter entered the room. "What is all that?" she asked, seeing the large tray Chrissy was carrying.

"Where's Detective Fortesque?" Chrissy answered, ignoring the question.

"He had to leave. What is all that?" she repeated.

"Coffee. Cream. Sugar. Cake. Soda for Chad."

"Chrissy, how nice of you! But Brett had to leave. There's been another murder . . ."

"Another murder . . . I didn't know there had been one murder." Chrissy put the tray down on the coffee table with a clunk.

"Oh, I'm sorry, honey. There was a body found at the public library this morning and . . ."

"But I was at the library this morning!"

"You were at school this morning," her mother corrected her.

"No, I was at the library. My adviser was having a hard time finding the college catalogs that I wanted because so many have been snitched from the school library, and so he went over to the public library to borrow some from their collection. I had a free period, so I went with him. He let me bring home Sarah Lawrence and Rhode Island School of Design since I helped. So I was at the library—right before it opened," she added when her mother didn't reply immediately. "It was really strange. The man that's there . . . you know who I mean . . ."

"Are you talking about Mr. Grace?"

"Yes. Well, he was on the phone when we got there, and he was angry. He was saying something about being disappointed in the person on the other end of the line and how he really felt that he had been led to believe something else. He was practically yelling."

"Really?" Susan absently took a sip of soda. "Did he say anything to you? Explain the call in any way?"

"No. He looked pretty embarrassed. Well, he would be, wouldn't he? He put his hand over the receiver and told us where the catalogs were and said he would be with us in a few minutes."

"And was he?"

"Oh yes. The catalogs were waiting on the reference librarian's desk—the one that's right next to the stacks—and we were just beginning to look through the first pile when he appeared."

"Then just a few minutes had passed."

"Yes."

"Did he try to explain the call?"

"Yes. And it was a little strange, too."

"Strange? In what way?"

"I'm not sure what his exact words were, but he said something about some patrons being more excitable than others—which didn't make any sense!"

"Why not?"

"I don't know. But I had a hard time believing that it was a library user on the other end of the line. And why would he yell at a patron?"

Susan wondered briefly about Charles Grace's marital status. She would have to find out about that. . . . But her daughter was talking.

"You are going to tell me who was killed, aren't you? Maybe it was the person on the other end of the line this morning. Maybe she came with a gun to kill him, and he grabbed it to protect himself and shot her first.''

"That might have happened except that the body in the library was a man's, and he was stabbed. It wasn't Charles Grace. I don't know who he was. I don't even think the police know his identity."

"You said something about another murder," her daughter reminded her.

"Yes. Jason Armstrong was found dead this afternoon— but I don't know anything else about that," she added as her daughter started to ask questions.

Chrissy stuck her finger in the cream-cheese frosting on the carrot cake she had brought. "Jason Armstrong is a hunk," she declared, licking off the luscious topping. "A bunch of us were talking about him at school the other day, and we were wondering why he married someone so much older than he is."

"So much old—" Susan gulped and stared at her daughter. Is this the way the girl and her friends characterized the very beautiful Rebecca Armstrong?

"Mother, his wife must be at least thirty-five years old. And Jason just graduated from University of Chicago two years ago."

"How do you know so much?"

"Mother, everyone knows that! It's in all the magazines and the newspapers. When they got married, she was called a cradle snatcher."

"By whom?"

"It was the headline in one of those newspapers at the grocery checkout." She had the grace to look embarrassed.

"Well, Chrissy . . ."

"I know," the girl interrupted. "But it is true that she must be a good ten years older than her husband. And he is fabulous-looking, and bright, and he must make a fortune. He could have had any girl he chose."

"Well, he chose Rebecca."

"And she killed him because he was getting bored with

her and starting to look at younger women.'' Chrissy seemed sure of her facts.

''Chrissy, no one knows who killed him, but you do know how murders are—everyone will have his or her own theory, and if we aren't careful what we say, innocent people might be hurt.''

Chrissy, a remarkably polite seventeen-year-old, could barely resist rolling her eyes heavenward. ''So why are you involved?''

''I'm not. Not at all. I just happened to find the . . . the body of the man in the library.'' She didn't have to wait very long for the reaction she was anticipating.

''Mother, how could you?'' Chrissy wailed. ''I'm busy applying to colleges. I still have to take my last SATs. My history teacher is driving me crazy. And you get involved in another murder. Your timing is terrible.'' She swung her hair over her shoulder and fled from the room.

Susan sighed and cut herself a piece of cake, but the doorbell rang before she could eat it. She hurried to the hall, grabbing the basket of candy with her left hand and opening the door with her right. The cries of excited children greeted her appearance.

''Trick or treat, smell my feet, and give me something good to eat,'' they shouted.

Susan passed the basket at this tasteful rhyme, commented on a few of the more clever costumes, smiled politely, and closed the door.

''What's Chrissy so upset about?'' Chad asked, appearing behind her.

''Where have you been?'' his mother asked, ignoring his question.

''On the phone. Did you know that there's been an arrest in the murder at the library?''

''No. Who . . . ?''

''I don't know his name. It was some homeless man . . .''

''What?'' Susan sat down hard.

''Yeah. Evidently he's been hanging around the library for

weeks, ever since it got cold, I guess. Anyway, he confessed to the crime.''

Susan remembered the words the man had spoken, the "everyone else belongs here." It couldn't be the same person, could it? But her son was still talking.

". . . I guess he went over to the Armstrongs' house and killed him, and then he went to the library and killed that man there. . . ."

"You guess? Chad, where did you hear about all this?"

"One of the kids on my soccer team called. His mother was down at the police station complaining about a parking ticket, and she heard the whole thing."

"What precisely did she hear?"

"She said he turned himself in."

"He what?"

"She was standing at the window talking to the police receptionist when he walked in and said that he was the murderer."

"That doesn't strike me as likely, Chad."

"Why not?" His adolescent voice squeaked.

"Because the Armstrongs just moved into Hancock last month."

"What does that have to do with anything?"

"That has everything to do with it," she said obscurely, reaching for the phone on the coffee table behind the couch. She dialed the number of the police station and sat back to wait for the answer. "Hello? Yes, I wondered if I could speak to . . . to Chief Fortesque. Well, when he comes in, would you tell him that Mrs. Henshaw called?" She hung up and looked at her son. "What's wrong?"

"I do not understand why you think every murder that happens in town is your own property. This one is solved. Why can't you just leave it alone?" And he turned and marched from the room.

Well, at least her family was unified, if only against her, Susan thought.

"Don't you just love adolescence? My husband says it's like living with your enemy."

Susan didn't have to turn around to know that her next-door neighbor was speaking. Amy Ellsworth had a distinctive voice, a cross between a chain saw and a dentist's drill was how Susan had come to think of it in the four months since she moved in. Of course, that was exaggerated, but the woman did whine. And since Amy believed that it was neighborly to just walk into the house without knocking, Susan was getting plenty of opportunity to decide just what obnoxious machine it sounded the most like on any given day. She bent her lips into a smile.

"Amy . . . hi."

"Don't think it gets any better. It only gets worse. When my youngest went off to college, he discovered that he could drive me crazy long-distance. He used to call when no one was home and leave plaintive messages on the answering machine—then when I called back, he was never there. And he never returned my calls. But the worst was the summer that my oldest went to Russia. He didn't write, he didn't call, for all we knew he could have been dead. I was suffering with my ulcer and didn't sleep the entire month of August."

Susan only half listened to this. She had worried and commiserated through each and every one of Amy's stories until she met the three boys she had been hearing so much about. The oldest was a Harvard-educated lawyer married to a Yale-educated lawyer with a brand-new baby who had slept through the night at one week and gave every appearance of continuing such exceptional behavior. The youngest was a junior at Dartmouth, in the top tenth of his class, destined for a full grant for graduate work in international affairs at Georgetown University. The middle child, the "problem child" as he was known, had gone off to UCLA determined to break into a career in acting. His second job was a stint in England with the Royal Shakespearean; the first had been the lead in the most popular sitcom of the season. Susan thought it a miracle that this woman sitting across from her had anything to do with raising these paragons.

"You heard about the murders." Amy rarely asked questions, and when she did, she didn't listen to the answers. She was most interested in her own opinions, her own life, her own words. She talked constantly. When she first moved in, Susan assumed she was lonely and hadn't discouraged the daily visits and phone calls, but as time went by, Amy didn't call her less; she just added her to the burgeoning list of people she contacted daily to keep them up-to-date on the state of her affairs.

"I had a horrible anxiety attack last night, and I didn't know why. Now I'm wondering if it could have had something to do with these murders."

Susan didn't bother to ask how the two could be related: she was sure to hear about it, so she had learned to save her breath.

"In fact, I'm sure it had something to do with it. It's frightening to think that some of us have been stalked by this homeless man and we didn't even know about it. We went about our business like always, never thinking about him lurking there in the background, ready to spring at the slightest opportunity."

"I don't think he did it."

"I was at the library a few weeks ago, and I'm sure he was watching me. I remember feeling funny when I was in the stacks. At the time, I thought I was just hungry from the diet I was on (have you noticed that I lost two pounds?), but now I think that it must have been him watching me. I was wearing my new plum-colored short skirt, I remember that. It was the same day the teenage boy at the gas station flirted with me while he filled my car. I guess I do look a little younger these . . ."

Susan had learned not to listen, but she couldn't help wondering about how ready . . . almost happy . . . everyone was to accept the guilt of that poor homeless man. That poor homeless man who could not possibly have done it, she reminded herself. "He couldn't have done it," she interrupted her neighbor.

". . . And, of course, you can always tell . . . what do you mean, he couldn't have done it?" Amy took a few seconds to adjust to the interruption of her flow. "Of course he did it."

"No, you see, the Armstrongs weren't here when those knives were sold. No one in their right mind would buy a set unless it was for a good cause, so I think we can rule out that they went to the store and bought them, so how did the homeless man get those knives? Even if he went to the Armstrongs' first, he wouldn't have gotten knives like that there."

"Oh. But he confessed."

"He confessed because he . . . well, I don't know why he confessed, but he didn't do it."

"Susan, he could have broken into someone else's house first and stolen the knives and then killed Jason Armstrong and . . . and that other man."

"I wonder if the police know who the other victim is," Susan mused, ignoring the first logical thing she had known Amy to say.

"I don't think he was a local person. . . ."

The phone rang before Amy had a chance to expound on this topic. Susan reached for the receiver. It was probably Brett.

It wasn't.

"Can you drive? I promised Steve he could take the car to football practice, and I totally forgot that we were running." The voice belonged to Linda Scott.

"We were?"

"Susan, don't tell me you forgot, too. Well, I suppose I'm glad you're as absentminded as I am. But I hope you're ready to go, because I have to rush today. There's no one here to greet the little monsters and fairies, and I don't want to come back after dark to discover the windows covered with soap and my porch awash in broken eggs."

"I don't . . ."

"Don't worry about me," Amy broke in, misunderstanding Susan's hesitation. "I have to leave now anyway. I can even let myself out."

"I . . ."

"Now, you know what you say to me when I start to make excuses," Linda nagged. "No pain, no gain. Let's get going, kid."

Did she say that? "Okay, I'll be over in ten minutes," she agreed, waving good-bye to Amy and hanging up. After all, there was no reason to sit here and hope that Brett would call. Who did she think she was? A policewoman? Brett had probably just been tolerating her presence years ago; certainly there was no reason for her to be involved in this particular murder. "Can you stay home and hand out candy while I run?" she asked her son, who would have been thrilled if he had known what she was thinking.

"Sure. We're not going out until after dark anyway. You said I could, remember?" he added quickly as Susan started to protest.

"Just don't leave until I get back," she insisted, wondering just when she had promised him all this. Certainly it was before these murders. Well, they would have time to negotiate later, she thought, hurrying up to her bedroom to change into shorts and an old T-shirt.

Running was new to Susan. She had put on her old aerobic shoes and tried out the local tracks in the middle of summer after spending the first six months of the year starting and stopping one diet after another. She was still waiting for a one-mile run to get easy. She was still looking forward to the day that she would travel around the track the twelve times that made three miles. She was still aching, sweating, panting. But she was still doing it. And she had decided that was all that mattered. Linda Scott had appeared to be a perfect partner for Susan. Linda was slightly more overweight and definitely shorter, so Susan had expected the run to be more difficult for her. But Linda was nothing if not determined, and she had been outrunning Susan for the last month and a half.

"I'm thinking of signing up for the Franklin marathon next week," she announced, getting into Susan's Maserati. "It's a ten K. I'm pretty sure I can do it. What do you think?"

"Great idea," Susan enthused. "When is it?" she asked, hoping she was busy.

"Next Saturday."

She was! "That's really wonderful. What time does it end? We're going to a brunch for some people at Jed's office, but I'd love to cheer you on at the finish line."

"I should be coming in around two in the afternoon if I run my normal nine-minute mile," Linda answered, smacking her watch. "I hope this damn thing is working right. I don't seem to be improving as quickly as I should be."

"Maybe it's the weather," Susan suggested, although they were in the middle of a beautiful autumn, and it was certainly easier to run now than it had been two months ago. But one of the purposes of a running partner is moral encouragement. "And I think your timing is getting a lot better. A whole lot better," she insisted, turning her car into the parking lot near the track.

"Not too busy," Linda said approvingly, getting out of the car. "Guess most people decided to stay home and hand out candy today."

"Or eat it," Susan said, joining her friend in some hamstring stretches.

"I heard about the murderer," Linda said, punching a tiny knob on her watch and nodding for Susan to start off. "It sounds to me like a serial killing. We were lucky he was caught so quickly."

"Serial killer?"

"Sure. Two murders in one day—what else would you call it? If he hadn't been caught so quickly, we might all be dead in our beds."

Susan knew she couldn't respond to that. She had to conserve her breath if she was going to make it a full mile and a half without stopping. She could, however, do a little thinking. At least, she supposed she could. Most of her time on the track so far had been spent trying to keep her legs going.

It had been just a few hours since the murders, and apparently everyone in town was ready to accept the confession of a stranger and be done with it. She rounded the second turn, thinking furiously. There was no reason to accept that poor, sad man as the murderer. Except, of course, that he had walked into the police station and confessed to the crime, she reminded herself as she started to breathe heavily. First lap complete. Five more to go.

There had just been something about him. . . . That was no way to decide a person's guilt or innocence, she reminded herself. But why would a person without a home, so far outside of this world, kill? Although, she had to admit, he could be homeless because of some sort of mental disability. Possibly he had killed Jason Armstrong because he was a famous face. Perhaps that murder was the incredibly sad result of a deranged mind. But the man in the library? Who was that man? She looked to see how far ahead Linda had gotten. Susan decided to slow down—just slightly.

Why didn't it get easier?

Second lap complete. And Linda was catching up.

"Who was the man in the library?" Susan managed to ask.

"No one seems to know—not someone from Hancock. You're not running very fast today."

"No. I missed lunch." Susan took a breath between each word as Linda sped off, apparently breathing with ease.

The third lap was usually easier. Possibly because its completion meant that she had gone halfway. Or because she was finally warmed up. Susan wasn't fond of people who told her that running was all in the head. For her it was the lungs that mattered. And her thighs. And her calves.

So who was this dead man? Was he connected with Jason Armstrong? Possibly employed by "This Morning, Every Morning?" Wouldn't Brett know about these things by now?

Had he called her yet? Would he call her? Was she ever again going to be able to breathe normally?

"Looking good today." The voice behind Susan was definitely male. Susan changed lanes to let the quicker runner have the inside of the track.

"Hey, Dave, what are you doing here in the middle of the day?" She slowed down in order to get the words out.

"That's one of the perks of running your own business; you can take off anytime you want. Of course, it's none too good for the cash-flow situation." David Pratt had inherited a chain of drugstores. They were evidently prospering, as his main problem usually was choosing whether to drive the Range Rover, the Jaguar, or the Ferrari to his gigantic "cottage" on Shelter Island, or to save his energy and charter a jet to fly either to the condo in Palm Springs (golf) or the condo in Aspen (skiing, the music festival, or just lounging around). The cash was apparently flowing just fine. "I heard that you found the body in the library."

Susan nodded. Fourth lap. About now she usually thought she was going to collapse. This was no time for anyone to try to hold a conversation with her.

"It must have been a shock."

Nod. Breathe.

"I also heard that you're friends with the new police chief. That you worked with him on a case some time ago."

Breathe. Nod.

"Does he have any ideas about who did it?"

"Arrest" was the only word Susan managed to get out.

"There's been an arrest? Already? Looks like we hired the right new police chief, doesn't it?" He looked pleased.

"Hi, Dave, are you going to run in the Franklin marathon?" Linda asked, tossing her hair over her shoulder as she passed them by. Dave was a rarity in Hancock: a single man. As such he got a certain amount of extra attention, and his presence required some extra primping.

"Sure am!" he called out his answer. "She's becoming

quite a runner, isn't she? And you're doing better, too," he added quickly, seeing the scowl on Susan's face.

Nod. Breathe. It was getting hard to listen now. And Dave had changed the subject, apparently finding Linda more interesting than the body in the library, although Susan seemed to remember that he was on the board that governed the library.

"She's certainly very attractive for her age," he was saying.

Why argue? Nod. Breathe. Was that a sharp pain in her left knee? The books all said to stop if it was a sharp pain, to continue in case of a dull ache. Breathe. Sweat.

"I must admit to admiring her for a long time. Years, I guess."

Linda must have some appeal that women didn't see. But Susan was too tired to be interested. Last lap. She knew she'd make it now.

"I think a lot of men were disappointed when she got married. Not that she didn't have a right to, it's just that one of our favorite fantasies had ended. It's all part of growing up, as my mother would say."

Susan watched sweat drip onto her new running shoes. She could barely hear him over the sound of her own breathing. The last two hundred yards. She pushed herself and crossed the finish line, still running. Out of the corner of her eye, she saw Linda wave, indicating that she had noted Susan's time. Linda was going for two miles today. Susan slowed down to a walk, holding the cramped muscle in her left side and trying to catch her breath.

"Look at her run. She's beautiful, isn't she?"

Susan looked from Linda to Dave. Was he crazy? Or . . . she looked over in the direction he was looking. Rebecca Armstrong was running around the track in white shorts and a turquoise T-shirt. Her gazelle-like legs easily took long graceful strides, her thin arms pumped gently, and those auburn curls swirled behind. So this is who he's in love with, not Linda. Susan was getting enough energy back to laugh at herself. "It's kind of strange that she would be here, isn't it?"

"Not really. She runs every day, you know. She's even talked about it on TV. I think she usually uses an indoor track at some athletic club in the city, but I've seen her here before—on weekends."

"I guess." Susan stood up straight. "It just seems like a strange thing to do right after your husband's death."

"Her . . . ?" Dave stopped walking and grabbed Susan's arm. "What are you talking about? The man in the library . . ." He shook his head. "He wasn't her husband. . . ." He stopped.

"No, of course not. Apparently no one knows who the man in the library was—not even his name. But Jason Armstrong was killed, too. He was found stabbed this afternoon."

"My God! I had no idea. Quiet, here she comes." Susan and Dave moved over to the grass in the middle of the track and watched Rebecca run by, flashing them her famous smile as she went.

Dave was the first to speak. "She doesn't look heartbroken."

"No, she looks wonderful," Susan agreed, watching as the woman bounded around the macadam. She was passing Linda now, and the two women evidently had enough breath left to exchange words. Whatever was said, it startled Linda; it was the first time Susan had known her to stop during a run. She was further surprised when Linda detoured across the field and ran to them, waving her arms and calling out something.

"She doesn't know! She doesn't know!"

"She doesn't know wha—Oh, no!" Susan gasped, turning and staring at Dave as the meaning of Linda's message became clear.

"Are you sure?" Dave asked as Linda reached them.

"I'm sure . . . That is, I'm almost sure," Linda panted.

"She . . . she passed me and said hi, and I said hi back, and then, without thinking, I asked how she was doing. . . ."

"And?" Dave prompted when she paused.

"And she said . . . She said 'great.' With a huge smile. She couldn't possibly know. Unless . . ."

"Unless what?" Susan asked.

"You two aren't letting me catch my breath," Linda complained, inhaling loudly.

"You can breathe later," Dave said unfeelingly. "Unless what?"

"Unless she knows and she took a bunch of tranquilizers and she's gotten flaky . . . Shhhh. Here she comes again."

"Finished so soon?" Again that beaming smile.

They all waited until Rebecca had trotted out of range of their voices. "She doesn't know." Susan spoke first, turning to the others. "And she isn't doped up on any sort of medication. No one could run that way and be high."

"So what are we going to do?" Linda asked.

"Do?"

"We can't just stand here and watch her run, knowing that her husband is dead and not telling her. It's wrong."

"You're right," Dave agreed. "Someone has to tell her. Linda . . . ?"

"I've never even met the woman."

"Susan?"

"I had a short conversation with her at the library this morning. Except for that, we've never spoken."

"Well, I've had all sorts of conversations with her in my dreams, but never in real life," Dave admitted. "I think it's up to you, Susan."

"But I can't do that! What am I going to do? Go up to her and announce that her husband was murdered? I can't do that!" she repeated.

"We have to do something," Linda stated flatly. "We all agree to that, don't we?"

"Yes, but . . ."

"Then you are going to have to do it, Susan. There isn't anyone else."

Susan looked from Linda to Dave and then to the woman happily circling the track. "Okay. If I have to do it, I have to do it. And I guess I'd better get it over with."

THREE

SUSAN THOUGHT SHE HAD A VIABLE PLAN: SHE WOULD run up to Rebecca Armstrong, casually asking to speak to her for a few minutes, and then the two of them would sit on the benches at the far side of the track, where, gently, Susan would relate the facts of Jason Armstrong's death.

Not a chance. In the first place, even by judiciously planning the start of her run, Susan had such a difficult time catching up with the other woman that, once at her side, she was out of breath and could hardly force out the necessary words. In the second place, Rebecca Armstrong had no intention of cutting short her exercise time. She was willing to talk, only they would do it while pounding around the macadam. She even chose the subject.

"You're not spending enough time warming up, you know. You could have problems with your knees or even shinsplints if you aren't more careful." Rebecca ran her fingers through her extraordinary hair as she offered this advice. "Who did you train with?" she continued.

" 'Train with?' " Susan repeated.

"Did you see the series we ran on women runners?"

"No, I must have missed that," Susan answered, thankful they were skipping her own background. "When was it on?"

"Early last summer. Maybe you were on vacation or something."

"Yes, we went canoeing. It's difficult to watch television

in the wilderness." She inhaled deeply. "I really have to talk to you. Really," she repeated for emphasis.

"Fine. I've done my miles. How about that bench over there?" Rebecca nodded toward the exact spot Susan had planned.

"Great!" Susan perked up, then cringed. This was no time to sound cheerful. She followed Rebecca to the bench.

"So? What can I do for you? I have a person who takes care of my own public appearances and charities—and you should talk to my husband if you want both of us . . ." Rebecca began, wiping her forehead on her sleeve and sitting down.

Susan knew that Jason Armstrong wouldn't be talking with anyone about anything. "No, it's nothing like that. I . . . I have some terrible news," and she told her as gently as possible.

Rebecca's reaction was the last thing she would have expected. The woman stood up, flung her hair back over her shoulders, laughed sarcastically, said, "So there are just as many crazy people in the suburbs as in the city," and jogged off without a backward glance.

David and Linda joined Susan so quickly that she could safely assume they had been waiting nearby.

"What did she say?"

"Where is she going? I could drive her. . . ." David began.

"She didn't believe me," Susan murmured.

"What?"

"She didn't believe me," Susan repeated as Rebecca got into her Mercedes. "She said something about crazy people living around here and took off. She doesn't know her husband was murdered."

They all watched the white car drive off.

"She'll find out quickly enough," David said. "It's a small town; she'll run into someone who'll tell her the same story pretty soon."

"Poor thing," Linda commented, standing up. "Well, I'd better be getting back to the trick or treaters."

"Me, too." Susan agreed. "I guess the police will notify her."

"You're probably right. They'll want to talk to her—even though this is one case where no one will suspect the wife first."

"Why not?" Susan asked, surprised by David's comment.

"Rebecca Armstrong isn't a murderer. Everyone knows that."

Susan was still considering that when she dropped Linda off at home. And when she followed a midget karate expert, a blue fairy with a runny nose, and a cowardly lion up the sidewalk to Kathleen Gordon's house.

"So where's your costume?" the woman who answered her knock on the door asked. She was slender and chic, with shimmering long blond hair. The little boy drooling on her shoulder was the only sign that life in the suburbs had changed Kathleen Gordon.

"This is my costume. I'm a suburban housewife. Not a bad disguise for the notorious head of an international spy ring, is it?" Susan answered, patting Alexander Brandon Colin Gordon, better known as Bananas ever since his birth last year, on the head.

"I've been bringing him to the door each time it rings. It's good stimulation for him to see all the children and their costumes."

"He certainly seems to be enjoying it," Susan said, smiling at the child, who was resting his head on his mother's shoulder, eyes closed.

"It's past his nap time. Come on in and have a cup of tea or a Milky Way."

"Have you heard about the murders?" Susan asked as they settled the child into his playpen, which was set up in the corner of the dining room.

"The what?"

"Shhh . . . You'll wake up your son."

"It would take an earthquake to wake him. He's a wonderful sleeper," Kathleen said proudly. "Come into the kitchen and I'll make some tea, and you can tell me what's going on."

"Just some seltzer. I've been running," Susan said, following her friend into the kitchen and explaining exactly what had been happening that day.

"So Brett's back" was Kathleen's only comment.

Well, that's an interesting reaction to a double homicide, Susan thought. "Yes," she agreed. Kathleen had worked with Brett Fortesque when she was an officer for the Connecticut state police. Susan had never known if their relationship had been anything other than professional. Not that she hadn't wondered.

"You don't think the homeless man did it" was the next thing Kathleen said. It was a statement rather than a question.

"No."

"You never think the obvious person is the murderer."

"So far I've been right," Susan insisted, finishing her Perrier. "Not that we really have anything to go on," she added quickly. "I don't even know who the man in the library is. And I don't know any more about Jason Armstrong than what I've read in *TV Guide*, so . . ."

"So you probably don't know very much about the murders," Kathleen began.

"And so you don't think I could possibly have any idea who did or didn't do it." They were good enough friends for Susan to be sarcastic.

"But I have faith that you'll find out the truth in the end," Kathleen assured her.

"Not that *we'll* find out?" Susan asked, with emphasis on the pronoun.

"Is that more trick or treaters?" Kathleen hurried to her door, not answering Susan's question.

"I'd better get going," Susan said, putting her glass in the dishwasher and following her friend out of the room. She paused beside the sleeping child, brushing wisps of hair back from his forehead.

"Perfect, isn't he?" Kathleen asked, coming back into the room from the front hall.

"Definitely. I'm going to head home. I don't know if Chrissy and Chad are passing out candy."

"Okay," Kathleen said, walking with her to the door. "Call when you find out more about the murders."

"You're interested?" Susan tried not to sound too excited.

"Of course. I'm just a little tied down these days, that's all. But I do get to the library once in a while, and I have been watching a lot—a whole lot—of early-morning TV since Bananas was born. He's an early riser, you know."

"Most babies are." Susan hated to destroy her friend's image of her child as unique, but the truth was the truth.

"But Bananas wakes up just in time for me to watch the Armstrongs every morning."

"What a talented child," Susan agreed. "Maybe he'll be able to help solve this murder."

Kathleen was laughing as she closed the door.

But driving home, Susan wasn't so amused. She was remembering the party last week where she had met the Armstrongs. Except that she hadn't, in fact, met them at all. Only guests who came early, stayed unusually late, or who were very aggressive managed to break through the crowd surrounding the famous couple.

Hancock is a friendly town, and it isn't terribly unusual for someone to hold a cocktail party to introduce a new neighbor, so Susan and her husband, Jed, hadn't been terribly surprised when an invitation appeared in their mail asking them to meet the Armstrongs at an open house held by a couple they knew well; the husband owned an advertising agency and was famous for the slogan credited with selling innumerable diamonds larger than a carat: "Prove you love her more than the one you married before." The agency where Jed worked had lost more than one account after the success of that particular sentiment.

The Henshaws had been surprised when they arrived at the party and found over two hundred guests milling around inside the large colonial home. The day had been rainy and bitterly cold; perhaps if the party could have spread out over the patio and into the yard, it would have been more successful. As it was, the guests were squashed inside, overflowing into bedrooms, the pantry, laundry room, and other places guests don't usually get an opportunity to enjoy.

Jason and Rebecca Armstrong had been seated on a large couch in the center of the living room. The idea had probably been that people would come in, be introduced, speak a few words, and then leave. Almost like being presented to royalty. Except it hadn't worked out.

By the time the Henshaws arrived at the party, the living room was filled with guests who had no intention of giving up their right to socialize with the rich and famous and were going without food and drink in hope of catching any pearls that might fall from the lips of these anchorpersons—or to impress upon them that they were not the only people of interest. Susan overheard one particular bore loudly expounding on his part in various civic affairs. He was not being listened to by a woman who hoped to interest Rebecca Armstrong in emceeing the fashion show her charity group was putting on to raise money for a very worthy cause; she was doing this by talking about the upcoming event as enthusiastically and loudly as possible. Amy Ellsworth, leaning across Jason's shoulder, claimed an intimate relationship with the wife of the head of the news division. Susan had peeked around the crowd, hoping to see how Rebecca and her husband were taking all this. The back of Rebecca's head revealed nothing; Jason had looked—incredibly, she thought—enthralled. Susan and Jed had nibbled on appetizers, greeted a few guests standing on the hallway stairs, given up hope of getting a drink, and gone home. Jed had wanted to watch a football game that afternoon anyway.

Susan had known a few minor celebrities in her time: a major league rookie had owned the apartment next to theirs in the city; an actor or two lived in Hancock, commuting to Broadway; a congressional representative lived on her block; her own cousin was a featured dancer with the American Ballet Theater. But she had never seen deference like that paid to the Armstrongs.

A group of preteens running between the houses dressed in rags, cork blackening their faces, reminded her of the opposite extreme of all this. It was interesting that children would still choose to dress as hobos and bums when the homeless problem had moved from fantasy to reality over the last decade. But less in suburbia than elsewhere, she reminded herself, turning the car into the driveway—right behind a white Mercedes. It displayed a vanity plate saying "SUNNY." It couldn't be.

Susan climbed out of her car and hurried up to the house. Scooting around the large jack-o'-lantern on the top step, she almost ran through the door. Chad, hearing her entrance, hurried out into the hallway.

"She's here!" They both knew whom he was talking about.

"In the living room?" Susan asked quietly.

He nodded yes, grabbing her arm. "She's crying, Mom. She just walked in the front door, crying, and now she's in the living room and she's still crying. I didn't know what to do." He looked very distressed.

"That's okay, Chad. I'll talk to her. Can you stay by the door and answer it for the kids?"

"Sure."

"But you don't have to stay here if you want to go out with your friends."

"We're not going out till nine or so, Mom."

Susan might have had something to say about that if she hadn't heard the loud sobbing in her living room. She entered the room and found, as she had expected, Rebecca Armstrong sitting on the couch, sobbing. Rebecca looked up at her entrance.

"You were right," she said, mascara running down her

cheeks. "I thought you were one of the crazies, but you were right. He's dead. Someone killed my Jason. You were right," she repeated, putting her head in her hands and wailing.

Susan didn't know the grieving woman well, but she couldn't just stand there. She sat down on the couch and put her arms around Rebecca, letting her, literally, cry on her shoulder. She didn't try to say anything until the tears had slowed. And then she didn't know what to say. But Rebecca spoke first.

"I'm sorry I doubted you. I . . . When you're on TV, you get attention from some insane people. And I don't know you. . . ."

"That's okay," Susan assured her, removing some of the woman's hair from her mouth. "You don't have to apologize for anything. How did you find out?"

"I went home, and there was a policeman waiting at the front door—he told me."

Why did you come here? Susan wanted to ask, but thought the question might be misunderstood.

"I didn't know where to go," Rebecca continued. "I don't know anyone in town . . ."—the image of the party where Rebecca had been invited specifically to meet people appeared in Susan's mind—". . . and I didn't know what to do. I was wondering if you would go to the police station with me. I have to go there to talk to them about what happened. And . . ."—she faltered—". . . I have to identify the body." She looked up at Susan. "Please. I don't know anyone else to ask. Would you please go with me?"

"Of course." It wasn't a request that she could decently refuse. "Do you want a cup of coffee? Tea? Maybe some brandy or something first?"

"No. I'd like to get this over with."

"Then why don't I drive?" Susan suggested.

"I'd appreciate that. I had a difficult time getting here," Rebecca said, standing up.

Susan led the other woman to her car, issuing quick instructions to her son as she left and wondering when she would get the chance to ask exactly how Rebecca had known where to find her.

Rebecca had stopped crying by the time they arrived at the police station, but she was so pale that Susan wondered if she was going to faint. She parked the car, and together they entered the building.

"We're looking for Detec . . . Brett Fortesque," Susan told the woman at the reception desk, unsure of Brett's title.

"So is everyone else today," the exhausted middle-aged blonde assured her. "This has been some Halloween," she continued. "And we still have tonight to get through. Do you know . . . ?" she began. But it looked as if Susan would have to wait to find out the rest of the question. The receptionist had just recognized Rebecca Armstrong and appeared unable to talk.

"It really is very important that we speak to Brett immediately," Susan stated, hoping to return to the subject at hand.

"And he really wants to see her," the blonde agreed. "Say," she dropped her voice to a whisper, "does she know that her husband was murdered?"

"Yes," Susan answered. "And you see how important it is that we see . . . ."

"Susan . . . ."

Rebecca had begun to sob again, and it was with much relief that Susan turned in the direction of Brett's voice.

"They're here to see you." The receptionist wasn't going to be cheated out of an announcement that was rightly hers.

"Why don't we all go to my office?" Brett suggested. "You had better answer that phone, hadn't you?" he added, glaring at the receptionist.

"I thought we . . . I thought I had to identify my husband," Rebecca said very quietly.

"You . . . ." Susan began.

"The policeman at my house," Rebecca explained. "He told me that I had to go to the police station to identify Jason. I think that's what he said."

"Why did you run away from him?" Brett asked.

" ' Run away?' " Susan repeated.

"I spoke to the officer assigned there myself," Brett assured Susan. "He said that Mrs. Armstrong drove up in a white Mercedes, got out, and greeted him, asking him what he was doing there. And he told her that there . . ."

"That there had been an accident," Rebecca interrupted, repeating the words in a shaky voice. "He said something terrible had happened and that Jason had been killed, and that I was needed down at police headquarters to identify the body. I'm sure that's what he said. And so, I'm here."

"Couldn't we just get this over with?" Susan asked, wondering how long Rebecca was going to be able to go on like this. Her paleness had increased, and her hands were shaking as she nervously tugged at a strand of long auburn hair.

"We have to go to the hospital to identify the body," Brett explained.

"Can't we do that now?" Rebecca asked, looking up at the handsome man.

"Well, I don't suppose there's any reason not to. Just let me make a phone call, and we can leave. You can wait in my office," he suggested. "It's more private and . . . quieter." He nodded at the phone, and Susan realized that it had been ringing almost continuously since they arrived. "Halloween is always a busy night for the police," he added, directing them down a long hallway to his office.

Susan followed Rebecca into a large room containing a desk, five gray office chairs, a table with a computer and a printer, and about forty cardboard boxes piled against the walls. "I just got here a few days ago, and my file cabinets still haven't arrived. But sit down. I'll go next door to make that call." He handed Susan a box of pink tissues from on top of the computer before he left.

Rebecca had seated herself in the chair nearest the door, and Susan went and sat down next to her, prepared to pass Kleenex if it became necessary. But Rebecca appeared calmer as she stared at the ugly beige linoleum floor.

"Can I get you anything? I saw a coffee machine out in the lobby. . . ."

"No. Nothing. I wish this were over. . . ."

"It's going to be difficult for you," Susan agreed. "Is there anyone you'd like me to call? A relative, or close friend, or . . . anybody? Someone you'd rather have with you right now?"

"No. No one."

"What about your husband's family?"

"There really isn't anyone," Rebecca insisted. "You see, we just moved here. I was born in California, and the show has been originating from there for years. We moved to New York for the new season—that's in September," she explained as though Susan was a visitor from another planet.

"I remember. But the rest of the show's staff moved with you, didn't they? Maybe one of them . . ."

"No. Definitely not one of them!" Rebecca startled Susan by her vehemence. "I would rather know what I'm dealing with before anyone on the show finds out about this. It's almost impossible to keep a secret at a television network, and anyone can tell you that a news department is a big-time rumor mill. I don't want anyone to know . . . to know that Jason is dead until . . . well, not right now."

Brett appeared in the doorway and ended their conversation. "We can leave now if you're ready, Mrs. Armstrong."

"Fine." She took a deep breath and stood up. "I'd like . . ." She looked at Susan strangely. "I don't remember your last name," she admitted.

"Henshaw."

"I'd like Mrs. Henshaw to go along with us," Rebecca ended.

"Of course, whoever you want," Brett agreed. If he thought this a little strange, he didn't say so.

In fact, no one said anything until they had driven the five or so miles to the local hospital and were waiting in a narrow, pea green hallway for the doctor in charge of the morgue.

"I wonder what's taking him so long?" Susan commented when the silence began to make her nervous.

"Her."

"Excuse me?" Susan looked curiously at Brett.

"This," he explained with a wave of his hand at the woman walking toward them down the hall, "is Dr. Penobscott. And this," he continued to the doctor, "this is Rebecca Armstrong."

"Of course. I'm a big fan of your show," the physician said, shaking hands before turning to unlock the door to the morgue. "Are we all going in?" she asked.

"Yes. I don't want to be alone," Rebecca said, removing Susan's last hope that she could avoid this task.

The tiny room did not have a wall of pullout drawers, as Susan had expected. It contained a few empty hospital dollies, some bulky equipment covered with gray drop cloths, and a table with the unmistakable shape of a body under a light green sheet. A fluorescent tube hung directly over the cadaver. It took only a few moments for Rebecca to identify her husband, which she did in a steady voice and without tears, and Susan was surprised at how quickly they were back in the hall.

"I'll have to ask you some questions now," Brett said, nodding good-bye to the doctor. "We can go to the station, or to your house, or wherever you would feel comfortable. I can drop Mrs. Henshaw off at home."

"Alone in that big house . . ." Rebecca started.

"I need to talk to you for only an hour or so, then maybe you could go to a friend's house."

"I don't have any friends around here. We just moved in." Rebecca repeated the story she had told Susan.

"Maybe a hotel," Brett suggested. "But I am going to have to ask you to stay in the area. Though I'm sure we can make arrangements for you to continue your broadcast . . ."

"And just where do you suggest I make my first appearance after my husband has been discovered murdered on Halloween? Some sleazy afternoon talk show or . . . I'm sorry. I know I'm acting terrible.'' Rebecca started crying again.

Susan put her arm around the woman's shoulder and led her out of the hospital. ''You're doing just fine. You're being very brave.''

''I'm just so scared,'' Rebecca sobbed.

''Why don't you go with Brett and answer his questions, and then he can drop you off at my house. You can stay in our guest room until you . . . you get everything straightened out.''

''That . . . that would be a big help.''

''Susan is a pillar of strength in Hancock,'' Brett added. ''She'll take care of you. Now, where would you like to talk?''

''The . . . the police station, I guess.''

''Maybe you could drop me off at home first,'' Susan suggested, getting into the back of the police car behind Brett and Rebecca. She had a lot to do if she was going to have a houseguest.

''Good idea.''

The Henshaws lived on the same side of town as the municipal offices, and the police car pulled up in front of the large colonial in only a few minutes. ''I'll be waiting here for your arrival,'' she said somewhat formally to Rebecca.

''Thanks,'' Brett called as he turned his car around. Rebecca stared straight out the window.

Susan hurried up the walk. It was dinnertime. She wondered if Jed's car was in the garage or if there had been some sort of problem on the road. She wondered if anyone in the family remembered the fresh pot of chili in the refrigerator that she had planned on serving tonight. She flung open the black-enameled door and smiled. Someone had remembered; the air fairly shimmered with essence of hot pepper. She pulled off her jacket, leaving it on the hall table near an almost depleted bowl of Hershey bars, and hurried down the corridor to the kitchen.

''Jed!'' Her husband, still in his gray suit, was standing in front of the stove, stirring a large pot with one hand and stuffing candy bars into his mouth with the other. He turned and smiled at her.

"Hi."

"You found the candy." Susan reached across the sink for a sponge. She'd wipe off the table before setting it.

"And the chili. I don't see how you keep this stuff from burning, though. Every time I stop stirring, it begins to scorch. I even had to change pots." He nodded at the large casserole sitting in the sink; crisp brown cinders of food clung to its bottom.

"I heat it up in the microwave," Susan explained, filling the dirty pot with water. She would deal with that later. "Jed, we're going to have company for a while. Houseguests. Well, actually, one houseguest."

"Someone fun, I hope." He popped the last of his candy bar in his mouth.

"Not under these circumstances."

"These circumstances?"

How was she going to explain? Well, they always said to start at the beginning. "Jed, have you heard anything about the murders in town today?"

Her husband turned and stared at her, eyes wide, mouth open. "I didn't know there was a murder, and you're telling me that there was more than one, aren't you?"

"Two."

"I assume the victims are no one we know."

"How did you know that?" She gathered together napkins, silverware, and glasses as she spoke.

"Because you don't seem at all upset." He turned off the burner under the chili. "Does this have something to do with our houseguest?"

"Her husband was one of the victims. Why don't I explain?"

"Why don't you? I'll set the table."

Susan told the story while he set the table, while she assembled a small Caesar salad, while he poured two glasses of imported ale, and while they drank the ale and ate the salads and bowls of chili. ''I was probably pretty stupid to invite her here, wasn't I?'' she ended.

''It may not have been one of your best ideas,'' he agreed vaguely. ''But I don't see what we can do about it now. When is she going . . .'' He was interrupted by the doorbell. ''I wondered when the evening onslaught of kids was going to begin.'' He put down his empty glass and stood up.

''Why don't I get it?'' Susan offered quickly, hoping it was children, but a quick glance at her watch told her that it could just as well be Rebecca. ''You can clean the table,'' she added, suddenly remembering that she hadn't done anything about the guest room, which hadn't been used since Labor Day weekend.

There were teenagers at the door, a high school group that included her own daughter. Chrissy was apparently dressed as a lady of the evening. Susan recognized the lacy silk camisole on her daughter as her own. She passed out candy, exchanged a few greetings with children she had known since their first day of kindergarten, and closed the door in Rebecca Armstrong's face.

''I'm sooo sorry!'' She pulled it open, realizing what she had done. ''Please come in.''

''Brett dropped me off. I told him there was no reason to wait around,'' Rebecca explained, entering the hallway. Jed's appearance caused a slight smile to cross her face. ''You must be Susan's husband. I'm . . .''

''Of course I know who you are,'' he hurried forward to assure her, shaking hands. ''Susan was just telling me about your terrible loss. I can't tell you how sorry we are . . .'' he continued, falling back on the conventions.

''It's good of you to put up with me,'' Rebecca cut him off. ''We . . . I don't have any close friends in town yet. You and your family are saving my life.'' She bit her lip.

''Would you like something to eat or drink?'' Jed offered as Susan turned to another group of children.

''No, thank you. I was wondering . . .'' She looked

around. "There are so many things I have to do . . . calls to make. My producer has to know . . . but I would love to lie down for a while. I'm suddenly very tired. Maybe if I could rest for a few minutes . . ."

"Of course, that's natural. I'll just show you the guest room." Jed led the way upstairs.

Susan saw what he was doing but wasn't in time to stop him. She just hoped no one had thrown a pair of outgrown soccer shoes in the middle of the bed. She returned to the group at the door. They were talking about the murders.

"I heard it was a gang killing. Probably something to do with a drug ring trying to get established in Hancock. The suburbs are the new market for big-time heroin and cocaine rings, you know," a mammoth scarlet butterfly insisted, antennae bobbing on her head.

"My father says there's already a lot of organized crime around. He says he never votes for an incumbent in office because they're sure to have been bought off during their first term," a pirate answered. Susan was amused to notice that his earring was real but the handlebar mustache wasn't. "Thanks, Mrs. Henshaw!" The boy returned his attention to what he was doing.

"Adam? I didn't recognize you with that costume!"

"How could you forget me!" He laughed. "I lit her back porch on fire during a Cub Scout meeting," he explained to the butterfly.

"Oh, Adam! You're terrible," his friend replied, obviously not meaning a word of it.

Susan smiled weakly and closed the door.

"She's lying down," Jed announced, returning to his wife's side. "She really is beautiful, isn't she?"

Susan stared at her husband.

"I mean, when her husband has just died, and you know that most women would look just horrible. . . ." He stopped just as Susan was beginning to doubt the sanity of having a beautiful widow for a houseguest.

"Maybe I'd better go up and make sure she has everything she needs," Susan suggested.

"She asked to be left alone. But you're right, she's going to need some things if she's going to stay here. I already suggested that and offered to go to her house and pick up some odds and ends."

"Odds and ends?"

"You know, toothbrush, nightgown, robe . . . She gave me the key to the front door." He held up a silver key chain.

"You know, Jed, I think I should run over to her house. I'll be better at picking out the things she will need. Don't you think?"

"Great." He handed her the key, knowing that she was looking forward to seeing the inside of the Armstrongs'.

She drove over to the house slowly, wary of the kids running door-to-door through the piles of leaves left at the curb for municipal pickup. She actually followed a rowdy group up the Armstrong driveway, her car lights picking out their gaudy costumes in the double beam.

"Trick or treat! Trick or treat!" the kids yelled, surrounding the car, laughing.

"I'm sorry, but this isn't my house. I'm just doing an errand for a friend. There isn't going to be any candy given away here tonight. Sorry," she repeated. But the children, unconcerned, were on their way to the next house.

Susan carefully walked up the brick path to the steps of the huge Victorian mansion. Dozens of tiny security lights set in the lawn had gone on at dusk, but the porch wasn't illuminated, and she was afraid of tripping. Brass lanterns on either side of the mahogany double doors clicked on as her foot touched the top step. What a nice idea . . .

Suddenly she jumped. Her heart was still pounding when she realized that mirrors had replaced the glass in the large oval windows set into the front doors. She had been frightened by her own reflection. Her hand shook as she fitted the key into the lock.

But the sight that met her eyes when she had found the

wall switches and turned on the lights gave her something else to think about. Expecting an entry hall, she was astounded to find herself in a three-story atrium. There were mosaics below, stained glass above, and a fabulous chestnut stairway connecting the two. Palms grew out of Oriental jardinieres, velvet seats lined the walls, and numerous doorways led in various directions. So where did they hide the toothbrushes? She started up the stairs, her steps silent on the thick Oriental runner.

The third door she tried led into what was obviously the master bedroom. Running along what appeared to be most of the back of the large home, almost a dozen floor-to-ceiling windows looked out into the darkness. The room was furnished with a huge Victorian bedroom set, covered with wooden curlicues. Fabric in a dozen different patterns covered walls, curtains, and pillows. A very talented designer had worked here. Three doors led from the room, and two large standing wardrobes and a marble-topped dressing table leaned against the walls.

Susan walked across thick rose carpeting to the dressing table and removed a hairbrush and comb, which she tossed onto the bed. She should have brought a suitcase, she thought, opening the drawers. She studied the large array of bottles and tubes, unable to decide what Rebecca might need. She selected two jars of cream and an almost empty bottle of cologne. These she also put on the bed. The wardrobe contained dozens of Porthault sheets, blankets, and other linens. She approached the nearest door looking for a closet. What she found was a dressing room lined with built-in shelves, drawers, and hanging rods. The space was wall-to-wall clothing. It took Susan only a moment to pick out a peach silk nightgown, then a minute to put it back on the shelf, deciding white flannel was more appropriate for the Henshaws' guest room. She found a Hermès overnight bag on one of the top shelves and, returning to the bedroom, put everything in it. She went back to the dressing room and added some underwear, socks, a moss green cotton sweater, and jeans. Then she left, her self-discipline not allowing for even a quick peek into other rooms. She had been in the house for less than fifteen minutes when she locked the front door behind her, smiling at her own reflection in the mirrors. And not screaming at the one-eyed monster that stood behind her. It was still Halloween, after all. He was just another trick or treater.

So why did he steal her purse?

FOUR

Proper Victorian gardens frequently boasted trellises, statues, rustic summerhouses, benches set in leafy bowers, ferneries, and an ornate pergola or two. Naturally, the Armstrongs' yard was equally well equipped. In fact, Susan might have discovered the person who stole her purse if she hadn't fallen over a hideous metal urn dripping dead coleus. She landed on a walk of crazy paving, shredding her stockings as well as her knees and palms.

"Hey! Are you all right?" a tall scarecrow called from the street.

"She's fine. She's getting up," his female companion assured him. "Don't embarrass her. People her age don't like to have attention drawn to their frailties. There was an article about it in *People* magazine."

They were joined by a noisy group of friends, and Susan was spared further pearls of wisdom from the celebrity press. She picked a dead leaf off her sleeve and grabbed the overnight case she had dropped as she fell. Her car keys she had, from habit, stuffed in the pocket of the suede jacket she wore. She would wait to get home before reporting the loss of her purse, she decided, hurrying to her Maserati. She was nervous, not knowing who might be lurking in the dusk, and she drove quickly—only to find a half-dozen cars blocking the entrance to her driveway. One was a police car, one belonged to Kathleen, and one was Rebecca's; the others she didn't recognize.

A hoard of tiny preadolescent Mutant Ninja Turtles stood expectantly by her open front door. A strange man was dropping miniature candy bars into their goody bags. This surprised Susan, but not as much as when that same man refused her entrance.

"But this is my house! I live here!" Susan protested repeatedly.

"So why don't you have identification?" he asked, barring her from her own hallway. "You drove here, didn't you? Do you always drive without your license?"

"I told you . . . Look, who do you think I am?" Susan asked, trying to make him see reason.

"I don't know who you are—and that's why you're not getting in. Go home, get some ID, and then we'll talk."

Susan had an idea. "Look, my purse was stolen. That's why I don't have my license. I was going to report it to the police. A man ran up behind me and . . ." She stopped, surprised by the grin on his face.

"Nice try. But, if any of that is true, you're going to have to take yourself down to the police station and make that report. I have other things to do." He nodded at the group of costumed children marching up the path. "I'm pretty busy here."

"You don't understand! I'm Susan Henshaw. This is my house. I bought those Reese's peanut butter cups that you're giving out."

"So why can't you prove it?"

"Ask somebody! Ask anybody!" Susan was getting desperate. It had been a long day and promised to be a longer evening. "Ask those kids! They know me. That tall girl in the . . ." She tried to figure out exactly what the costume was supposed to represent; it consisted mostly of lacy underwear worn over ripped black leotards through which a lot of skin covered with goose bumps was shining. "You know me, don't you, Hazel?" she asked.

"Sure I do" came the obliging reply as the girl tripped down the steps.

"You reporters will stop at nothing to get a story, will you?" He watched the children walk back down the street. "Corrupting young children. It's terrible."

"Corrupting young children!" Susan screeched. The young innocents were almost naked from behind. "What do you mean? Who do you think I am? Do I actually look like a reporter?"

He peered at her. "Not really. You do look more like a housewife, to be honest."

Susan gave up. She had better things to do than hang around and be insulted. Besides, it was her house, and she knew where the outside stairs to the basement were located. She hurried back toward the street, making a detour as she got to the high privet hedge Jed had cultivated for years. She inched along behind it until she arrived at the side of the house. From here it was a straight line to the basement door. She stopped to look in the living room window.

Rebecca Armstrong was perched in the middle of the largest couch, her feet on the antique sleigh Susan used for a coffee table. She was surrounded by men, apparently all trying to help relieve her grief. Surprisingly, Charles Grace leaned over the couch, a solemn look on his face and a box of Kleenex in his hands. Rebecca was flanked by two young men whom Susan didn't recognize. One held her hand, and the other had just offered his immaculate linen handkerchief to the cause. Jed stood at the rear of the room holding a crystal snifter and a bottle of Napoleon brandy. He looked embarrassed.

As well he should be, Susan thought, leaning closer to listen through the glass. Rebecca was telling the story of how she and Jason had met.

". . . And he ignored me. I can't tell you how long it had been since someone ignored me in a situation like that. After all, the only reason I go on these publicity tours is to meet people, and the only people who come to the events come to meet me—it's definitely not for the ambience! This thing took place in the studio of a thirty-year-old television station

in Utah—high school locker rooms have more ambience—
and smell better!

"You'd be amazed how many people think it's bad luck
to marry someone with your own last name. Hundreds of
people took the time to write and warn us of some sort
of upcoming doom when the story of our engagement
came out. But Jason and I aren't superstitious—that is, we
weren't. . . .'"

Fresh handkerchiefs appeared in response to her renewed
crying. Jed poured the brandy and then drank it himself.
Susan crept on around the side of the house; she had read the
story in *TV Guide*.

"I don't blame you at all. In your position, I'd probably
end up doing this myself."

Susan almost screamed as Amy Ellsworth appeared at her
side.

"Calm down! They're going to hear us. And how are you
going to explain sneaking around in the dark, looking in the
windows of your own house?"

Susan found her voiced. "Amy! What are you doing
here?"

"Shhh!" She pulled Susan away from the window. "Susan, listen to me! I may have mentioned that I know the wife
of the president of the news division at Rebecca's network"—only about a dozen times that Susan personally knew
of—"and I think you would be wise to leave everything in
their hands. They're professionals, after all. . . ." She took
a deep breath and grasped Susan's hands, digging her long
scarlet nails into the sensitive flesh. "Susan, your hands,"
she cried, noticing the raw flesh in the light from the window.

"I'm okay. I just tripped over a flowerpot and fell. It's
nothing," Susan said quickly, pulling free. "And Rebecca
is in a terrible situation. She knows no one in town,"—Susan
remembered that Amy had been at the party, but she chose
to go on—"and she has no one to depend on in a crisis. Jed
is merely doing what he can to comfort her," she insisted.
"I'm sure I don't have to worry about . . . about anything."

"For someone who's all alone in the world, those network people sure appeared fast enough." Amy's smile was smug.

" 'Network people?' "

"The two men who were sitting with her on the couch, and a couple of others. I think one is handing out candy at the front door, as a matter of fact."

"How do you know where they're from?" Susan asked, wondering why it was so difficult to get information from her.

"That's the way they introduced themselves," Amy insisted. "I came over earlier to help out, and that's what they told me when I answered the door. Jed was busy in the kitchen. And Rebecca had insisted on some privacy—upstairs—and the bell rang. I thought a good neighbor would help out, and, anyway, I assumed it was more trick or treaters. . . .."

"But it was these men," Susan prompted, knowing that Amy could get sidetracked more easily than most people.

"Yes."

"They just rang the bell, and when you opened it, they announced that they were from . . ."

"From the network is how they put it—as though there was just one." Amy nodded enthusiastically. "I thought it was a little strange myself. Of course, they did tell me their names, but I was so nervous—with Rebecca Armstrong being here and all—that I'm afraid I forgot them right away."

"And what did Rebecca do when she saw them?"

"She was obviously relieved. She looked as though a tremendous burden had been lifted from her shoulders."

"Really?" Susan remembered how anxious Rebecca had been to keep the news of her husband's death from her colleagues. Things weren't making sense. "Did she say anything?"

"Well, of course, she ran over to them and started talking immediately, but we—Jed and I—thought that we should leave them alone, and the doorbell was ringing again. . . .."

Susan thought she could guess exactly who had insisted

that Rebecca have some privacy. "I really have to go now, Amy. I have some things to do immediately," she lied, hurrying off to the basement door. If Amy thought it was an unusual way to enter the house, and she probably did, Susan didn't give her a chance to talk about it.

In a few minutes, Susan had climbed the stairs and entered her kitchen. She found Kathleen Gordon there, pouring Jamaican Blue into the electric bean grinder.

"I hope you're making a full pot. I'm exhausted," she said, more relieved than surprised by her friend's presence.

"Where did you come from?"

"The basement. I was banned from my own house by a strange man at the front door," she added, and went on to explain what had been happening since she last saw her friend.

"You've had a busy afternoon, haven't you?" Kathleen said when Susan was finished, pouring her a cup of coffee. "I can answer some of your questions, though. For instance, I know why those men are here. They're here to make sure no one says or does anything they're not supposed to."

"What? I thought they were from the network: producers or cameramen. . . ."

"They are from the network, but they're not producers—they're the first line of defense."

Susan gave Kathleen a puzzled look.

Kathleen explained. "Look, I've only had a bit of experience with this type of thing, but when I was working in the city, I was assigned to a few cases that involved large corporations. No matter what the case was—murder, suicide, embezzlement, organized crime, whatever—the first response to any crisis was that the public relations department formed a wall around the people involved."

"A wall?"

"First they show up and offer to help. Then you can't find the people you want to speak with. They don't even answer their own phones—all calls are channeled through the public relations department. And the PR department is full of people trained to say nothing in two thousand words or more. There's a lot of senseless activity, there are articles printed in the friendly press, but nothing new is learned. Nothing.''

''I don't think it will be like that this time,'' Susan said, arranging sugar and cream next to cups and saucers on a large mahogany tray. ''After all, both Rebecca and her husband worked in news—they're always talking about it on the air. Surely news professionals won't be that bad. After all, they're always trying to find out the truth about people.''

''So who sent out the two men in your hall? They're not reporters,'' Kathleen reminded her as the smell of fresh coffee began to overpower the remains of the chili.

Susan just sighed. ''What I'm really wondering is how they knew about the murders.''

''Rebecca didn't call them?''

''I don't think so. She told me she didn't want anyone in New York to know about Jason's death. . . .''

''She couldn't have thought she was going to keep it a secret.''

''I know. But she was upset. I don't think she was thinking clearly.''

''Well, she can't be blamed for that—they've only been married for a few months, and there was no reason to expect that he would die. . . .''

''Why don't you even consider the possibility that she killed him?'' Susan protested. ''In any other case you would. The wife is usually the first suspect.''

Kathleen was silent for a moment, pouring coffee into the ceramic pot that Susan offered her. ''I'm not sure you're right about that,'' she said slowly.

''Think about it,'' Susan urged. ''Think about those tell-all books by family members of stars. Obviously being a celebrity doesn't necessarily mean exposing your true self.''

''Brett doesn't think she's the murderer.''

''That's right! I forgot that I saw his car in the driveway. Where . . . ?''

''He got a call a few minutes ago and had to leave. He

was probably going out the front door when you were coming in the basement. I was making coffee for him, actually.''

"Kathleen . . ."

"It was interesting to see him again," she continued without waiting for Susan to go on. "It will be interesting to have him living here in Hancock."

Now what did that mean? Susan didn't have time to inquire; Jed hurried into the room.

"I—good, coffee," he approved after getting over his surprise at seeing his wife. "Rebecca was just saying that she would have some coffee."

"I'll . . ."

"She likes it with cream and sugar—two teaspoons," he interrupted his wife. "We should probably offer some to those men, too," he added vaguely.

"I have everything here." Susan pointed to the heavy tray. "Why don't you take it on out? But don't give any to that man answering the front door!"

"Why on earth not?"

"He wouldn't let me in the house! You wouldn't believe . . ."

"I would," Jed disagreed, taking the tray from her. "The stories that the press make up—the lies—just to get close to celebrities—Rebecca has been telling us all about that. I think they're probably right to be cautious. Not that they should have kept you from your own house," he added, seeing the look on her face. "I know you're having a rotten day, Sue. Maybe you'd like a drink or—or something."

"What I would like is to sip some cold wine while sitting in a warm bubble bath, but it looks like that moment is still hours away. Maybe I should pull some croissants from the freezer or something. . . ."

"Why don't you let me do it," Kathleen suggested. "I think you'd better tell someone official about how you were mugged at the . . ."

"What?" Jed put down the tray so hard that two of the

cups lost their handles. "Why didn't you tell me about that? Were you hurt?"

"I'll take the coffee out," Kathleen said to the embracing couple. They didn't bother to respond.

"I probably should report this to the police," Susan said, after she had told her story and Jed had exclaimed over her skinned hands and knees.

"Definitely. It's hard to believe that it's just a coincidence that you're mugged on the Armstrongs' front porch on the same day that Jason is murdered there. Although I've never believed that old saying about the guilty man returning to the scene of the crime . . . still, it could have been the murderer who grabbed your purse."

"But why? My purse didn't have anything to do with the Armstrongs."

"Let's think a second. You said you were hit from behind. I don't suppose the man could have thought you were Rebecca. . . ."

"Thank you for not comparing her hair, hips, and everything else with mine. And the answer is that it certainly wasn't that dark—and there was the porch light as well. It comes on automatically when someone approaches. Besides, the man could probably see more than my back." She explained about the mirrored doors.

"But you really couldn't see his face."

"No, he was wearing a large mask. Or she, if it comes to that. Although it was pretty tall for a woman."

"But . . ."

"But it could have been," she agreed with what she didn't give him a chance to say. "Why don't you get back to our guests, and I'll call the police."

"I . . ."

"I'll be out in just a moment." She picked up the phone. "Really."

"I'd feel a lot better if you'd put some first-aid cream on your hands." Jed was hesitant to leave.

"I will. There's some in the drawer here. I'll be right out," she said as he left the room.

Brett, found quickly at the nearby police station, was gratifyingly concerned that she had been mugged, interested that it had happened on the Armstrong porch, and incensed that she had not been allowed to enter her own home. Susan found herself explaining that none of it mattered, that she was all right, really. She hung up, smiling and thinking that he was going to do just fine as the chief of a small-town police department. She was staring into the bottom shelf of her freezer, wondering which of four rectangular packages contained croissants, when Charles Grace entered the room.

"Can I get you something?" Susan asked when he didn't say anything or even acknowledge her presence.

"I was looking for a private phone." He didn't waste any energy smiling. "But there seem to be people in every room of your house."

"You mustn't think it's usually like this . . ." Susan began before she could stop herself. She hated being made to feel that she was doing something wrong when, in this case at least, she certainly wasn't. She considered the phones in the rooms upstairs and then dismissed them. Rebecca was using the guest room, and her own bedroom wasn't much cleaner than she expected her children's were. "There's an extension in the laundry room in the cellar," she offered. "It's right down those stairs. If you wait a minute, I'll show you the way."

"I'll find it myself." He opened the door she had indicated.

Susan shrugged and returned to her puzzle. The first box was certainly too heavy for pastry.

The librarian's call must have been short; he returned to the kitchen while she was rewrapping a large chunk of uncleaned squid, clams, and blood worms that her son and husband had bought when preparing for a deep-sea fishing expedition that bad weather had canceled. Susan went ahead with her job, finding and putting the croissants in the oven, before turning and again offering to help.

"Did you get through?"

"Yes. It . . . it was a local call."

"Oh." Susan was embarrassed. "That's not what I meant. I just wond—is there anything else you need?" she finally asked.

"No." But still he didn't move.

"Then why are you here?" She was afraid she sounded as exasperated as she felt.

"I wondered if you could come to the library tomorrow to speak to me. It's important," he added, probably in response to the surprised look on her face.

"Of course . . ."

"I usually lunch at twelve-thirty. Come to my office." Then he turned and hurried from the room.

Susan stood next to the stove, blinking. She had always thought that Charles Grace was a strange man, an unlikely combination of nerd and tyrant, but why did he seem to think it so urgent that he speak with her? Why was he at her house? The timer rang as she decided that this was one of the smallest mysteries she had to worry about. She tossed the croissants on a tray in what she hoped was an artful manner, grabbed an unopened bag of candy bars from on top of the refrigerator, and headed to the living room. The crowd was still there. And its focal point was still Rebecca.

"I thought some of you might be hungry," she announced, setting down the tray.

"Starving," one of the network men agreed, reaching for sustenance.

"The coffee is enough for me," Rebecca said, cradling the cup against her chest. "But thank you."

"You look tired. Did you get a chance to lie down?" Susan asked.

"No. I feel so . . . so strange . . . almost disoriented." Rebecca ran one hand through her fabulous hair.

"I picked up your things from your house. Why don't you

go upstairs and get ready for bed? I can bring you a snack there," Susan offered. "Go on. Rest is the best thing for you."

To her surprise, Rebecca's colleagues joined in Susan's urging, and, in a few minutes, she was headed upstairs to the guest room. The network men commanded Susan's attention as soon as Rebecca had left.

"I'm sure Rebecca can find everything by herself, so why don't you just sit down and rest yourself for a few minutes? We're all sorry about the confusion that kept you out of your own house earlier, but we do need to talk to you, Mrs. Henshaw . . . and your husband, of course."

"I think I'd better be going." Charles Grace stood immediately, understanding the not-too-subtle hint. "I'll see you at lunch tomorrow?" he added, picking up his coat.

"Yes. Of course."

Jed looked curiously at his wife but said nothing. Kathleen offered to escort the librarian to the door, stating that it was time she herself was leaving.

"We need to figure out some sort of strategy here," one of the men said when the Henshaws' guests had left, not bothering to introduce himself.

" 'Strategy?' " Susan was surprised by his choice of words. "I think she'll be okay once the initial shock has worn off. . . ."

"I'm thinking of the press and the public. We have to protect Rebecca. Famous people are in a more vulnerable position than the rest of us, as you surely understand."

Susan nodded sagely, thinking of the warning Kathleen had given about these men and wondering what was coming next.

The other, older man was speaking. "It was truly wonderful of you and your family to open your home to Rebecca in this crisis—not many people would have done it."

"And there aren't many people that Rebecca would feel comfortable with in a situation like this. You've really received a compliment here,'' his partner joined in. ''How long have you been friends?''

''Uh . . . we only met today,'' Susan answered after a short pause.

The men exchanged what she was sure were meaningful glances, except that she didn't know what they meant. ''Then you don't know very much about her professional life . . .'' one of them began.

''We don't know very much about her life at all,'' Jed interrupted impatiently. ''We don't watch television in the morning, unless there's something important going on in the world that we're anxious to hear about, so we're not exactly major fans of the Armstrongs. But we will certainly do anything we can to help any of our neighbors who are unlucky enough to experience a tragedy like this one.''

''I'm glad to hear that, because this problem isn't as simple as it might look at first glance. You see, Rebecca is going through a terrible crisis. A terrible tragedy has occurred in her life, and we are here to try to make sure that the results of this don't affect her permanently.''

''I don't understand,'' Susan said, wondering if anyone could lose their husband and not have the event affect the rest of their life. Even if she remarried, Rebecca would always feel this loss, no matter . . . Her thoughts were interrupted.

''She's going to want to take some time off from the job—hell, everyone will expect her to take some time off—but we're here to see that she has a job to come back to.''

''I don't understand. Surely the network isn't going to fire her because her husband was murdered,'' Jed stated.

''No one at the network would ever want to take Rebecca's job from her—she's been the premier morning-show hostess on television for almost a decade now—but you know what happens to people when their Q score drops.''

''Yes,'' Jed said, ''we do.''

''We do?'' Susan, amazed, looked at her husband with a puzzled expression on her face. She certainly didn't know what was being talked about. It couldn't possibly have anything to do with G spots (not that she had ever really understood that one either), could it?

"Q scores are simple, Sue. They've been used by television and admen for years. It's a measure of audience recognition—the higher the score, the better known the personality. And in television, the better known you are, the more desirable you are. People like to watch familiar faces."

"But won't all this publicity make Rebecca more familiar?"

"There is such a thing as a negative Q score as well. The right publicity is good for people. The wrong can kill them."

Susan had the sense not to take that statement literally. "So what do you want me . . ."—she glanced at her husband—"or rather us, to do?"

"Nothing."

"What my colleague means is that we want you to keep doing what you're doing—giving Rebecca a place to stay, taking care of her, listening to her stories. . . ."

"What we don't want you to do is talk to the press, or your neighbors, or your cleaning woman, or your minister, or anyone about Rebecca or anything that has happened to her," the more abrupt of the two interrupted to say. "And we want you to make damn sure that your kids don't say anything to anyone either. Remember that Kissinger boy and Nixon's trip to China."

Susan opened her mouth to defend her children, but Jed beat her to it. "Chad and Chrissy aren't small children, they're teenagers—young adults—and I'm sure if we explain the situation to them, they will have the maturity to understand the need for discretion. But they are certainly too old to be ordered around." As if they had stood in line and taken orders when they were young, Susan thought, but refrained from speaking. These men were making her angry. Jed was still talking. "I also think you're misjudging my wife and myself. We brought Rebecca into our home to help her—and we will help her. But we certainly won't let her presence hurt any of our family relationships—or endanger any of us. You may not be aware of it, but my wife was mugged at the Armstrong house while running an errand for Rebecca.''

''That is exactly the type of thing we don't want to press to know.''

''I hope you're okay, Mrs. Henshaw,'' the more moderate man interrupted his companion. ''We had no idea you'd been hurt this evening. I wish''—he looked pointedly at Jed—''that we could convince Rebecca to go to a hotel in New York City. She would be comfortable there, and we could look out for her without endangering anyone.''

''Have you suggested that?'' Jed picked up immediately.

''Of course we have,'' said the man Susan was coming to think of as the bad PR man. His tone of voice implied that he thought the Henshaws had been underestimating him—and that he was tired of it.

''For some reason Rebecca is determined to stay away from her colleagues in the city. We suggested that she occupy the network's suite at the Waldorf for a week or two, but she refused. She said she didn't want to talk with any of her colleagues—at least not right now.''

''That's strange,'' Jed commented, almost to himself. ''I wonder if there is someone in the city that she doesn't want to see.''

Chad's noisy entrance changed the topic. Ignoring the man at the front door, he sloppily dumped the large plastic Gap bag full of candy on the polished surface of the delicate antique table in the hall and barged into the living room. ''I heard you were attacked,'' he cried out to his mother.

Susan was gratified by his distress and maternal enough to try to relieve it immediately. ''I'm fine. Someone stole my purse, but I didn't get hurt, and there wasn't even very much money in it,'' she assured him.

''How did you hear about it?''

''I ran into one of the girls in my class down at the diner. She has a friend who saw it happen. I couldn't believe it,'' Chad answered the public relations man. ''Everything happens to my mother. Everything.'' He didn't sound thrilled by the fact.

''Well, the important thing is that no one got hurt,'' Jed said, trying to redirect his son's anguish. ''Now that you're home, why don't you take a shower and wash some of that makeup off. . . .''

''I just stopped in to dump my loot and get another bag. You didn't think I was ready to come home, did you?'' Chad's voice got shriller as he protested.

''It's late . . .'' his father began.

''But I promised Chad he could stay out till eleven tonight,'' Susan surprised her son and husband by saying. ''After all, Halloween only comes once a year, and he has finished his homework. I'll just get you another bag.'' She got up, and her son followed her from the room and back to the kitchen.

''Listen, what exactly did the girl who saw me get mugged say to you?'' she asked, rummaging in a drawer full of plastic bags. ''Is this one okay?'' She held out a large Saks bag.

''Yeah. Fine.'' He took the proffered object. ''She just said that someone came up from behind you and grabbed your purse and that you fell down when you ran after him.''

''Did she see where the mugger went?''

''She said he ran back behind the Armstrong house. One of the guys she was with was going to try to catch up with him, but they thought it was just a prank—not a serious mugging, I mean. Why do you want to know all this?''

''Because it may have something to do with the murder,'' she said slowly, assuming he was going to object to her involvement.

But he surprised her. ''Okay. If I hear anything else, I'll tell you about it.'' He started for the door and then turned back, a grin on his face. ''You know I don't like you messing around in these murders, but I guess a person has the right to find out who stole something from them. Besides, I owe you for letting me go back out tonight. Bye. I'll be home by midnight.'' And the door slammed behind him.

"Midnight?" Susan didn't have time to object. There was a strange woman entering her kitchen. She was wearing a green-plaid bathrobe and carrying one of Susan's antique Spode cups and saucers in her hands.

"I wonder if it would be an imposition if I asked for some Earl Grey tea?" the woman asked, apparently right at home. "I always have a cup before going to bed."

FIVE

The woman, whose name turned out to be Hilda Flambay and who was also from the press department at the network, got her Earl Grey tea, and Susan took a quick shower long after midnight. (The chilled Chablis would have to wait for another day.) She and Jed did manage to grab a short private conversation, deciding only that next year they would go anywhere rather than spend Halloween in Hancock. They were discussing it again the next morning.

"What I'm having trouble with is that you agreed to let that woman stay here without telling me," Susan repeated for the third or fourth time.

"A lot had happened. I already told you that I wasn't thinking. Can't we forget about Hilda for a while?" he asked, handing his wife a cup of the coffee he had just brewed.

"I find it a little difficult to forget about people when they're sleeping on the Hide-A-Bed in my den." But she took the coffee and sipped it gratefully. "Thanks. Yesterday was awful, and I'm not sure today is going to be much better. I suppose I should spend some time with Rebecca, but I have no idea what she might want to do. And I should speak with Brett again about the mugging. . . . Did I tell you that Charles Grace asked me to meet him in his office for lunch?"

"You're kidding. Maybe that's why he was here last night. I never figured out how he got in. I just looked up, and there he was. . . ."

"You didn't let him in?" Susan was so surprised that she

stopped stirring the large bowl of pumpkin muffin batter she held in her arms.

Jed shook his head. "I didn't let anyone in. Right after you left, Brett showed up. He asked one of the network people to keep an eye on the front door. After that, there was no reason for me to answer every time it rang."

"You mean that man let Charles Grace into my house and he wouldn't let me in?" Susan angrily filled the greased muffin cups.

"I guess Charles Grace had identification, hon."

Susan just sighed and shoved the pan into the oven. "Did he explain?"

"Who?"

"Charles Grace. Didn't he say anything to anyone?"

"I don't think so. Rebecca was talking and crying, and the three network people were trying to comfort her and making a bunch of phone calls—Charles Grace seemed to be the least of our problems. Those look pretty good," he added. "I guess having people in the house is going to make a lot of extra work for you."

"It usually does—but that's not what I had in mind," she added. "I just don't understand these people. Rebecca is upset, so I can't blame her, I guess, but Hilda seems to think absolutely nothing of asking for special favors or making extra work. I gave her some printed sheets—Ralph Lauren and brand-new—and she explained that she really preferred sleeping on white cotton."

"And you ran right back up to the linen closet and found a set," Jed concluded.

"I know!" Susan admitted her own culpability. "But I want guests to be comfortable, though apparently she thinks I'm the maid or something. . . ."

"She *is* a rather determined lady . . ." Jed began.

"No, she's a bitch," Susan said flatly. "And, worse than that, she's one of those people who thinks that a woman who chooses to stay home and raise a family is inherently inferior to all professional women."

Jed had heard his wife's opinions on this particular subject before. He knew the only thing to do was nod and look sympathetic. Not that he wasn't. He had no illusions about raising children and running a house; his wife had worked and worked hard. She had also finished speaking.

"Well . . ." Jed searched around for a less emotional subject and found one. "I guess the kids had a good time last night. Chad has enough candy to feed an army, and he was teasing Chrissy about her new boyfriend, and she was blushing like crazy. Did they make it off to school on time?"

Susan poured orange juice into a glass pitcher and laughed. "Yes. Chad filled his backpack with candy and said something about saving money by not buying lunch in the cafeteria, and Chrissy sipped some tomato juice and sort of floated out the door in that new sweater she bought last weekend. I don't think much of their diets, but at least they're involved in their own lives—I really wish we could keep them out of this mess."

"Hmm." Jed's agreement was rather absentminded. "You don't happen to know when she's going to leave, do you?"

"Rebecca or Hilda?"

"I think where Rebecca goes Hilda will follow."

"You're probably right. I have no idea. I think it would be awfully rude to urge her out the door," Susan said, joining her husband at their kitchen table. "You didn't seem to mind having her here last night," she reminded him.

"You know, in person, she's pretty hard to resist. She's beautiful and has lots of personality, and right now, of course, it's hard not to feel sorry for her. But when she's not right here . . . I don't know. I guess I'm not explaining very well, am I?"

"No, but I think I know what you mean. Aren't you going to be awfully late for work?"

"I called and explained that something had come up. You know, it's going to be rather strange when the word gets out that Rebecca is staying here."

"I suppose so. . . ."

"You suppose so. Susan, you may not be a big fan of morning TV, but a lot of the country is. Jason's murder is going to be big news. . . . Looks like we have company," he added, getting up and opening the back door. Brett Fortesque stood on the doorstep.

"I know it's early, but I thought you might be interested in what was dropped off at police headquarters sometime during the night." He held up a dirty brown leather bag.

"My purse!"

"Dropped off . . . ?" Jed began the question as his wife leapt up and ran to the door.

"Come on in," she urged. "Have some coffee. Tell us about it."

"I'd love some coffee, and there's not much of a story. The purse was apparently tossed on the mat in front of the door sometime in the early-morning hours. Between four and five A.M., as far as we can pin it down . . . Thanks." He accepted a steaming cup from Susan. "It's filthy, but it's also pretty full. But you'd be the only person who can tell us if something's missing."

Susan was rummaging around in the bag as he spoke. "It looks like everything's here—as far as I can tell, that is. I'm not terribly organized when it comes to my purse. I just dump stuff in and hope it will be there when I need it. But the big things are here: wallet, makeup bag, comb, notebook, checkbook. . . ." She poured everything out on the table. They grabbed to keep pens, breath mints, tubes of lipstick, and a silver pillbox from rolling to the floor.

"Every time she does this, it reminds me a little of those cars at the circus that dozens of clowns pop out of," Jed commented, picking up a Swiss Army knife that had toppled into his lap.

"I don't think anything is missing," Susan said.

"Do you happen to remember how much money you had in your wallet?"

"I'd just cashed a check for two hundred dollars the day before," Susan muttered, opening the red leather envelope and counting the bills inside. "Let's see. I had picked up Jed's shirts at the cleaners, been to the grocery store and the pharmacy—oh, no, I charged everything there—but I also paid cash for getting a couple rolls of film developed, and I filled the car with gas. There's seven dollars in here—that's about right. I don't think anyone took anything." She began to restore order to her handbag, tucking a tiny ceramic frog into the side pocket. Jed and Brett exchanged a look, but neither of them asked. "It seems strange that someone stole my purse, didn't take anything, and then returned it to you, doesn't it?"

"It does indeed," Brett agreed. "I think we can assume that the mugging was a diversionary tactic rather than a theft."

"Meaning?"

"Meaning that your wife's purse was taken to throw her off guard rather than for monetary gain."

"Maybe the mugger got disgusted with how little money was in it," Susan suggested.

"If the motive was money, wouldn't he . . ."

"Or she," Susan reminded him.

"Or she have at least kept what was in there? Besides, the pillbox has some value and maybe even these?" Brett suggested, pulling tiny earrings made of pearls and emeralds from the messy pile.

Jed raised his eyebrows at his wife.

"Yes, they're . . . they're beautiful, aren't they? Jed gave them to me for Christmas last year. They are a little heavy, though," she explained to her husband. "But I'm sure they're worth quite a bit, so you're probably right," she continued to Brett, slipping the jewelry into the pocket of her short denim skirt. "But I wonder why the purse was brought to the police station. Why not just dump it into a garbage can or throw it in the ocean?"

"Good question."

"But no good answer?" Susan asked, filling everyone's coffee cups.

"No way of knowing what is the correct answer, at least," Brett explained. "That's why I was hoping that something had been stolen. Then, at least, we could guess what the thief was after."

"Maybe that's why nothing was taken. To confuse us," Susan suggested.

"Might be, might not be. We're going to have to wait and find the answer to that one. I do think, though, that we can assume the mugging had something to do with Jason Armstrong's murder."

"I thought you were asked not to talk about the murder with anyone." An angry Hilda Flambay stood in the doorway. She turned her attention to Brett. "And I don't know who you are, but if you repeat anything about this murder to anyone, I can assure you that it will do you absolutely no good. . . ."

"I'm Brett Fortesque . . . the chief of police here in Hancock, Miss . . . ?"

It would be rude to grin at Hilda's discomfort. Susan did it anyway.

But Hilda recovered quickly. "I apologize. If I had known who you were, I certainly wouldn't have spoken the way I did. You probably understand as well as anyone the need for discretion in a situation like this."

"Maybe a little better than anyone," Susan suggested, still smiling.

"I'm Hilda Flambay." She offered her hand to Brett.

"She's from the network," Susan added.

"My boss sent me here to help Rebecca, and the Henshaws have been very generous in allowing me to stay with them while she's here. I don't know what we all would have done without them." She smiled warmly at Jed. "But I would appreciate speaking with you, Chief Fortesque. I know you must be absolutely swamped right now. . . ."

"Actually, I was going to ask for a few words with you."

"Then why don't we go to the living room?" Hilda suggested, opening the door. "And maybe," she added, "Susan would bring us both some coffee?"

What else could Susan do? She brought the coffee. When the muffins were finished, she brought them on a tray with butter and three flavors of jam. And an hour later she repeated the process when Rebecca got out of bed and joined them. Susan was still seething as she parked in the lot by the library, ready for her meeting with Charles Grace.

Oh, well, she thought, at least he wanted to speak to her and wasn't looking for maid service.

Apparently he wasn't even looking for her, she discovered when the woman at the checkout desk explained that Mr. Grace had been needed urgently at the town office and had asked Susan to excuse him if he was a little late.

There are, of course, worse places to wait for someone than in a library. In fact, the library was one of Susan's favorite places. She headed over to the magazine section. Maybe this month's *Runner's World* could tell her what to do about aching hips.

"Checking out the scene of the crime?"

Susan found that she was looking at the woman who had been crying in Charles Grace's office yesterday. If only she could remember her name . . .

"Marion Marshall," the woman identified herself, possibly realizing there was a problem.

"Of course . . . I'm so terrible at names." Susan offered the standard excuse.

"You're Susan Henshaw. I've read your name in the paper—you investigate crimes . . . murders." Marion whispered, either because it was the habit of her profession or because she was embarrassed to be overheard talking about such matters.

"Yes," Susan answered, running her hand through a pile of magazines.

"Can I help you find something?"

Susan was surprised by the offer. "No, thank you. I'm just

looking," she answered as though she were on a casual shopping expedition.

"Well, just let me know if you need me." Marion wandered back into the stacks.

Susan continued to browse, keeping one eye out for Charles Grace's return. She was very hungry and thinking about giving up on her appointment and returning home for some lunch when Marion Marshall reappeared at her side. "I know this sounds strange, but I really need to speak with you—privately."

"Of course." Susan had become accustomed to that particular statement over the past few years. "But I'm waiting for an appointment right now."

"It will only take a few minutes. We could borrow Mr. Grace's office. I'm sure he wouldn't mind. . . ."

"As that's who I'm waiting for, I think we can take the time to talk. As long as you don't mind if I break it off when he gets here."

"What time was your appointment for?"

"Ah . . . noon."

The other woman glanced at her watch. "It's not even quarter after yet. Mr. Grace probably won't be here till twelve-thirty. He's usually late. We're all used to it. In fact, we laugh about it."

Susan didn't generally find amusement in people wasting her time, but she didn't think this was the moment to mention it. "Then we have a while, don't we?" was all she said. She insisted on leaving a message with the librarian at the desk before following the other woman up the stairs to Charles Grace's tower office.

Once there, Susan sat down in the chair provided for visitors, expecting Marion to take the one at the desk. Instead she wandered over and stared out the window. Susan waited patiently. This, too, didn't come as a surprise. People frequently insisted on talking to her and then, apparently, couldn't figure out how to start. Usually all they needed was a little time.

"Most people don't understand Mr. Grace." Marion surprised Susan with her choice of topic.

"Maybe they don't know him all that well," Susan suggested when Marion didn't continue.

"Well, of course that's true. He's only been in Hancock for a few years. But in such a short time, he's done so much for the library." Marion sat down and leaned closer to Susan. "I came here six years ago, right out of library school. It was an entirely different place then." She grimaced. "It's not just that the building is different—that's not what I meant." She stopped talking, and Susan wondered if she had forgotten exactly what she was talking about when she realized that they were no longer alone. Charles Grace had joined them, mounting the stairs too quietly to be heard.

"Mrs. Henshaw, I'm so sorry to be late. I hope Marion has been entertaining you?" He looked at his employee without smiling.

She didn't appear to notice the omission. "I . . . I was just speaking with Mrs. Henshaw . . ." she began.

Susan was surprised by Marion's nervousness. After all, they hadn't been talking about anything particularly noteworthy.

"I appreciate your interest, Marion, but I think Mrs. Henshaw and I had better be left alone now. I have some very important things to discuss with her, and also a very busy afternoon ahead. If you don't mind?" He nodded down the stairs.

Marion scurried from the room, reminding Susan of a chubby mouse. Some women really shouldn't wear gray. And no one should be so subservient! She turned her attention to Charles Grace, but her expression betrayed her feelings.

"You're probably thinking that I was rude to poor Marion," he said as the door at the bottom of the stairs clicked closed. "But, believe me, that is the only way to deal with her. I'm afraid that she has gotten to be something of a problem. You must understand, I'm the only single male here and, of course, an authority figure to the poor girl. She has developed a schoolgirl crush on me. It's only become a problem recently—the other librarians have noticed it—it would be impossible not to notice it. She's always offering to help me with something or other, she stays around every afternoon until I am ready to leave, walking me to my car like I'm a schoolboy. . . . She even baked these cookies for me,'' he added, taking a tin from his drawer and laying it on top of his desk. "I know I should be more understanding, but it is quite annoying and making my job substantially more difficult than it has to be! I'm afraid I am becoming very intolerant.

"You don't mind if I eat in front of you,'' he continued, unwrapping a huge corned beef on rye. "I have so little free time in my day.''

"No, I've . . . I've eaten already,'' Susan lied. Certainly she had had the impression that he was inviting her to lunch with him, but what could she do now?

"Then perhaps we should get right down to business.'' He took a huge bite from the sandwich.

Susan waited while he chewed carefully. She had always guessed that there had to be someone who listened when the advice to chew each bite one hundred times was given; how unfortunate Charles Grace had to be the one. The question of whether she was going to starve to death while he ate his lunch was becoming more interesting than what he had to say.

"In fact,'' he continued after swallowing noisily, "some of the other girls have come to me and suggested that she needs psychiatric help. She is really complicating my management of this library, and, to be completely honest, I don't know what to do about it.'' He took another enormous bite.

"Is it Marion that you wished to speak to me about?''

"Heavens, no!'' He forgot himself long enough to speak with his mouth full. "I make it a policy never to speak about personnel matters outside of the library.''

"Well, then . . .'' Susan began again, wondering just what he thought he had been doing.

"I do, however, believe in making exceptions to rules after I have considered whether it is absolutely necessary, whether there is any other way to deal with a situation. And if there isn't, I believe in going ahead and speaking freely." Swallow. "You do understand, don't you?" Bite.

"No." She waited for him to chew and swallow.

"It was no accident that man was killed in my library."

"No?"

"No." The subject interested him so much that he stopped eating for a minute. "You've probably heard what people are saying."

"I've been busy," Susan answered. "I can't say that I've heard anything. I don't even know who the victim was."

This appeared to startle Charles Grace. "I thought the police told you everything." He sounded as if he was accusing her of lying to him.

"I can't imagine why you thought that," Susan said. "I have helped the police with one or two murder investigations, but I certainly have no official standing with the department."

"I thought you and the new police chief were very close."

"I think you've misunderstood. I am not close to Brett Fortesque—in fact, until yesterday, I had not seen him for more than three years. And, to be honest, Mr. Grace, I still don't know why you wanted to speak with me today."

He stood up so abruptly that only some quick action kept his sandwich from falling to the floor. "In that case, I'm afraid I have called you here unnecessarily. I misunderstood the situation. It looks like you won't be able to help us after all. Perhaps I should stop wasting your time and wish you good day."

"Perhaps you should." Susan didn't bother trying to keep the anger from her voice. As she left the room, she noticed that Charles Grace's distress at Marion's offerings didn't extend to spurning them. He was happily munching on cookies as she slammed his office door behind her.

She walked out into the startled faces of those in the building. Once again she had broken the traditional silence of the library.

Marion Marshall hurried to her side. "You weren't in there very long," she said.

"It turned out that we didn't have much to say to each other."

"I have a lot to say to you. I'm on my lunch break now. Will you join me? We could eat on one of the benches down by the pond. I bring my own lunch, and I always bring more than enough for two—in case someone forgets theirs," she added. Both women glanced up at Charles Grace's office. "Please," Marion begged.

"Okay. If it won't take too long. I have a house full of guests."

"Oh, I promise you I'll take up as little of your time as possible."

Why was it that Susan always felt as though she were talking to an overly mannered child when she was with this woman? But it was best to hurry. She noticed Amy Ellsworth leaning against a computer talking with someone whose back was to her. Amy was always explaining how busy she was, but Susan had noticed that she seemed to have more than enough time to do what her mother would have called talking everyone's head off. Susan certainly didn't have time for that now. Marion pulled an old-fashioned straw picnic basket from behind the desk, and Susan followed her outside.

The library was a couple of thousand feet from the duck pond. As a convenience to the citizens of Hancock and to protect the lawn, three trails had been devised leading from the building to the path around the water. A half-dozen willow trees leaned toward the water, and geometric beds of autumn chrysanthemums completed the picture. The town had constructed numerous benches from which to view it. Marion led the way to one almost hidden in the trees.

"No, wait!" She stopped Susan from sitting down. She pulled off the calico cloth that had been covering the basket and unfolded it, spreading it across the bench. "There's a

lot of pollen in the air, as well as bird . . . uh, bird efflu-
ence,'' she explained delicately, gesturing for Susan to sit.
''Now, I have cold avocado soup, crab salad, cheese and
rolls, green salad with raspberry vinaigrette, and made-
leines.''

''Is this a special occasion? Your birthday or something?''
Susan asked, accepting the silverware and napkins offered.
Apparently Marion always carried a spare set.

''I just like to come prepared. Like the Girl Scouts, you
know.''

Susan was just beginning to know. It looked to her like
Marion was truly always prepared for a guest. And, possibly,
sadly, always hoping that Charles Grace would be that guest.
Marion's next words were to prove her wrong about that.

''Actually, I was hoping I would get the chance to talk
with you today.'' She busied herself laying out the elegant
(china, not plastic) meal, and Susan waited until she was
ready to speak again. ''I need something from you, Mrs.
Henshaw.''

Susan was glad to see that Marion didn't emulate her boss's
mastication habits. ''Thank you.'' She accepted a full plate
gratefully. ''What do you need?''

''There's only one way to say this, and that is just to say
it.'' Marion took a deep breath and followed her own advice.
''I know you're friends with the new chief of police. I . . . I
hope you'll speak to him. Tell him what a wonderful person
Mr. Grace is, and how the murders yesterday had nothing to
do with him or the library that he has worked so hard to
create!''

Now Susan took some time to chew her food. (The crab
salad was wonderful!) ''You think Charles Grace has something to do with the deaths,'' she said finally.

''No, of course not. But Mr. Grace has enemies who will
use this event to take his job away from him, to run him out
of Hancock!''

Susan thought this was a strange conversation, but she did
need some information. ''Did you see the murder victim

when he was still alive?'' she asked, pulling the crust from a roll and tossing it in the direction of a large gander.

''Oh, yes. He even spoke to me. I was at the front desk, checking out books, when he came up and asked about the library.''

''He lived in Hancock?''

''I don't think so. I'd never seen him here before, and I do usually recognize most of the people in town. But he was interested in the library. You know, the new building and all. He asked how long it had been open and how a small town like this managed to build something so spectacular. We're always getting questions about it. The library is really special.''

''Did he ask about anything in particular?''

''Just some general questions about what books were shelved where.''

''Which you pointed out to him.''

''Of course. That's what we're here for. Mr. Grace believes that service to the public is very, very important.''

''So he didn't head straight back to the aisle of the stacks where he was found.''

''I don't know. The Halloween party in the children's department ended, and there was so much confusion with the children running around and screaming and trying to find their mothers. I just didn't pay attention anymore. I'm sorry.''

''Well, you couldn't have known that he was going to be murdered.'' Susan stuffed the last of the roll in her mouth; that goose was beginning to look slightly menacing. ''Do you remember anything else that he said—anything at all?''

''No. And I thought about it all night long! Mr. Grace doesn't like the staff to gossip—he says it's a demeaning habit—but I couldn't help but listen to what's being said this morning, and more than one of the librarians noticed him wandering around yesterday morning. . . .''

''You mean he was here for a while?''

''I probably saw him at the desk half an hour before you found him,'' Marion answered. ''And he could have been here before that. I didn't see him enter the building. He could have been here ever since we opened the doors at nine o'clock, for all I know. It was a very confusing day. Do you think that goose is going to attack us?''

Both women stared as the hissing animal stretched out its wings and elongated its neck. ''He doesn't look too happy, does he? Maybe we should move,'' Susan suggested, grabbing up her lunch and the half-full picnic basket.

''Yes.'' Marion threw the last three rolls at the animal, grabbed the cloth they were sitting on, and they fled.

''We could just sit here. On the edge of the bridge,'' Susan suggested as they came to that landmark. ''Or maybe we should keep moving?''

''I think we gave him enough food to keep him busy for a while. I just wish I hadn't wasted all last night making potato rolls. Store-bought would have been good enough for a bird.'' She took the basket back from Susan as they strolled. ''Have a cookie.''

''Thanks. Have you spoken with Charles Grace about any of this?'' Susan asked, munching on a lemon bar.

'' 'Spoken with' him?''

''Asked him if he was the murderer?''

''Of course not! How could I ask that?''

''But you're accusing him of . . .''

''No, I'm trying to protect him. We have to figure out a way to make sure someone else is convicted of this crime— or no one. Murders go unsolved. Why can't this be one of those?''

Susan saw tears in her eyes. ''Is this why you were crying in his office yesterday? Because you thought he had killed the man?''

''Of course not. I told you. I don't deal with this type of thing very well. I've always hated the sight of blood.''

Susan got the impression that perhaps Marion wasn't being completely truthful, but now wasn't the time to push. She had already gotten a lot of information for one day. ''Look, as much as I appreciate the lunch, I don't think I can help you. I want to find the truth. And if Charles Grace is the murderer, then he shouldn't be allowed to get away with it.''

Marion grabbed Susan's hands. ''But there's that homeless person who confessed. Now, if we all just sit back and do nothing, he can take the blame—and he probably deserves it. You don't spend as much time around homeless people as I do. When I first wanted to be a librarian, libraries were sacred places . . . repositories of knowledge, my favorite college professor used to say. Now they're filled with all these smelly people who probably can't even read. They sit around all day pretending to look through magazines and books, they listen in on what everyone says, they even use our bathrooms to bathe in! It's disgusting. They would be better off in prison. They belong in prison, away from decent people. Away from . . .''

Susan had heard enough. She handed Marion the basket. ''That was a wonderful lunch, and I appreciate you sharing it with me, but I don't agree with you. Who knows why that poor man is homeless? Who knows what things he has had to endure that you and I probably, fortunately, can't even imagine? If he confessed to a crime that he did not commit, he still shouldn't be convicted of it. And I am going to do anything I can to help him.'' She turned and started back up the hill to the parking lot.

Susan was furious. She was as confused as any person living in the nineties. Recession, inflation, drugs, violence . . . she read the papers, she knew about them all. Sometimes she even managed to accept her own inability to sort out the problems, to contribute in some way to the solutions. But she had not become numb, and she had no intention of ignoring this obvious injustice—and stupidity. She was still fuming when David Pratt flagged her down.

''Hey, slow down. Or are you getting in some extra jogging time today?''

Susan slowed down. ''I'm sorry, Dave. I didn't see you. I was . . . I was thinking about something.''

"About the murders, I'll bet. Everyone in town knows that you're our favorite amateur sleuth."

It sounded a little like the promo for one of a dozen TV shows. Susan was still trying to think of a response when one became unnecessary.

"I have to run. I'm late for a meeting with Charles. We have to figure out what sort of public statement to make about the body in the stacks yesterday."

It sounded like a mystery novel, but Susan had another question. "Why you?"

"Me? I'm chairman of the library board, didn't you know?"

"No, I didn't know you were chairman. You're going to have some job, aren't you?"

"Oh, it won't be so bad. This is going to be an overnight sensation. Good thing that homeless man confessed, though, isn't it?"

SIX

SUSAN WAS USHERED INTO A MINUSCULE ROOM CONTAINing two folding chairs and a battered metal cabinet. The cabinet's doors were slightly ajar, and she spied rolls of toilet paper and bottles of fluorescent commercial cleanser.

"This is usually used for storage. Hancock is too small for an interrogation room. And, happily," Brett added, "there's not much call for one either."

Susan smiled nervously. She was beginning to regret the upcoming interview. Just what had she gotten herself into? Why was she so avidly defending a man with whom she had exchanged less than a hundred words, a man apparently unwilling or unable to fit into society, a man who had confessed to two murders that she was convinced he did not commit?

"You don't have to go through with this, you know." Brett had rightly interpreted her mood.

Susan smiled at him. "I think I do. The poor man has been locked up here. . . ."

"Hey, don't feel too sorry for the guy. This isn't San Quentin, you know. He's been staying in a room bigger than this one with a portable TV and a radio. He has clean sheets on his bed, a daily shower if he wants one, and three decent meals a day. It was so busy last night that he got my dinner—I'd sent out for shrimp in lobster sauce from a Chinese place someone recommended. We all stop in to talk with him. In fact, he and the night dispatcher are involved in some sort of

95

endless chess game. Believe me, this man probably hasn't lived so well in years.''

"And he won't live this well if he's convicted of a murder," Susan reminded him.

"True. And, I have to admit, he won't be living like this for much longer. The only reason he's here and not in the county jail is some sort of construction problem that they're having over there. Soon as that gets cleared up, we'll be sending him out of town to await trial.''

"Where he won't get Chinese food and chess games.''

"Probably not," Brett admitted. "But, you know . . .''

"I know. He just might be guilty.''

"You're the only person who insists upon his innocence, you know. Even the public defender will probably be trying for some sort of variation on a manslaughter conviction.''

"What about everyone here? What about the chess player?''

"They all think he did it—even the chess player. The guy doesn't talk much about his past, but when he does, it appears to be a tale of minor brushes with the law, drug and alcohol abuse, time spent in some of the Northeast's less enlightened public mental institutions. Sadly enough, there's nothing new or unusual about his story in this day and age.''

"Surely most people who go through what he's been through don't become murderers," Susan insisted.

"Of course not, but most don't confess to it either. Look, no matter what he does, no matter who he's talked to, he hasn't changed his story. He still says that he killed both men.''

"And he still won't talk about how he is supposed to have done it—at least that's what you said on the phone," Susan reminded him. "He won't explain how he got hold of the knives, doesn't explain how he selected his victims. . . .''

"No. You're right. He only says that now he's confessed, and it's time for us to get to work and discover what actually happened and convict him of it. He may just be very clever, you know. Unless we learn an awful lot during this investigation, there's no way we're going to get a conviction on this one.''

''And you're hoping that whatever I learn from talking with him—if I learn anything talking with him—will help your case?''

''If he did do it, do you want him to go free?'' Brett calmed her rising indignation.

''No. I guess not.''

They were both silent for a moment.

''He's not a very appealing guy—you're not romanticizing him, are you?'' Brett asked. ''Because if you are, you're going to be disappointed.''

''I've seen him around. I talked to him in the library. I don't think . . .'' Susan began.

''I'll be in the room with you,'' Brett announced. ''I can't trust this guy.''

''But that won't work! How will I get him to admit that he's lying about the murders when you're here?''

''Look, we can try it with me standing out in the hall with the door slightly cracked. But I think you're taking an unnecessary risk.''

''Why unnecessary?''

''Because this guy isn't going to change his story for you. He wants this investigation to go on. He's probably enjoying the attention or something. I suppose a psychiatrist could explain it. And if this gets to court, probably a half dozen are going to get a chance to.'' He stood up.

''Why do you keep calling him 'this guy'? Why don't you use his name?''

''Because,'' Brett began, opening the door, ''he won't tell us his name. I'll get him now.''

Susan had about five minutes alone in the room to think about the man who had said everyone would blame him for the murder in the library, who had confessed to two crimes that she was sure he didn't commit . . . the man who refused to disclose his name.

She shouldn't have been surprised to find his ragged clothing replaced with clean jeans, a chambray shirt, and running shoes. His hair was still long, still shaggy, but shampoo had revealed reddish highlights, and it was tied back in a pony-tail. Shaved and rested, he looked as if he belonged in sub-urbia. Susan, mannerly as ever, smiled.

It wasn't returned. The man sat down in the empty chair, took a fresh pack of Newports from his pocket, and lit up.

Susan, slightly unnerved, heard herself start to babble. "Thanks for seeing me."

He shrugged, cigarette ash falling to the floor. "I'm not too busy these days." His tone was sarcastic.

"I wanted to talk to you—to understand what you said to me in the library yesterday after the first body had been dis-covered. I don't know why you've confessed—unless you were beating them to the punch or something—why would you confess to murders that you didn't do?"

"Didn't I?" The man neither smiled nor frowned, and his voice was flat, as nearly without expression as possible.

"I don't believe you did," Susan insisted, appalled at how artificially hearty she was sounding.

"You weren't there when he died. How could you know?"

"He?" Susan paused on the word. "Are you saying now that you only killed one man?"

"I ain't saying that at all. I confessed to killing two men, so I must'a killed two men. And that's all I'm saying about that." He flicked the still-lit cigarette into the corner, where it hit the cement floor and was left to smolder.

Nothing was going to catch fire. Susan successfully re-sisted the impulse to get up and stamp on it. The man lit another. Susan took a breath and decided to try a different track.

"How long have you lived in Hancock?" she asked, just as she would have a newcomer at a neighborhood cocktail party.

" 'Lived?' " A slight wrinkling around the eyes might have suggested either amusement or anger at the question. "Are you under the impression that I am the type of man who is content to sleep in the same bed each night? To wake up looking out the same window each morning?''

"I . . ." She began apologizing immediately. Her stupid questioning had offended him. She was furious at herself.

"Don't worry, lady. Guy I used to know in a New York shelter used to talk like that. Me . . . I'm glad for any bed anyplace. My life doesn't need more adventures."

"Then . . ."

"But I'm not confessing to murders that I didn't do just to get a place to sleep. I'm not that desperate. Not at this time of year." He took a long drag on his cigarette. "Now, middle of February's something else again," he mused.

Susan waited, hoping he'd continue.

"So why all this interest in me? You one of those do-good women who makes big pots of smelly soup and brings them down to the shelters on weekends? This your way of doing something about the homeless problem?"

"I . . ." In fact, Susan had been cooking for a shelter for a couple of years now. The fact that he seemed to know unnerved her, and she couldn't think of anything to say.

"Listen, lady. I got a chess problem to work out, so if you've got nothing better to do than ask me questions that I ain't going to answer, that don't mean I have to sit here and listen to them." He got up.

Susan wondered where he had learned to play chess. She must have been thinking about that when she heard herself ask another question. "Have you ever lived anyplace nice? Someplace pretty?"

That stopped the man, and as he seemed to think about an answer, Susan envisioned him as a small child, eating an after-school snack at a table with a blue-and-white-checked cloth, geraniums in the background. . . . But he was answering.

"Sure did." He almost smiled. "I hate them shelters— disgusting places full of crime and idiots—and soon as it got a little warm last spring, I made myself a house along the highway. Some truck had dropped a big pile of flattened, waxed corrugated boxes near the side of the road, and I took a couple of dozen of them up to this clearing under the trees and built a nice little hut. It was even waterproof, because of all the waxing, see?'' He was staring at a blank wall as he spoke. ''Well, one night it got pretty warm, really warm, in fact, and in the morning I woke up early 'cause there was all this bright light around me. When I pushed back the piece of board covering the front of my hut, I found I was in the middle of a garden of sorts, surrounded on all sides, and even up above, with branches covered with yellow flowers. They smelled real sweet, and I could see the sun shining on the Hudson River through spaces in the flowers.'' He stopped for a moment to remember. ''That was beautiful, real beautiful. You see''—and he looked straight at Susan—''things ain't always as bad as people think.'' And, without another word, he walked from the room.

When Brett returned after the few minutes it took to lock up his prisoner, he discovered Susan still sitting, staring at the chair where the homeless man had been. ''Not quite what you expected?'' he asked, touching her gently on the shoulder.

''I . . .'' She took a deep breath. ''You expect me to have changed my mind, but I didn't. I still don't think he's a murderer.''

''Well, if you find some absolute proof to the contrary, you will let me know, won't you?''

Susan heard the dismissal in his voice. She didn't agree with him and she had wasted his time; she didn't blame him for being annoyed with her. ''Of course,'' she said quickly, standing up. ''I'll let you know anything I discover—even if it convicts him.''

Brett smiled, and together they walked to the front door. ''You know, there is one thing I don't understand here. . . .'' Susan slowed down, looking at him curiously. ''Who mugged you on the Armstrongs' front porch? This man had already confessed to the murders. He claims complete credit for the stabbings. . . .''

"You think my purse being stolen wasn't a coincidence?"

"I don't like coincidence. Especially not in a crime as serious as murder." He looked at her sternly. "I'm not saying I agree with you about this; I'm only saying it's something that bears thinking about.

"Now you take care of yourself," he added, opening the door for her. "And thanks again for taking Rebecca Armstrong in. Having her here in town might actually speed up this investigation."

Susan hurried down the steps and toward the parking lot. She had gotten the message. Start her investigation with the mugging and work quickly. She climbed into her car and put the key in the ignition. She had only one question: How?

Well, she decided, the scene of the crime was the classic place to start, and since she didn't have any other ideas, it was as good a place as any other. She headed home; she would have to think of an excuse to get the key from Rebecca.

Possession of the key was the last thing she should have worried about; it was in her hand almost before she got through her front door. That and a list of items that Rebecca apparently needed to make it through another day. Susan didn't even bother to nod to the network people (who had multiplied and were beginning to crowd her living room) before she set off on her hunt.

The key chain Rebecca had urged upon her was elegant and distinctive. Few keys hung from its sterling ring. Susan had been informed which one was for the front door, but she was interested in what had happened on the porch, so she paused to search the lawn and surrounding property first.

The porch fronted the house and then swung out, jutting into the yard before continuing on down the side of the building. Susan walked around the entire area, moving around the freshly enameled white-wicker furniture and numerous pots trailing petunias and impatiens. She was wondering what miracle had allowed this particular area to remain frost-free so late in the year when she realized that the plants had a light coating of dust—on their silk petals and leaves. She moved closer to the ornate rail that surrounded the space and then peered over the edge into a line of hedges that had been placed in the lawn, full grown, to landscape the house. There was a space between the plants and the building where the mugger could have hidden while waiting for her, but any footprints had been covered by drifting leaves. Besides, Susan reminded herself, how had the mugger known she was going to appear? She slowly strolled the shiny green floorboards and thought this out.

Since the person couldn't possibly have known that she was going to be here, he must have been waiting for someone or something else. Probably for Rebecca, but Susan couldn't make much sense of that. She was getting chilly. She'd explore the rest of the yard later. She inserted the key in the lock and gulped back a scream.

"Susan! What's wrong? It's me."

The apparition behind her turned into her next-door neighbor, and Susan's heart returned to normal. It was the first time in months that she found herself glad to see Amy Ellsworth.

"Rebecca thought of some other things that she needed, and I volunteered to come on over and help you get them."

Susan suspected that Amy was more than slightly interested in seeing the inside of the house, and though she would have preferred looking around alone, there was nothing she could do about that now. She turned the key, and they were inside.

"What's on your list?"

Susan hadn't, in fact, had time to look at the sheet of paper that Rebecca had shoved in her hand. She stopped in the large atrium entryway, and while Amy chattered on about how much it must cost to keep such a space heated in the winter and air-conditioned in the summer, she pulled the list from her jacket pocket and studied it.

There were about thirty items written in bold block letters with a black wide-point fountain pen. Everything from a special herb tea to a particularly personal piece of underwear was listed. If only directions had been given for finding these things, Susan thought.

"What's yours say?" she asked Amy.

"Not much. Two colors of lipstick, a white nightgown, and some slippers, and a few other odds and ends."

Sounded like Rebecca was going to add some class to her temporary residence, Susan thought, before deciding that she was being bitchy. "She wanted me to bring some special food items, so I'm going to start in the kitchen."

"Good idea," Amy enthused. "I'll come with you."

They prowled through the halls together, opening doors to bathrooms, closets, and even a small room apparently reserved exclusively for a phone and two fax machines before finding the kitchen. It was every bit as impressive as Susan had expected it to be. The prominent colors were evergreen and white with lots of copper and butter yellow accents thrown in. A huge green Garland stove stood against one wall, opposite banks of industrial refrigerators. Cherry cabinets surrounded the appliances, and everywhere there were marble countertops, brass rails, and an extraordinary collection of gourmet tools. From a duck press to an imported espresso machine, this place flaunted all the necessities of the good life.

A more prosaic needle in the haystack came to Susan's mind as she considered finding a box of tea here. Well, she knew where she kept tea: in a convenient cupboard, right next to her stove. She walked across the room and grabbed the shiny brass pull. An exemplary collection of wineglasses stood before her. She sighed, why should she get lucky? She started to systematically search the large room, opening cupboard doors and examining the contents. The room was organized as no kitchen she'd ever been in. Like was gathered to like. All the glasses were in one place, all the spices, all the pots, all the pans. But nothing was in a spot convenient for cooking. The glasses stored by the stove were a case in point. So were the shelves of various expensive vases (wedding gifts? or an annex to Steuben's warehouse?) sitting conveniently by the upright freezer in case anyone wanted to throw a couple of frozen peas into one. She would have commented on this strange arrangement to Amy if she could have gotten a word in edgewise, but Amy had been chatting away ever since the two of them had entered the room. Stumped, Susan decided that she might as well listen.

"Of course," Amy was saying, "they probably don't know how to cook. I wouldn't expect them to, would you?"

Susan did expect it. She expected everyone over the age of fourteen who knew how to eat to be able to cook something, but she decided not to mention it. She looked at the list. "Was there anything that you would expect to find in the kitchen on your list?"

Amy appeared surprised. "No."

"Then we may as well head on upstairs, don't you think?"

"No, I don't. I want to see the living room, and I want to see the dining room." Amy hurried out of the kitchen, as though afraid Susan might try to thwart her curiosity.

Susan, with a backward glance at a shelf crowded with imported coffee (no tea of any kind), followed.

"This really is something, isn't it? Not that I like Victorian myself. Too much like the junk my grandmother had in her apartment. But this is really very grand, isn't it?"

The two women were standing in the middle of an extraordinary room, full of museum-quality antiques artfully displayed. Susan was impressed, too. She was still impressed fifteen minutes later when they had finally covered the first floor and were mounting the stairs to the bedrooms. Impressed but curious: where did these people go to slop around in jeans and watch TV? The house was so formal, ornate, and delicate. She'd be afraid to sit down in some of the chairs for fear of breaking them, and she wasn't large.

The bedroom was familiar territory, and she ignored Amy's chatter while collecting the wardrobe that Rebecca had requested. She even found the desired two sheer negligees, one peach, one lime green. Susan wondered briefly if these fabulous items had been splurges for Rebecca's trousseau or if Rebecca had always slept (or whatever) like this.

"Be sure to pick up that tea. Rebecca mentioned it to me specifically."

"What?"

"The tea. I thought you knew about it." Amy looked confused. "Rebecca told me that she wanted some sort of special tea that she always had before she went to bed. She said it was near an electric pot in her dressing room. . . . "

"Why didn't you tell me before? I assumed it was in the kitchen. Didn't you wonder what I was hunting around in there for?"

"Not really," Amy answered vaguely, picking up plates from the bedroom mantel and looking at the manufacturers' names on the bottom.

"What did you think I was doing?" Susan asked impatiently.

Amy shrugged. "Looking around, I guess." She focused on Susan. "You can't tell me you haven't been curious about this house. Everyone in town has been talking about it ever since it was announced that the Armstrongs were going to move in."

"Yes. I was interested, but I do have more important things to do right now."

"Well, of course, you have houseguests. But how much trouble is that? You just throw on a little more food at mealtimes and provide some clean sheets. . . . " She shrugged as if to show how casually she accepted these things.

Susan didn't believe it. Amy was always telling other people how easy it was to do something, but when it came to doing them herself, she was always too busy with some nebulous task to actually accept the responsibility for any work. Susan returned to the job at hand, folding and packing everything in two more Vuitton suitcases. The tea she found behind an elegant tiny screen on top of an Oriental lacquered chest. It was packed in an ornate rosewood box inlaid with sterling silver. Susan carefully picked it up and sniffed at the contents. It smelled like no tea she knew, but she shrugged, wrapped it in a silk scarf, and placed it in a suitcase before she snapped them both shut. Picking them up, she went back to the bedroom, expecting to find Amy there. Stupidly expecting to find Amy there, she decided. She should have known that Amy, her curiosity unsatisfied, would have wandered off. There was nothing she could do but follow her.

She certainly didn't plan on carrying these things alone. She dumped the suitcases near the door and headed out into the hall. The rooms were arranged around the opening for the atrium, and it was easy to circle the space, opening door after door, to see if she could find Amy. When she did, she was so surprised at the location that she forgot to be angry with the other woman for holding her up. Amy was standing in the middle of a completely modern media room. The large space contained wall units with six television screens, numerous VCRs, speakers, and monitors. Seated in front of all these electronic marvels were two modern leather couches, set at angles to a coffee table cum control panel of buttons, knobs, and switches. On the walls behind the viewers, a huge abstract hung over a well-supplied see-through acrylic bar. The only colors in the room were the browns of the woods and the various beiges of the carpet, the unusually textured suede-covered walls, and the couches.

Susan felt as if she had turned the corner at the end of the eighteen hundreds and landed in the twenty-first century, somehow leaping through time and avoiding the intervening hundred years. "It's impressive," she commented, still staring. How long had it taken Rebecca and Jason to learn to control this equipment? She still had to look through the guidebook before setting her own, substantially simpler, VCR. "Isn't it?" She looked at Amy. The other woman had been unusually silent.

"Did you hear anything?" Amy asked, walking back toward Susan.

"No. What did you hear?" Susan thought of her mugger. Was he (she?) back?

"I thought . . . something out in the hall." Amy seemed unusually hesitant. "Did you let anyone in while I was looking around?"

"No. And I think we should be very careful." Susan moved closer to the door that had swung closed behind her. She picked up a bottle standing on the bar and slowly, carefully, opened the door.

"Maybe you shouldn't do that. Maybe we should call someone for help. There's a phone."

There were, in fact, four phones. Susan, surprised at Amy's good sense, smiled a little weakly at her. "Good idea." She let the door swing closed again.

Amy had picked up the receiver and was busy punching buttons. Little red lights lit up, but apparently she didn't make her connection. "Damn! Let me . . ." She tried again.

"What . . . ?"

"Wait a second. I've gotten through; it's ringing." Amy waved her off.

Susan waited anxiously and was surprised when Amy hung up without saying anything.

"Nobody home," Amy explained without Susan asking. "Maybe I should try the police station."

"You certainly should!" Susan had assumed that was what she had been doing. "Dial nine one one. Who were you calling before?"

"My house. I thought I could get through to my husband. He wasn't feeling well and he didn't go into the city today, so I thought he might be there."

Susan didn't say anything. What was the point? Valuable time had been lost. There was nothing she could do about it now. Apparently, from Amy's conversation, she had finally gotten through to the police station and was explaining their predicament. It took more time than necessary, as Amy insisted on adding insignificant details and suggestions as to how the person she was speaking to should deal with this situation. By the time Amy had hung up, Susan thought her molars had probably been stripped of their enamel. She stopped grinding and tried to smile. "Are they sending someone?"

"The new police chief is out in his car somewhere nearby. The dispatcher called him on their two-way radio. He's going to hurry right over here." Amy sounded nervous.

No more so than Susan felt. "You didn't tell him to be careful. Whoever is out there could be armed. Brett could be in danger."

Amy, typically, brushed aside concern directed at someone beside herself or her family. "He's the police chief. He's sure to know what to do. Besides, it's his job to protect us. We pay his salary, after all."

Susan, ignoring this, had opened the door slightly and was trying to listen for Brett's arrival—or the intruder's departure. She didn't hear anything. Amy, still in the middle of the room, chewed on a cuticle, a worried expression on her face. Susan wasn't sure how long they remained in these positions. She was so relieved when she heard the front door open and Brett's voice calling out that everything else seemed to vanish.

"Who is that? What's he saying?"

But Susan didn't hang around to answer Amy's questions. She ran out the door toward the stairs. "Brett! Be careful! We heard something. We think someone else may be in the house!"

"Susan? Susan, is that you? Are you all right?"

"Yes, but . . ."

"I heard what you said. Don't worry. I'm not alone. If there's someone here, we'll find him."

Susan was so happy to see Brett that she had to resist running toward him. She felt more than a little foolish at her reaction. She was too old to believe in knights in shining armor. She looked back, hoping Amy hadn't noticed her behavior, but the other woman had moved toward one of the two windows in the room and was apparently peering down at something in the backyard.

"Can you see my man?" Brett asked, appearing in the doorway.

"I see one man," she answered slowly.

"One is all there is. I didn't think it smart to yell that out, just in case we were overheard by anyone. But, to tell the truth, I think we're alone. Did you call the station right after you heard the intruder?"

"No, I . . ." Amy seemed embarrassed, so Susan helped out.

"Amy called home first. She thought someone might be there to help us," she explained.

"But when I didn't get any answer, I called the police station right away," Amy assured him. "I spoke to this really nice woman and told her what was going on here, and she said you were out in your car and she called you."

"And here I am." Brett smiled reassuringly. "But I think enough time has passed for us to assume that anyone who was here has left by now. Why are you two here?" he added.

"Rebecca asked me to pick up a few things for her, and Amy offered to help . . ." Susan began and then, realizing that Brett probably didn't know her neighbor, she introduced them.

"So you offered to help," Brett said to Amy, shaking her hand. "That was very nice of you. Mrs. Henshaw had an unpleasant experience here yesterday. I can certainly understand why she wouldn't want to be alone."

Susan didn't bother to correct Brett's impression of Amy's motives. And Amy eagerly jumped on the bandwagon. "Susan told me about the mugging and, of course, I felt I just couldn't allow her to do this errand alone. I wanted to help Rebecca, too, of course. I had a lot of errands to do today— running a house can be such hard work, and my husband is a lawyer with a large Wall Street practice and doesn't have time to help me at all, I'm afraid—but . . ."

A squeal from the two-way radio Brett held made further conversation impossible.

"No one out here, Chief. I've gone over the grounds twice.

Want me to hang around until you leave? Or stay and guard the place?''

''Thanks, Bob. We're fine here. Just carry on with whatever you were doing before this call came in,'' Brett ordered, and then flipped off the machine. ''Looks like our intruder has gotten away.''

''If there ever was an intruder,'' Amy surprised Susan by saying. ''Maybe we just got carried away. There are probably a lot of big limbs brushing against the house, and that's probably what Susan and I heard. We just thought there was someone outside. After all, two men have died and Susan was mugged here yesterday. You know how we women are. . . .''

''No, how are we?'' Susan angrily interrupted Amy's speculations.

''Well, Susan, even you have to admit that we were pretty scared by one small noise. . . .''

''That's because so many strange things have been going on, not because we're women,'' Susan insisted.

''Maybe, but . . .''

''In fact, it would be a little strange if we weren't a little spooked under the circumstances. . . .''

Just when Susan thought Brett (who was smiling broadly) was going to insert some thoughts of his own, the phone rang.

There was an extension on an ornate papier-mâché table in the hall and, at Brett's nod, Susan, who was closest to the instrument, answered. Her husband was on the other end of the line.

''Jed! Hi. Yes, we're fine. I know we've taken a long time, but it was difficult to find a few things, and we've had one or two interruptions.'' She waited while he explained his reason for calling. ''I don't understand. I was there this morning, and he was completely disinterested in talking to me. Did he mention that?''

Amy and Brett moved off down the hall so they could chat without interrupting Susan's call.

Jed was trying to explain what the beginning of his afternoon had been like. ''Look, I left work right after that meeting this morning, thinking you probably needed help at home with Rebecca and all these network people. . . . Did you say something?''

Susan assured him that he hadn't heard the curses that she was, in fact, muttering, and he continued.

''Anyway, when I got here, Rebecca said that you had gone over to her house to pick up a few things for her.'' (Susan stored away this interesting definition of ''a few things'' but didn't say anything.) ''And since you seem to have forgotten lunch, I went out to the deli to pick up some sandwiches. I don't know when Mr. Grace started calling, but when I returned, that woman . . . Hilda . . . said that he had been trying to get hold of you for a while. They're working hard at some sort of scheme to keep Rebecca's reputation intact, and she seemed a little miffed that she had to take personal messages for you . . .''

''Then she can just move into a hotel. She is, after all, living in our home, Jed. That woman has a lot of nerve and . . .''

''Right.'' Jed interrupted before Susan really got going. ''So, anyway, I called the library, and Charles Grace was absolutely insistent that he speak to you as soon as possible. He was most emphatic. He said it was urgent.''

''I don't suppose he suggested it was a life-and-death situation?'' Susan asked rather sarcastically.

''He didn't say anything about that, but he said it was very important. He wants to see you at three P.M.''

Susan looked at her watch. Three forty-five. ''And what did you tell him?''

''I said I'd try to find you and pass on the message.''

''Well. You did.''

''Are you going to go?''

''I'll see. It depends on what's happening here. We thought we heard a prowler, and the police have been here checking it out, so I really don't know what's going to happen. But if

Charles Grace calls back, at least you can say that you passed on the message.''

"What about Rebecca's things? Apparently she really needs some of them.''

Susan thought of the see-through negligees now packed in the expensive luggage. "I can send them home with Amy if I decide to head downtown.''

"Okay. And, Sue . . .'' He paused, and Susan, assuming he was going to tell her to be careful, started to construct reassuring phrases. "Where do we keep the honey mustard? Rebecca says she can't eat ham on rye without it.''

SEVEN

Susan had no trouble resisting the urge to run out and purchase honey mustard. In fact, she would have had trouble discovering such a need inside herself. She didn't particularly want to speak with Charles Grace either; she was still mad about the snub she had received from him earlier in the day.

On the other hand, he might have some information essential to the case, she reminded herself as she drove to the library. She was wondering what had changed since noon, when he had claimed to be too busy to keep the appointment he had insisted on last night, when she almost ran into a large black Jaguar.

Susan was tired. She felt that it had been a long day, and it was barely four o'clock. That was the only excuse she could make for saying what she had just said to a complete stranger. Only the driver wasn't a complete stranger. The driver turned out to be David Pratt. Happily he was amused by Susan's vocabulary.

"You don't happen to be a longshoreman, do you?" he asked, leaning out his window and grinning at her.

"Sorry about that. It's been a difficult day, and now Charles Grace wants to see me at the library for some obscure reason."

"Me too. And the reason is insurance."

"What?" Susan looked in her rearview mirror to see who was honking so loudly.

"He's worried about the town's insurance policy. He's afraid the family of the man killed at the library is going to sue. At least, I think that's what's worrying him. He called an emergency meeting of the entire library board. I didn't know you were a member, though."

"I'm not. . . ." Susan glanced at the car passing her. The driver was apparently more than slightly irritated by her conversation. "He just called my house and asked to see me."

"You're lucky. You probably won't be tied up all afternoon. In fact, I'd appreciate it if you would be sure to tell Linda that I'm not going to make it to the track when you see her."

Susan glanced at her watch. "I'd forgotten all about running," she admitted, thinking how quickly this glitch had appeared in her plans. "I'm supposed to meet her in fifteen minutes." She glanced over her shoulder into the back of the car. A sweatshirt and sweatpants belonging to her son lay across the seat; he had brought them home from school to be washed, and they hadn't made it to the laundry room yet. A pair of Chrissy's running shoes were on the floor. Susan made her decision. After all, Charles Grace apparently hadn't worried about wasting her time. "Listen," she urged David, "why don't I go to the track and deliver your message to Linda? Then I'll run my mile and head back to the library. You could tell Charles that I'll be there as soon as possible."

"Fine with me. I'd better get going, or I'll be late. See you there—I have a feeling this meeting is going to go on forever. How that man can talk once he gets started." The loud engine of the Jaguar drowned out his words, and Susan stepped on the accelerator and headed toward the track.

There wasn't a whole lot of space in the front seat of her sedan, and she was busy struggling to get her son's sweatpants tied tightly when Linda drove into the parking space beside her. Susan opened the door and pulled on the black running shoes.

"Great-looking new outfit," Linda called over her shoulder, taking long loping strides toward the track.

The two friends had developed a routine that suited them both. Unless they shared a ride to the track, they didn't speak until the end of their respective runs. When they got to the field, Linda liked to stretch for a few minutes, then do some mental exercises that were supposed to get her "psyched" for the task ahead. Susan just tried to reserve her strength. After the run, however, they usually chatted for a few minutes—once Susan had caught her breath. Today, however, they had guests.

"Hey, how long have you been here?" Susan asked, sitting down next to Kathleen Gordon. Bananas was toddling around the grass in the middle of the track, chasing a sparrow.

"Just a few minutes. You're getting better, aren't you? Faster, I mean."

Susan mopped off her forehead. "I don't think so. But I'm going farther each month, and I keep telling myself that's all that matters."

"It is." They both watched as Linda ran by. "You were going to talk with the homeless man," Kathleen began when they weren't likely to be overheard.

"I did," Susan said, and then related that conversation, the suggestions Brett had made, and what had just happened at the Armstrong house.

Kathleen was silent for a few minutes, watching her son and, presumably, thinking over the events of Susan's day. "Has Rebecca given any reason for not returning home?"

"Maybe she would find it painful?" Susan suggested. "After all, Jason was found dead on the front porch. He was probably killed there, in fact."

"Did she see his body?"

"She identified it at the morgue. . . ."

"But did she see his body when it was lying there in front of her home?"

"No. At least I don't think so. I think she came home from here yesterday and found a policeman on her front lawn who told her about it."

"And then what did she do?"

"She drove over to my house." Susan paused. "It still doesn't make a lot of sense, does it? I mean, it's not as though we were friends or anything. I met her at that party and then spoke briefly with her in the library yesterday morning when the first body was found, but it's not as though we really knew each other at all."

"Did she explain?"

"Oh, yes. She said that she knew no one in town, which is probably true. She hasn't been here very long, and everyone said that with her work schedule, we weren't going to be seeing her much anyway."

"But she was at the library yesterday morning."

"And she runs here once in a while. I haven't seen her before, but David Pratt has a crush on her, and he says she has worked out here in the past."

"But she was at two places where you were on the day that her husband was killed—for the first time since she moved to town."

"I know it sounds like that, but I don't see how the three things could be related," Susan protested.

"They might not be," Kathleen said, getting up and taking something out of her son's fist before it went into his mouth. "Or she might have been trying to get in touch with you."

"In the first place, why would she want to be in touch with me? She didn't know that her husband was going to be killed, she didn't know that she was going to need a place to stay. . . ."

"Maybe she knew exactly that."

"What?"

"In the first place, maybe she knew that her husband was going to be killed because she was going to kill him. That's not impossible, is it?"

"I don't know," Susan said slowly. "I don't know where she was when he was killed. I do know that she was running around this track afterward without a care in the world, but I suppose that could just have been an act.''

''Maybe it wasn't. Maybe she killed him, eliminated whatever problem he was causing her, and once he was dead, she really didn't have a care in the world.''

''Maybe . . . Although, if I murdered someone, I think I'd be pretty nervous about it afterward. But what you're saying makes some sense. Maybe the first murdered man was connected with her job in some way.''

''Maybe. But networks are pretty big organizations. They wouldn't necessarily have met. Did she say that she knew him?''

Susan thought for a moment. ''No. I don't think she said anything about him at all.''

''Is she the person who told you his identity?''

''No. In fact, she didn't say anything about him at all yesterday morning in the library. I know the police didn't connect them right away because Brett said he didn't interview her—and he interviewed all the people who were important or who were thought to be possible suspects.''

''But no one could know who those people were right after the murder. Unless someone was standing over the body with a knife in his or her hand.''

''No, the closest person to the body was me, I'm afraid.''

''You do tend to be lucky like that, don't you?'' Kathleen asked, smiling.

''Yes, but I don't call it lucky.''

''But your experience with murders is probably the reason you have this houseguest, don't you think?''

''I . . . I really hadn't thought of it like that,'' Susan answered as Linda, watch in hand, came to a stop in front of them.

''That last mile was slightly under eight. Not bad for an old lady like me, right?''

''Not bad for anybody,'' Kathleen said. ''In fact, it's great. How many miles a day are you doing?''

''A minimum of two. Usually four.''

"Fantastic. How long have you been running?"

"A few months. Same as Susan."

Susan wandered over to where Bananas had seated himself and was happily picking pieces of grass, throwing them over his shoulder and onto the top of his head. "Having fun?" she asked him, squatting down by his side.

The child answered by heaving grass into her face. "I'll take that as a yes." Susan laughed and pulled him into her lap.

Bananas giggled and threw more grass at her. The two of them kept each other amused while his mother and Linda chatted together. Susan was thinking about Kathleen's last statement. She supposed what Kathleen was saying was that Rebecca wanted her to investigate this crime—except that didn't make any sense. As far as she knew, Rebecca believed that the man who confessed had committed the murders. Or did she? Susan really hadn't had a chance to speak with Rebecca about that. She hadn't, in fact, had a chance to speak to her about anything. Rebecca kept her so busy running around playing hostess and doing errands that the two women really hadn't spoken seriously at all. Was that intentional? Was she being distracted for a reason? She was thinking so hard and Bananas was so busy that neither of them noticed that they were no longer alone.

"I wonder where David is?" Linda sat down and tucked a piece of clover behind Bananas's left ear.

Susan started. "I forgot! He's at a meeting of the library board. Charles Grace called it—something about insurance. David asked me to tell you, and I just wasn't thinking. I'm sorry."

"No problem," Linda assured her. "He's doing a lot more for that library than he expected to when he accepted the job."

"Really?"

"Yes. He's not a great worker, you know. It's probably a good thing he inherited all that money because I don't think he's much of a businessman either. I'm surprised Charles

Grace chose him. There are a lot of gung ho accountants in town who would love to muddle around in the library's books and look important.''

''Does this meeting have anything to do with the murders?'' Kathleen asked.

''In an indirect way. I think Charles Grace is afraid that the library is legally responsible for someone being murdered there. Or that there's going to be a lawsuit or something.''

''And the library board is what?'' Kathleen asked.

''Actually, I'm not sure . . .''

''I am,'' Linda broke in, handing Bananas back to his mother. ''It's the governing body of the library. It's all volunteer work, of course. Hancock is pretty much run by volunteers. But they do have the legal right to make decisions that affect the library in a very real way—like the Board of Education and the schools. David is chairman of the board. He has been for the past few months.''

''So they will have some real decisions to make concerning how the news of the murder is handled or what to do if someone does sue.''

''Definitely.'' Linda confirmed Kathleen's suggestion.

''He wanted to see me,'' Susan muttered.

''Who?''

''Charles Grace. It was a little strange, in fact. Last night he came to the house and insisted that I come to the library and talk to him this morning, but when I got there, he was too busy to bother. Then while I was at the Armstrongs' house, he apparently called my home a few times. He told Jed that it was very important that I come to the library right away. Obviously, I didn't think it was all that necessary to rush over there. After all, the last time I did, he didn't even bother to talk with me,'' she answered Linda's raised eyebrows. ''And I thought I'd go on over after I ran,'' she added.

''Bananas and I were on our way to the library,'' Kathleen surprised her by saying. ''He's very fond of books, you know.'' She didn't admit that, primarily, he liked the way they tasted.

"Maybe I'll see you there," Susan said, standing up. "I don't know how long the meeting will last. Probably I'll get there and Charles Grace will be too busy to see me again."

"Well, it's worth a try, isn't it?" Kathleen asked, as they all headed toward their parked cars.

"I suppose so. It's stupid to be so sensitive about being ignored."

"You don't like Charles Grace, do you?" Linda surprised them both by asking.

"I never really thought about it," Kathleen admitted.

"Neither did I, but now that I'm seeing more of him, I don't find much to like either," Susan agreed.

"David says the board has to spend too much time defending him. That if he got along with the public better, they would have a lot less to do."

"That's funny. The other librarians insist that he believes service to the public is the most important part of a librarian's job," Susan said.

"Well, apparently that's not the way he acts. But I don't know much about it all. David is very discreet," she added.

They said good-bye at their cars and then backed out and headed in the same direction.

The town of Hancock must suddenly be full of enthusiastic readers, Susan decided as she entered the parking lot. It was the first time she'd ever had to search for a spot for her car.

The Hancock Public Library prominently displayed an official sign from the office of the Hancock fire inspector notifying the public that no more than three hundred citizens were to inhabit the first floor of the library at any one time. Susan thought it was a good thing no one was counting. The large area was jammed. She headed to the front desk as quickly as the crowd would allow, only to be told by the woman there that Charles Grace was in a board meeting and had left word that he was not to be interrupted for any reason. Susan thanked her for the information, smiled politely, and left, determined to interrupt Charles Grace whether he wanted to be interrupted or not. The man was going to go down in her personal history as having a whole lot of nerve.

The library's meeting rooms shared the downstairs area with the children's section. Susan hadn't had any reason to visit them until now. There were three conference rooms. One had the door closed, and the other two were full of women sitting around. Susan, who had spent a lot of time in meetings of one group or another ever since her children had begun nursery school, didn't get the feeling that either group was official in any respect. That left door number three. She hesitated for a minute, attempting to overcome her reluctance to be rude, and then opened the door to the third and final room. David Pratt was sitting at the head of a large walnut table, smiling. At the other end, the end closest to her and to the door, Charles Grace sat, scowling at her entrance. Susan ignored his expression and walked right in, closing the door behind her.

"Excuse me," Susan offered her apologies to the rest of the group, "but I got a message that Mr. Grace wanted to speak to me—urgently."

"Then you are certainly welcome to join us." This from David.

"I really don't think that's necessary," Charles Grace leapt in. "I can speak to Mrs. Henshaw later."

Did this man think she had nothing to do but wait around for him? "I'm afraid that will be impossible," Susan argued. "I have a lot of things to do. . . ."

"I understand Susan has Rebecca Armstrong staying with her." David offered an explanation for her insistence.

Everyone at the table turned and stared at Susan, possibly admiring the social coup she had pulled in having such a famous guest. Susan wondered if she should offer to sell off bits of her guest-room carpet to the highest bidder. (Somewhere in her dresser drawer she still had a few square inches of hotel carpeting that, possibly, Paul McCartney had walked across in 1965. It had been sold as a part of a fund-raiser for some charity or other.)

"Well, I don't need to see you now," Charles Grace insisted. "In fact, the problem that I had, the one I needed you for, has gone away. So there's really no reason for you to stay here. No reason on earth," he repeated, looking stern.

Susan was rather taken aback, but before she could think of anything to say, David Pratt solved her problem. "Perhaps you would like to stay for a bit? The library board's meetings are open to the public. Although we don't usually draw much of a crowd. Or even a solitary spectator. Maybe you'd like to be our first?"

Susan would have melted from that charming smile if she had been susceptible; briefly she thought about Linda's reaction to David. Then, returning to the subject at hand, she sat down in one of the chairs lining the walls, choosing to ignore the head librarian's frown. "Thank you." She smiled back at David.

"We were trying to decide the question of a lawyer." Charles Grace tried to get everyone's attention back to the subject at hand. "And I believe I was speaking, Mr. Pratt."

Susan listened for a few minutes to the pros and cons of the library hiring its own lawyer versus using the one the city had on retainer. But it didn't take long to see where the question was taking them. In fact, it quickly became apparent that the library had no funds for such an expense, and as the town's lawyer was probably the best one for the job anyway . . . Susan thought that the board members around the table were just letting the librarian blow off some steam. She wondered if this happened often and then, watching the group, decided that it probably did. The board members looked as if they were becoming less and less tolerant as Charles Grace rambled on and on, making a point and then arguing against it. Susan suppressed a yawn. No wonder no one came to these meetings!

Suddenly the door opened to reveal Amy Ellsworth, arms full of papers, purse open, glasses askew. "Sorry I'm late. I had to do some errands for Rebecca Armstrong. She's staying in my neighborhood, you know, and I just don't feel that I can refuse to help in any way possible.'' Her concerned glance fell on Susan, and she had the grace to look embarrassed. ''Of course, most of the work is falling in the lap of this woman. . . .''

''I think we can talk about that later, can't we?'' Charles Grace interrupted impatiently.

Susan worked her lips into what she hoped looked more like a smile than the hangover from recent dental work. Amy beamed at everyone in turn and sat down in the last empty seat at the table.

''I have the notes of our last meeting with me if anyone wants to bother with that now.'' She checked the expressions of her fellow committee members, but Susan noticed a lack of enthusiasm for the suggestion.

''That will be completely unnecessary,'' Charles Grace insisted. ''This is, after all, an unscheduled meeting. I think we can be a little looser than we might be under ordinary circumstances.''

''Good. So who has been taking notes?''

''I'm afraid no one thought of that.'' David broke the news of this oversight as gently as possible. ''But I think the last hour or so can be summed up in a few words. Something like 'a quorum of the board met on the morning of November first to deal with the possible legal problems connected with the death of an unknown man in the library the previous day, etc., etc.' ''

Charles Grace turned pale. ''I can check this all out with you later, of course.''

''Of course.'' Amy, who had been writing furiously in an elegant leather-covered notebook, agreed to his suggestion, and the group got back down to business.

Susan wanted to concentrate on the discussion this time, but it became more and more absurd. Amy's late entrance offered Charles Grace the chance to reiterate all the points he had made previously. And while she took more notes than necessary, the remainder of the members of the committee either became irritable or dozed off. Susan was more than a little bored, and it would be more than a little impolite to get up and leave. If only she had been secretary of the group—then she could have made out a grocery list while pretending to take notes.

The meeting was going on forever. Susan had given up hoping for an interruption when she remembered the instructions of the librarian at the desk, so she was surprised (all right, she'd admit it, she was thrilled) when a loud knock sounded on the door.

She was even more surprised when it turned out that Marion was the intruder. She would have thought that the one person who would never ignore an order from Charles Grace had done just that.

"I certainly hope there is a good reason for this interruption, Marion." Susan didn't have to be looking to know who had spoken.

"That phone call. The one you've been waiting for. I thought you would want to know about it." Marion seemed intimidated by her boss's words. As he meant her to be, Susan thought, getting angry. She didn't know who made her the maddest; Charles Grace for the way he treated her, or Marion Marshall for the way she accepted that treatment.

Charles Grace stood up as his employee scurried from the room. "I suppose we'll have to break this up now. . . ."

"I really must speak with you." Amy Ellsworth was busily gathering up pieces of paper that had fallen from her notebook as she spoke. Extraordinarily long nails hampered her at the task.

"We can correct those minutes lat—"

"About something much more important—and more urgent," she insisted, picking up her notebook and hugging it to her chest. "It's private, and I do have to get home soon," she added as if Charles Grace had asked for some of her time instead of the other way around. "Maybe we could go to your office?'' She walked out of the room, apparently assuming that she would be followed.

Charles Grace glanced around, nodded at his committee members, and left.

''Well, that was rather abrupt.'' Susan leaned across the table to David Pratt. ''I wonder what that phone call is about—he was so insistent that he not be interrupted.''

David laughed and moved closer to her as the rest of the committee either made their ways to the door or spoke casually together. ''You didn't really believe that business with the phone call, did you? That's one of the oldest business ploys in the world,'' he added, seeing the surprised look on Susan's face. ''Charles Grace didn't want the meeting to go on forever—he had, after all, made his point more than a half-dozen times—so he had ordered his secretary to interrupt with news of 'an important call' at a prearranged time. Everyone does it.''

Susan didn't bother to correct David's impression of Marion's job description. ''I guess that's why he didn't rush right out to answer the phone.''

David laughed. ''Yeah. He's not really all that good at big-business tactics, is he? Not that he would have to be in a place like this, I guess.''

''No, this isn't exactly IBM, is it?''

''Sometimes you'd think it is, the way he acts.'' David had lowered his voice before speaking.

''Like what?''

''Everything is a crisis. Take today, for instance. There was no real reason for this meeting. Charlie could have called us all up individually and made his point, but he loves to hear himself talk.''

''I wonder why he called me,'' Susan said. ''I didn't talk to him, but Jed said that he insisted it was urgent. I'm getting a little tired of this,'' she added, then explained what had happened earlier in the day.

''Interesting.''

''Interesting?'' Susan repeated, puzzled. ''Why's that?''

"He's calling meetings, worrying about lawyers, panicking. . . . It almost sounds like he doesn't believe that the man who confessed is the killer. Well, think of it this way," he added, seeing the puzzled look on Susan's face. "If the man who confessed is convicted of the murders, that will be it. No one will have to look any further into all this, the library won't be involved. But if it turns out that he didn't do it, there's going to be a full-scale investigation. Who knows what that will turn up."

"What . . . ?"

"I don't know," he answered the question before she had a chance to ask it. "And I can't imagine what there could be. After all, as we were just saying, this isn't IBM. There's this audit coming up, and no one has bothered to do anything about that. And no one is getting very excited about it if they do care."

Susan didn't say anything, but she didn't agree. Just because the reward looked insignificant didn't mean it wasn't of major importance to someone. David spent his time doing business deals; he might be surprised to discover the type of thing people would have—and have—murdered for. "You don't have any idea what sort of skeletons are hidden in the library's closet then?"

"No. I try to steer clear of that type of stuff—internal personnel matters, petty likes and dislikes, professional jealousies. . . . Charles Grace asked me to join the board and help with the financial affairs of the library. And, let me tell you, with state, federal, and local funding regulations, tax matters, and the outstanding balance on the mortgage of this new building, I don't have a lot of time left over to worry about all the rest."

"Who deals with that? The personnel matters and everything?" Susan persisted.

"Everyone else on the board. You could ask Amy. She usually has her finger in everyone else's pie." He frowned. "She's not necessarily all that reliable, though. She exaggerates. You know?"

"I do. What about the librarians? Do you have much contact with them?"

"None. And, having spent more than a few hours involved with their idea of bookkeeping, I can't say that I want to." He looked at his watch.

"Don't let me keep you," Susan said quickly.

He smiled. "Anything you want to find out about this place financially, just let me know."

"I will," she assured him. They walked upstairs together and separated near the checkout desk. But she had something to do before leaving. Even if Charles Grace didn't say what he had wanted to see her about, he was going to explain exactly why he couldn't find the time to talk when he was the one who kept insisting on it. Susan opened the door and marched up the stairs to Charles Grace's office.

Her entrance might have been more effective if there had been anyone around to see it. As it turned out, she was more surprised than surprising. The room was a mess. Worse, she thought irrelevantly, than her son's bedroom, and that took a lot of doing. What yesterday had been an orderly office now looked as if an invading army had moved through. Papers were strewn everywhere in such disorder that Susan checked to see if one of the windows had been left open. The drawers of file cabinets were ajar and more papers spilled out, books were strewn around, falling open in such a way that their spines were surely cracked or damaged. Susan was quickly losing any illusions she might have had about librarians. She glanced around one more time, turned, and walked back down the steps. There was nothing here for her. Except . . . She looked more closely at the mess on Charles Grace's desk. Just what was her library card doing there?

Susan did what she did next without thinking. The card was hers; she grabbed it, tucked it in the pocket of her jacket, and headed down the steps. And since it was hers, why was she so nervous and relieved that no one seemed to have noticed her presence in the old bell tower? She hurried out of the building and back to her car before looking at the card again. When she double-checked, it was indeed the card identifying her as a patron of the Hancock Public Library. The card was new. All cards had been reissued on the date of the dedication of the new building. The cards displayed each library user's name, address, identification number, and magnetic code strip. They were decorated with an artist's idea of how the new building would look once the recently planted blue spruce trees (thirty-five of them, each over three feet tall, one hundred and seventy-nine dollars apiece, planting extra) towered above the eaves.

Susan placed the card from her pocket on the dashboard of the car and opened her purse. She pulled out her red wallet and glanced through the slots that held her credit and membership cards. It took only a few moments to be sure that this card was indeed hers and not a duplicate. She replaced everything and leaned back against the leather upholstery, staring at the small square of cardboard in front of her and biting her lip.

There were a lot of explanations for this, she reminded herself. Probably she had left her card at the desk after checking out some books, and one of the librarians had put it away to give to her at a future date. Probably Charles Grace was going to return the card when he saw her this afternoon. That made sense and was the most likely explanation. Although there were others.

The most ominous of the others was making Susan very nervous. What if, she asked herself, this card had been in her wallet where it belonged until yesterday afternoon? What if it had been removed from her wallet when her purse was stolen at the Armstrong house? What if her purse had been stolen just so someone had access to her library card? The thought was so absurd that she couldn't continue. But it led to a more likely explanation. Maybe the mugger had gone through her wallet, had accidentally gotten her library card in with his or her own things and then, today, had tried to use it to check out books. Realizing that it wasn't his or her card . . .

It was pointless. Too much speculation and no facts. Susan was startled out of her reverie by a loud knock on her window.

"Hey, open up! We're freezing out here!"

Susan popped a button to release the automatic door lock, and Kathleen and Bananas slid into the front seat. "I forgot his hat, and it's getting colder. His poor little ears are starting to turn red." Kathleen explained her anxiety. Bananas, apparently unaware of any possible damage to his extremities, burped happily, said, "hi yo,"—his standard greeting to all, near and dear and stranger alike—then popped the thumb of one of his mittens into his mouth. His mother patted him fondly. "What do you think about the identity of the first victim? It's something of a surprise, isn't it?"

"Isn't what?"

"That he worked at the same network as Jason and Rebecca . . ."

"I didn't know that! Who was he? What did he do?"

"I don't know his name. He worked in the public relations department."

Susan briefly considered the crowd in her living room for the past twenty-four hours. There were more of them? Just how large was the public relations department? "Who told you all this? And why don't you know his name?"

"One of the librarians . . . a Marion Marshall . . . told me that the victim had been identified by his prints this morning. She didn't remember his name, but she said that he had worked for the network until about a year ago. Then he joined a firm of public relations consultants."

"So he left the network before Jason went on the air?"

"Yes. Although he spent the last few years working very closely with the staff of 'This Morning, Every Morning.' "

"He would know Rebecca."

"Probably."

"But she didn't recognize him yesterday morning."

"Really? Are you sure she saw the body?"

That made Susan pause. "No," she admitted, "I have

no idea at all whether or not she saw the body. Let me think. . . . I don't remember seeing her around when I was in the stacks. In fact, I was pretty upset and not noticing anything, so I don't think I would have seen her if she hadn't spoken to me. And we weren't anywhere near the body then. We were by the refreshment table in that area with all the couches.''

''That's a really nice feature in the design of the new building. Very luxurious,'' Kathleen mused. ''Why did you leave the scene of the murder?'' she asked, returning to the subject.

''Oh, well, the police came, and their men started examining the body, taking pictures, that type of thing, so everyone was asked to gather in one area. There was food left over from the Halloween party in the children's library, and it was brought up and put out on a long table there. That's when Rebecca spoke to me.''

''And you'd never talked with her before?''

''Never. The only other time I'd seen her in person was at that party a few weeks ago. In fact, I haven't watched TV in the morning since I was nursing Chad, and she wasn't on that long ago. I keep thinking the conversation is going to get around to her work, and I'm going to have to say something intelligent and . . .'' She paused. ''And I'm going to have nothing to say—not that we talk that much.''

''Why not? She is living in your house,'' Kathleen said, rearranging her son's weight in her lap as he had fallen asleep.

''She's always surrounded by those men. And I always seem to be out doing errands for her.'' She turned and looked Kathleen straight in the eye. ''Nothing about this setup makes much sense to me,'' Susan said.

''I can't disagree with you,'' Kathleen said. ''But maybe once you've figured out exactly why Rebecca Armstrong wanted to stay with you, you'll understand a little more about what is really going on here.''

EIGHT

SUSAN COULD HAVE RETURNED TO THE LIBRARY AND
tried to speak with Marion Marshall. She should have gone
to the grocery store and shopped for dinner. Instead she drove
home, walked through her front door into her living room
and, ignoring the irritated stares of those working there, she
insisted upon speaking to Rebecca Armstrong. Immediately.
And privately.

"That's an excellent idea. Just let me dash upstairs and
change, then we can talk," Rebecca agreed, rising to her
feet.

Susan was so surprised at this response that she didn't
question the other woman's apparent need to dress for the
interview. "I'll be in the kitchen," she called up the stairs
after her guest, and hurried from the room before anyone
suggested that she turn on the Mr. Coffee. She had expected
to find her kitchen a mess, but, although a quick look revealed empty coffee canisters and a dishwasher full of mugs,
cups, and saucers, every counter had been wiped clean and
everything else put in its place. Susan was wondering what
a glance in her freezer might suggest for dinner when Rebecca reappeared.

"We got takeout from the deli for lunch, and I told everyone to make sure this place was cleaned," she said, pulling
her hair back and tucking it into a terry headband. "I know
we're imposing, but we don't have to trash your home. I'm
afraid our standards get to be pretty low when we're travel-

ing. Why, I've edited pieces on the destruction of the environment in a three-by-five-foot room holding two people and over fifty half-full, gummy, cigarette- and coffee-crusted Styrofoam cups.'' She was heading for the door to the garage as she spoke. ''What's the matter? Did you forget something?'' she turned and asked when it became apparent that Susan wasn't following her.

''I . . .'' Susan realized that Rebecca had changed into shorts and a T-shirt. There were running shoes on her feet.

''I don't think I'll need sweatpants. I usually run in shorts until it's well below freezing,'' Rebecca continued, apparently not recognizing Susan's confusion. ''We are going to the track, aren't we?'' she added impatiently, holding the door for her hostess.

Susan ignored her right knee as it gave a warning throb of pain. ''Sure, I . . . I just wanted to get some tissues,'' she added, yanking at a box in the corner of a cabinet.

''Good idea. I noticed yesterday that the cold weather was making your nose run.''

Susan smiled and followed Rebecca to her car. But Rebecca apparently had no intention of driving. ''My car is fairly recognizable. I thought maybe we could take yours?''

Susan reminded herself that Rebecca could hardly have known that her husband was going to be murdered when she selected such distinctive vanity plates. Together they walked to Susan's Maserati. She would drive slowly; it would give them a chance to talk.

''Did you hear that the first man murdered yesterday—the man found in the library—worked at your network?'' She wasted no time before getting to the subject. ''In the public relations department,'' she added when Rebecca didn't answer.

''Do the police know his name?''

''I suppose so. I haven't spoken to Brett yet. This information came from someone else. All I know right now is that he had worked in the public relations department and then, about a year ago, he left and joined a private consulting firm. He worked on 'This Morning, Every Morning'—at least that's what I was told.''

''Mitch Waterfield.''

''What?''

''Mitchell Waterfield was his name,'' Rebecca repeated quietly, obviously upset.

''You knew him?''

''Of course. He was at the network for years—long before I got there. He worked pretty much exclusively for 'T.M.E.M.' three or four years before he left.''

''So you knew him pretty well?'' Susan glanced over at her passenger in time to see her shrug one shoulder. ''There must be a lot of people working on that show,'' she suggested.

''Oh, there are.'' Rebecca's response was more enthusiastic this time. ''Producers, editors, gofers, cameramen, sound men, makeup men, unit managers . . . Maybe you'd like to come into the city and watch a show go on the air. I'm sure I could arrange something when this is all over.'' She stopped and sighed. ''If I have a job when this is all over.''

''Surely . . .'' Susan began.

''There are no 'surelys' in television.''

''But you must have a contract!'' Susan recalled an article in the *Times* that, while mainly reporting the immense sums on-the-air personalities were paid for what looked like only a few minutes of work, had mentioned contracts more than once.

''Oh, they'll pay me for the next two years, four and a half months. My agent has seen to that. But I may not be able to get a job in any market larger than Sioux City when this is over.'' She was silent a moment. ''My first job was in a town smaller than that. My hair was done by the local hairdresser. My clothing provided by a locally owned department store. They both got full-screen credits. I looked like hell. I had to sneak into the station at night to cut my own demo tape. Otherwise I'd never have gotten out of there.''

" 'Demo tape?' "

"A sampling of my work. In this business you can sit tight and hope a plane crashes in your station parking lot or that someone assassinates a presidential candidate while he's visiting your town, and then maybe, just maybe, the networks will arrive, and, while they're doing body counts or interviewing the grieving widow, someone important will notice you and your work and give you a chance to move up. Or, you give up on fate, make a lot of demo tapes of your shows and send them out to whoever might look at them."

"And that's not easy?"

"It is now that half the people you know own air-quality video cameras, but years ago it wasn't. There were no small privately owned cameras; everything had to be done in a studio with professional equipment. And it had to be done by professionals. I had a friend who worked the night shift running the old movies that used to be put on the air after the network signed off for the night. He used to run duplicates of my tape for me—on borrowed stock, of course."

"And that's how you made it to the network? I thought I had read that you came from Los Angeles?"

"Just the last stop along the way," Rebecca explained. "Also Albuquerque, Denver, and Memphis."

"You worked hard." Even Susan heard her own words as an embarrassing understatement. She continued quickly. "And I don't see why you should have to give up everything you worked for. After all, it certainly wasn't your fault that someone murdered your husband—or anyone else who worked on your show," she added, knowing that wasn't true if Rebecca was the murderer. But if she was, Susan supposed, she would have a job anyway. If her agent was as good as she claimed, Rebecca Armstrong might end up the most highly paid prisoner in American history—at least for two years, four and a half months of her life sentence.

"Actually, there are probably going to be some people who will say that I had an affair with Mitch Waterfield."

It was terrible timing. Susan had just steered her car into

the parking area beside the track. "And did you?" she asked, putting her foot down slowly on the brake pedal.

"No, but he was a very close friend. In TV land, there are lots of people who can't accept any relationship without a prurient twist. Right before I met Jason, I had a hard time breaking up with a man I'd been with for years—Mitch helped me through that. So we spent a lot of time together, and since he wasn't seeing anyone seriously, we didn't worry about what sort of interpretation people put on the relationship. . . . I generally spend about five minutes warming up."

"Huh?" Susan was startled by the change of topic.

"You know—stretching." Rebecca got out of the car.

Susan followed. "I don't do that enough," she admitted. "I'll follow your lead." And we can continue to talk, she added silently.

Rebecca seemed to have the same thought. They walked briskly to the track as she continued her story. "I was, embarrassingly enough, in love with a married man for more years than I enjoy remembering. I suppose it was just the same old story." She stopped by the fence surrounding the track, bent over, and clutched her ankles.

"He promised over and over to leave his wife and family, but he never did," Susan suggested, trying to imitate Rebecca's moves. Apparently Susan's ankles were farther away—or maybe her arms were shorter?

Rebecca seemed surprised by Susan's words. "Not at all. I was with him because he wouldn't leave his wife and family. I didn't want him to commit to me."

"And Mitchell Waterfield helped you during the breakup?"

Rebecca touched her forehead to her knee before answering. "Oh, he helped during the relationship, too. It had to be hidden, of course."

Susan considered out-of-the-way restaurants, back entrances to apartment buildings. She didn't consider introducing her forehead to her legs. "So how did he help?"

"He made sure that my name and pictures were seen with

the men I was publicly dating—there was a politician, a successful businessman or two, and a writer. And that I got lots of interviews in places like *Vanity Fair* and *Vogue*, where I could talk about the virtues of playing the field before settling down to start a family, etc., etc. That truly is the same old stuff.'' She stretched her arms over her head. ''But people still want to read it. Ready to run?''

''Sure. But I'm going to take it slowly. I've been having some trouble with my right knee.''

''I'll push the first three miles, then I'll slow down, and we can chat for the last mile or so.'' Rebecca punched a few buttons on her watch and took off.

Susan trotted behind. Way behind. She needed to think about something besides her poor aching legs. What had Kathleen said? Find out why Rebecca wanted to stay with the Henshaws, and she'd know a lot more about everything? She'd have to approach that subject when they were together again.

If she lived that long. There was an unoccupied bench by the side of the track. Susan couldn't resist. She sat down and rubbed her knee. An injury was a legitimate excuse to rest, wasn't it?

Not, apparently, to Rebecca. ''Run through the pain,'' she called out as she passed by.

Fortunately she ran so quickly that Susan didn't have time to think of an appropriate answer. An appropriate civil answer; a number of less-than-polite responses did come to mind. But, she reminded herself, she had to find out more, had to take advantage of this opportunity. She got up and resumed her slow trot around the track.

''He must have been in town to see me,'' Rebecca called out, passing Susan.

That was an inspiration. Susan tried to catch up with Rebecca, quickly realizing it was a hopeless cause. But there was, after all, more than one way to skin a cat. She slowed down to await the next time Rebecca ''lapped'' her.

''When . . .'' She gasped for enough oxygen to speak.

"When did he tell you he was coming to Hancock?" she managed to call out.

Incredibly Rebecca could run backward almost as well as forward. "He didn't tell me. I had no idea. I was absolutely shocked when I saw him lying there on the floor. . . ."

Rebecca halted suddenly and put out a hand as if to steady herself on some nonexistent nearby object. Susan hurried to her side, afraid that she was feeling faint.

"You did see him!"

Rebecca didn't answer.

"I wondered if you had seen him," Susan continued. Then she realized that Rebecca had not only seen the body, but she had chosen not to help identify it. Susan stared at Rebecca Armstrong.

Rebecca grimaced. "I didn't know what to do. When I saw him lying there . . . I just didn't know what to do," she repeated.

Susan returned to the bench without speaking. Rebecca followed close behind. When they were both seated, Susan wasted no time asking polite questions. "So what did happen yesterday morning? Do you know who killed Mitchell Waterfield?"

"No. I know *I* didn't." She answered the last question first.

"Did you discover his body?"

"No. At least I didn't see him until after you screamed. . . . Maybe I should tell you everything from the beginning."

"Why don't you?"

"I was there to pick up my library card—and to try to explain tactfully to the man who runs the library . . ."

"Charles Grace?"

"Yes. I'd forgotten his name. Anyway, since we moved to town, Mr. Grace had left a half-dozen messages on our answering machine requesting that Jason and I might like the opportunity to get better acquainted with Hancock and its people and contribute to the community. . . ." She pulled a stray lock of hair behind her ear angrily. "If you know him, you must know how damn pedantic he can be. Anyway, he wanted us to get involved in some sort of fund-raising activity for the library."

"And you were going to 'tactfully' turn him down?"

"At least put him off. Jason and I are . . . were . . . Look, I know celebrities can do a lot for charities, but if we did everything everyone asks, we'd have no life of our own. I recognize a responsibility to the community I live in, but Jason and I both wanted time to decide where to get involved. Where we could do the most good."

"Of course. So you went to the circulation desk . . . or to the tower office?"

"The circulation desk. The woman working there found my new library card and gave it to me. We talked for a few minutes. She told me how much she enjoyed 'T.M.E.M.' and I told her how happy we were that we had found a place like Hancock to live in. You know," she ended vaguely.

Susan nodded. She didn't and she did.

"And then you screamed," Rebecca continued. "I turned and ran toward the sound. Half the people in the library did, too, of course. In fact, the librarian I was speaking with almost leapt over the circulation desk—and it's certainly more than waist-high. When I got to the stacks, I was with about twenty other people, but I'm taller than most, and I could see through a gap in the shelves of books. In fact, I could look right into Mitch's face." She faltered for the first time since starting her story.

"You recognized him immediately?"

"Yes. I could see his face clearly from where I stood. Anyway, I could hardly believe it. I hadn't seen Mitch for over a year—we invited him to the wedding, but he wrote that he was going to be on vacation or something that week— and here he was lying on the floor of our new local library with a knife in him. I had no idea what to do. Luckily, in the excitement, no one was paying attention to me, so I just backed away from that part of the building and took some time to think.''

''And?''

''And I decided to shut up, keep what I knew to myself, and see what happened. After all, all I really knew is who he was, and surely the police would find that out easily enough. I didn't think I was doing anything wrong. But, of course, I just wasn't thinking. I should have known that the police would discover Mitch's connection with 'T.M.E.M.' almost as soon as they identified him. There was never any way I was going to stay completely uninvolved in his death.''

''Of course, you didn't know that the same person was going to kill your husband.''

''No, of course not. I . . . I don't think that I could have prevented that by telling the police I knew Mitch, do you?''

''I don't see how.'' Susan tried to reassure her.

''Actually, I didn't get asked very much. The officer who questioned me is a big fan of the show. He did almost all the talking.''

Gushing, Susan suspected. ''What did he ask?''

''Actually he asked if I knew anything about the murder, and, of course, I told him no—because I didn't. Then he told me what he liked about 'T.M.E.M.,' and I thanked him and that was it! I didn't actually lie.''

And you didn't actually tell the truth. But Susan kept that thought, among others, to herself. ''What did you do then?''

''Well, I hung around for as long as possible. I did want to know what was going on. After all, a friend of mine had been murdered. But the police were politely firm about everyone going on about their business, so I left.''

''And?''

''And I did some errands.'' She shrugged. ''You must know how it is when you move into a new house. There have been about a hundred errands each day. I went to that decorator's shop down by the river to see if some pleated shades we're having made had come in, and I went to a framers in the mall on the highway to check out matte colors. I went to

Hancock Hardware to pick up paint chips, I dropped off some dry cleaning, and then I went home and changed to run."

"And, of course, you didn't see your husband at all."

Rebecca frowned, then bit her lip. "I've been thinking about that. I parked behind the house and went in the back door. I left that way, too."

Susan tried to remember the design of the Armstrongs' driveway. "But you had to pass the front of the house, didn't you?"

"Yes, of course."

"And Jason wasn't there? He wasn't sitting on that bench that the trick or treaters found him on?"

"I don't know," Rebecca began slowly. "The porch has so much damn clutter that I'm not sure I'd have noticed if there had been a dead elephant lying across the threshold of the front door. I honestly can't say for sure that he wasn't there!"

Susan digested the information for a minute before asking another question. "Where was Jason supposed to be yesterday? Were you surprised to find that he was at home in the early afternoon?"

Apparently her question surprised Rebecca. "I have no idea. We don't check up on each other. We both had a free day, and we were both doing what we needed to do."

It didn't sound like any newlyweds Susan had known, but Rebecca continued.

"We had reservations at the Four Seasons for dinner with some old friends. Jason eats breakfast but I don't, so I left him a note reminding him of it when I left. He was still sleeping the last time I saw him."

Both women were silent for a moment.

"I guess I should go to the police station and explain all this, shouldn't I?"

"Probably," Susan agreed.

"I need to tell everyone back at your house about it, too," Rebecca added.

"Your public relations people don't know the truth?" Susan was amazed.

"Of course not. Do you think I trust them?"

"But you told Mitch about your affair."

"But Mitch was different. He was a friend," Rebecca explained, getting up. "In television, it's a real good idea not to mistake colleagues for friends." She began to sprint around the track. "Aren't you coming? I have three more miles to go," she called over her shoulder, not interested in whether or not Susan responded.

Susan had no intention of running anymore today. She sat and watched and wondered about a person who would continue to exercise regularly despite the murders of her husband and her friend the previous day. Extremely self-disciplined? Extraordinarily self-possessed? Neurotically self-centered? A combination of all three or something else entirely? For some reason, Susan couldn't even begin to make any judgment about Rebecca's character. Of course, she hadn't known her very long, but still, in the past, Susan had found that tragedy is usually very revealing. But Rebecca never seemed to drop her public persona.

Susan turned her attention to the track. Rebecca, arms up, legs stretched to cover the macadam as quickly and efficiently as possible, looked like an illustration of the ideal woman runner. As she watched, Rebecca was joined by three other women. Suddenly, Rebecca's entire body changed; from confident athlete, she became the stricken widow. Her shoulders dropped, her eyes fell, it looked as if her hair lost some of its sheen. After a few minutes of conversation, Rebecca jogged slowly back. (To the tempo of an unheard funeral march? Susan wondered.)

"There's no way I can do this today. Those women practically accused me of being a heartless bitch. Let's get out of here," Rebecca suggested.

They headed around the track and back to Susan's car. As they passed the other women, Rebecca slumped slightly. Susan didn't know if it was an intentional gesture or not. But when they were almost at the car and, certainly, far enough away not to be heard, Rebecca spoke.

"Damn them! Don't they know that if I stop for a day, if I don't keep at it, someone else will have my job? And I won't let that happen! Jason wouldn't have wanted that," she added, almost as an afterthought.

Susan unlocked the car, and they slid into their seats. As they backed out of the parking space, Rebecca angrily pulled the band out of her hair. "Damn," she repeated. "Do you know anywhere I can rent a treadmill? I guess I'm going to have to avoid the public until after the funeral." She leaned back in the seat and closed her eyes.

"When's that?"

"What?"

"When's the funeral?"

"Oh, they think it should be on Monday. The police need to do an autopsy, and that gives Jason's family time enough to get out here—maybe someone can convince them to stop in the city and get some decent clothing. Poor Jason. He would have hated it if he'd known that his mother was going to be at his funeral—in all her polyester glory."

"His family is from the Midwest?" Susan asked.

"His family is from nowhere Indiana—nineteen fifties style. I've never been able to figure them out. I go on publicity jaunts all over the country. Everyone's chic these days. You can buy decent clothing in Plains, Georgia, for goodness' sake. But Jason's mother and his sisters are practically an illustration for the word hick."

"And his father?" Susan hoped Rebecca wouldn't think she was prying.

"He's dead. He died a few months after Jason was born. So Jason was raised by his mother and three older sisters. How those women managed to produce an intelligent hunk like Jason is beyond me."

"Really?" Susan hoped it was an encouraging word. She had just realized that she knew almost nothing about Jason Armstrong.

"Hmmm." Rebecca's eyes were closed, and she was resting her head on the back of the seat, but she kept talking. "Jason must have been born asserting his independence—it's the only explanation I can think of. When I flew out to visit them, we spent the first night of the visit going through the family albums, and from the beginning he was different from everyone else. The pictures when he was just a toddler show this little blond boy standing as tall as possible in front of four dumpy short women. They all look alike—really—let me tell you, when the girls (they call themselves 'the girls'—can you believe it?) turn gray there will be absolutely no way to tell any of them from their mother. But Jason always stood out.

"He won all the awards in high school and was captain of every sport, and they took a picture of the entire group each time. You can watch him grow up in those albums. Jason just got smarter, stronger, and better-looking. They just faded farther and farther into the background of the pictures."

"They must have been very proud of him," Susan suggested.

"I suppose." Rebecca admitted it was a possibility. "But he outgrew them. He went off to college, and they stayed behind. He changed and grew, and they didn't. By the time he arrived at the network, he had nothing in common with them."

"Did they attend your wedding?"

"Well, we certainly couldn't *not* invite them, could we?"

Susan wondered if that meant Rebecca would have liked to. And Jason?

"But we kept the wedding party very small. Only one attendant each—so Jasmine and Jonquil and Juniperberry or whatever the youngest sister's name is—didn't feel left out for not being asked to be bridesmaids."

How sensitive of you, Susan thought, turning a corner. They were in the process of covering every street in town to get home, but Susan didn't care. She was learning too much to end this trip.

"We did buy them appropriate outfits, however. And I convinced my own hairdresser to make the time to cut and style their hair. Jasper—the youngest girl, I can never remember her name—looked quite nice. The other two were impossible, and his mother wouldn't even think of altering her gray bun. She claims never to have had a haircut. She brags about being able to sit on her hair, it's so long. Only who would want to sit on such a stringy, lank old thing? Ugh." She opened her eyes and glanced at Susan. "You probably think I'm not being very nice, don't you? But they were holding him back. And Jason was very ambitious. He planned on being one of the anchors of the evening news one day— in prime time." She closed her eyes again. "Fortunately, *People* magazine didn't include a picture of that woman in the article they wrote about us—just a tasteful photo of the small farmhouse he grew up in."

"Rebecca . . ." Susan paused a moment, reluctant to ask any questions that might stop her talking. "What about your family? Will they be coming to the funeral?"

"I don't have any family. My parents died when I was in college—an auto accident—and my only brother and I haven't spoken to each other in almost twenty-five years."

Susan noticed that Rebecca didn't appear distressed by this break with her brother. Perhaps he wasn't photogenic either.

"Isn't it taking an awful lot of time to get to your house?"

It was lucky Rebecca had her eyes closed. They had been circling four large blocks for a while now. "Almost there," Susan lied cheerfully, turning the car in the right direction. Time to ask the biggie. "Rebecca, why was it so important for you to stay in my house? After all, you didn't even know . . . Damn!"

"What's wrong?"

"We're being pulled over by one of Hancock's finest." Susan steered her car to the curb and glanced at her passenger. Was Rebecca relieved by the interruption?

Rebecca was smiling. "It's Brett," she said, turning around in her seat. "Isn't this convenient? I'll just tell him about Mitch right now. That will make things so much easier.''

''Isn't he going to think it strange that you didn't admit to knowing Mitch before?''

Rebecca shrugged. ''That officer didn't really ask me if I knew him,'' she insisted. ''I know a little about this type of thing, Susan. The networks get sued all the time. You never answer questions that aren't asked. You never volunteer information.''

It wasn't her problem, Susan decided, opening the car window as Brett walked up. ''Am I getting a ticket?'' she asked sweetly.

''There's no legal minimum speed in Hancock—at least none that I know of'' was the answer. ''I hope I didn't really scare you. I pulled you over because I saw that Mrs. Armstrong was your passenger. I'd like to speak with her—if you don't mind,'' he added to Rebecca. ''I can drive you to wherever you were headed at the same time.''

Rebecca opened the door and got out of the car. ''Anything I can do,'' she assured him. ''Jason would have wanted me to help your investigation.''

As she drove off, Susan, looking in her rearview mirror, saw that Brett was staring at Rebecca's long bare legs as he helped the bereaved widow into his patrol car. She wondered where they were going. She knew where she was going, where anyone with unexpected houseguests went: grocery shopping.

Susan didn't like shopping without a carefully prepared list. She'd found that trying to organize a full meal in her head usually led to a second trip to the grocery store. ''Keep it simple,'' she advised herself, following a grocery cart into the store. She didn't even know how many people were going to be around for dinner. She headed toward produce. Salad was good and simple: three kinds of lettuce, two varieties of mushrooms, cherry tomatoes, maui onions. . . . Surely there was good Danish blue cheese in the refrigerator at home, and there were olive oil and vinegar in the cupboard. Spaghetti was easy and quick, and she had made James Beard's marinara sauce so many times that she had the list of ingredients in her head. Let's see, she needed ground beef, ground pork. . . . She headed for the butcher.

Susan was at the checkout, unloading three loaves of Italian bread and the aluminum foil they would be wrapped in when they were transformed into garlic bread (Chad would like this meal even if no one else did!), when Amy Ellsworth snuck up behind her.

NINE

AMY ELLSWORTH DID NOT, IN FACT, MAKE ANY EFFORT at all to surprise Susan. It was just that when Susan was particularly busy, she worked hard to avoid people like Amy, people with too much time in the day.

"Susan! Do you believe how frantic everyone has been ever since the murders?" she cried loudly, bumping Susan with her grocery cart. "Oh, I'm sorry. Did I . . ."

"I'm fine," Susan insisted, continuing to unload her groceries onto the conveyor belt. "I . . ."

Amy was watching intently. "I'll bet I can guess what you're having for dinner. But don't you think spaghetti made with ground meat is sort of nineteen-fiftyish? Why don't you make a pasta primavera? Just toss some vegetables in oil, a little cream sauce. . . . What could be easier?"

Susan continued to unload her cart, thankful Amy couldn't see her face. "So how was your conversation with Charles Grace?" she asked casually.

"Susan! That was confidential committee business. I can't talk about it with just anyone—or just anyplace." She glanced around the grocery store; the expression on her face suggested that she saw spies everywhere, you just never knew. "Although there is something I would like to speak with you about. I think," she lowered her voice, "that maybe someone is out to get Charles Grace."

"To . . . you mean to kill him?"

"Kill . . . ?" Amy squealed. One or two of the women

around them glanced in their direction; most of the shoppers
were in too much of a hurry to finish, get home, and start
cooking to bother. Amy lowered her voice anyway. "What
are you talking about? You must have murder on the brain.
This is something much more subtle. I suspect a conspiracy."

Susan had to pay for her groceries. The conspiracy theory
would have to wait until later. Except Amy wasn't very good
at waiting. "You won't believe what has been going on,"
she insisted, starting to unload canisters of diet meal mix.
"Chocolate crème, cherry vanilla . . . these women are trying to ruin Charles Grace, and I don't think we should let
them! Strawberry swirl . . . It's going to be difficult to convince people that it was all an accident, a coincidence, of
course, but when you consider most popular novels today, I
don't think it's so unlikely . . . I thought I'd bought banana
mint . . . Oh, there it is!" She swept down upon the missing
container and reached across the cart for Susan's arm. "Don't
leave without me. This is really important!"

"I have to get home and start dinner. Why don't you come
on over, and you can tell me all about it?"

"Excellent idea. Who knows who might be listening in
here?" Amy glared at the woman behind her, getting only a
blank stare in return. "I'll be there as soon as I can," she
called to Susan's retreating back.

Susan waved over her shoulder and continued on her way.

Amy didn't show up while Susan was stirring tomato
sauce, and she didn't show up while Susan was telling Jed
about finding her library card, but Susan wasn't worrying
about Amy. She was too busy worrying about where Chad
was and what he was doing.

She was still worrying later while her husband and guests
were consuming the meal she had prepared. They were five
at dinner. Rebecca had brought Brett home with her. Hilda
Flambay was the only other representative of the network;
the rest of the public relations department had disappeared.
Chrissy had called right before they all sat down and ex-

plained that she had been invited to eat at a friend's house, but everyone was halfway through the meal and Susan still hadn't heard from her son. Jed said not to worry, but Susan did. Chad was not without his faults, but he was very prompt and always called to explain if he was going to be delayed.

So where was he? Susan swirled pasta around her fork and ground her teeth.

"You're not eating."

Susan started. "Excuse me?"

Brett was leaning across the table. "I just noticed that you weren't eating. It's very good, too," he added, glancing at his empty plate.

"Let me get you some more," Susan insisted. "And there's more garlic bread."

"I'd love some. This is the first home-cooked meal I've had in ages—and only the second meal I've managed to get today."

Susan passed the platters and the bread basket and explained her mood. "I'm sorry. I was just wondering where Chad is. He never misses a meal without calling and . . ."

"Oh, you don't have to worry about him," Ms. Flambay insisted. "His coach scheduled an extra soccer practice. He'll be home around eight-thirty."

"I . . . How do you know?" Susan asked.

"He called this afternoon. I was busy talking on the other line and simply forgot about it. Good thing you mentioned him," she said, seeing no need to apologize for her oversight.

"You should have told me about Chad's call earlier. I can't imagine that you thought it wasn't important," Susan said.

"Heavens, he's not a small child," Hilda protested. "I assumed you wouldn't panic over him being a little late for dinner."

"I am not panicked," Susan began, and then gave up. So what if Hilda considered Susan overprotective? Chad was safe and accounted for, and that's all that mattered.

"Well, I certainly don't blame you for worrying." Brett

spoke up while placing two large hunks of garlic bread on the side of his plate. "Some pretty strange things have been going on in the last two days. Murders, muggings, reports of rampant obscenity . . ."

"Sounds like it would make a successful miniseries," Hilda muttered, taking a sip of her wine.

"Obscenity?" Jed asked. "Is Jesse Helms coming to town or something?"

"No, this has to do with the library—I don't know that much about it. There was a pile of messages on my desk about some sort of obscenity at the library. I didn't get a chance to sort through them. I guess I'm a little tired. I probably shouldn't be saying anything about it."

"Does this obscenity charge have anything to do with Jason or Mitch's deaths? Because if it does . . ." Hilda began.

"I don't see how it could," Brett answered, accepting another helping of spaghetti. "It's just a few elderly, conservative women who apparently haven't come to terms with some of the conventions of the modern novel—such as explicit sex."

"And they're planning to burn the books in the town square," Hilda suggested.

"No, but they want the head librarian to resign," Brett answered.

The library again! Susan glanced at Brett. Could this be a coincidence? She knew that Brett didn't feel any more comfortable with coincidences in a murder case than she did. And, of course, this might be the crisis that was apparently obsessing Charles Grace. If, that is, Charles Grace was the type of person who would take the time to worry about his own job during a murder investigation. It didn't take Susan more than a second to decide that he was just that type. Amy Ellsworth was probably in the middle of it, too. This situation had all the ingredients of something Amy would enjoy: prurient interests, character assassination, and censorship.

"Book burning? Censorship?" Rebecca mulled over the words. "Might be an interesting story here," she suggested.

Jed refilled his guests' glasses with wine. Susan took a sip of hers and considered Rebecca. The consummate professional, Susan decided. The day after her husband was murdered, Rebecca was working to maintain her appearance and considering possible story ideas for the show. The suggestion seemed to strike other people in other ways.

"On 'This Morning, Every Morning'?" Amy Ellsworth appeared in the doorway to the room. "You're right! It would be a wonderful story! Significant, topical, important . . . On the other hand, it has to be handled in just the right way. You certainly wouldn't want to damage Charles's career. After all, these women are really just archaic. A lot of very fine literature has graphic sex. Where have these people been all these years? And poor Charles!" Amy pulled a spare chair up to the table between Susan and Brett and sat down. "He says something like this could end his career."

"I don't understand . . ." Susan started.

"Apparently I've been getting calls about it all day," Brett interrupted. "Why don't you tell us all about it—unless you think that would be indiscreet."

"Not really. And a piece on 'T.M.E.M.' "—Susan noticed that Amy had immediately latched onto the show's nickname—"would certainly help Charles."

"We don't do pieces to help people," Hilda spoke up. "News is always a search for the truth. . . ."

"Shut up, Hilda." Rebecca spoke up. "This is a dinner table, not a courtroom; you don't have to do your shtick here."

"Would you like a glass of wine, Amy?" Jed already had a crystal goblet in his hand, anticipating her answer.

"Yes, that would be lovely," she said gratefully, and paused to catch her breath before beginning her story. "Well, let me see. Charles Grace called me early yesterday morning. It was very early—hours before the library opened. I had just gotten out of bed; I hadn't even had time to shower. I hadn't even glanced at the *Times*, and I always manage to read it first thing every morning—even if I only have time to peek at the headlines. I think it's very important to stay up-to-date. . . ."

"So Charles Grace called very early, did he?" Brett nudged her back to the topic at hand.

"Yes, and he said it was urgent that we speak. Naturally I told him I would get to the library as soon as possible."

"He didn't suggest meeting somewhere else?" Susan asked.

"No. In fact, I suggested that we meet at the inn for breakfast—it being so early and everything—but he said he had a full day scheduled and needed to finish some paperwork. Meetings, I guess, and, of course, there was the Halloween party."

"He mentioned the Halloween party?" Brett asked.

"I'm not sure. He did mention Halloween because that reminded me that I hadn't bought my candy yet, and so, of course, I did that, and what with showering, errands, and everything, I turned out to be late, and we didn't get a chance to talk after all."

"You didn't?" Susan was confused.

"Well, you didn't expect us to discuss it with a dead body lying on the floor, did you?" Amy replied. "I just explained that I had numerous errands to run, didn't I?"

"So when did he tell you about this?" Brett asked gently.

"Last night. He called me on the phone. It was very late, and I could see that my husband didn't like it, but I felt it was very important to listen. The poor man was obviously distressed. It was my duty as a library board member and a friend.

"Well, the poor man hemmed and hawed. It was obviously very difficult for him to talk. But I reassured him that he could tell me anything, that I would keep his confidences and do anything I could for him. You know the types of things people say." She looked around the table. Susan wondered if anyone had missed the manner in which Amy kept confidences, but she said nothing, and after a minute Amy continued.

"Well,"—Susan was beginning to wonder if Amy knew how to start a sentence without using that particular word— "it took him the longest time to get the words out, and then he talked around in circles for a few minutes, and I couldn't imagine what he was talking about. And when he did finally explain, I felt so bad for him. . . ."

"What," Rebecca asked rather coldly, "was his problem?"

"He was hurt by his own generosity," Amy said dramatically.

"What happened?" Brett asked calmly. Susan was impressed. She was resisting an urge to pour her wine over Amy's head—barely resisting.

"Well, Charles believes in public service. He knows that it's an old-fashioned idea, but that doesn't make it any less valid. So he expects each librarian, no matter what his or her position, to serve the public. So," she hurried on, glancing at Susan, "when people ask for recommendations of what to read, he helps them. Of course, it is impossible for him to know exactly what the other person is looking for without knowing that person. For instance, when I want to read a good mystery, I want something with English villages and vicars and tea parties; another person might think a good mystery needs a lot of blood and S & M sex stuff. You know?" She looked at Brett.

"Tastes vary," he agreed.

"Yes." Amy nodded vigorously. "So when people come to him, he can only guess at what they might like to read. Also, he's a very busy person. He doesn't have time for a whole lot of reading, so he has to trust the reviewers—and who knows who they might be." She spoke as though she suspected all reviewers of sliding along on their stomachs leaving a trail of slime behind, Susan thought.

"And this problem has something to do with the books he's been recommending to people," Brett suggested.

"His problem is the books he *had* recommended," Amy corrected him. "You see, it seems he suggested some novels with some pretty strange or . . . uh, exotic . . . sex scenes to some of the elderly women in town.''

"How many?''

"What?'' Amy stared at Brett.

"How many times did this happen to how many elderly women?''

"Well, I don't actually know. It couldn't be too many, could it? I do know,'' she continued quickly, perhaps feeling the irritation level in the room beginning to increase, "that the women had come to him the day before, complaining about his suggestions, and that very night the husband of one of the women had called Charles at home demanding that he resign or face public censure—at least, that's how Charles explained it.''

"That's crazy,'' Rebecca commented.

Apparently the story wasn't destined to be on "This Morning, Every Morning,'' Susan thought. "It does seem to be a rather drastic response.''

"Just how explicit were the books?'' Jed asked.

Amy winced. "Very. At least that's what I understand. Charles explained that he hadn't read the books—that he had no idea.

"He wanted to make sure I understood that this wasn't a question of censorship. The library has some very explicit books on the shelf. There are the traditional marriage manuals, of course. And they have some of the more current sex books in the paperback section. There's one on what every mistress should know that has some unusual suggestions about oil of wintergreen, and apricots, and other rather exotic ideas—and no one has objected to that book. It's just that these women expected something different when Charles recommended the book.''

"Apricots?'' Susan wondered if she had been spending too much time in the fiction department.

"It sounds to me as if a few people have been making mountains out of molehills,'' Jed suggested. "Surely it isn't serious enough to bother the chief of police over.''

"I assured Charles that the library board could deal with it, not that we haven't been terribly busy, what with funding the new building and now this dreadful murder. But Charles is so sensitive, and I'm afraid this is hurting him terribly. These women are talking to everyone. He says you wouldn't believe the dreadful phone calls he's been getting lately."

Susan was wondering if the call her daughter overheard had anything to do with this when she heard the front door open. "Chad? Is that you? We're here—in the dining room," she called out.

Her son appeared in the doorway. Mud dripped off the boy from his hair to the tops of his socks. He was shoeless.

"Maybe you would like to take your shower in the basement," his mother suggested. "That's why we had the bathroom added beside the laundry room," she reminded him.

"But I'm starving. The coach let us go late, and lunch at school was disgusting today. Just let me get a snack in the kitchen first."

"Please clean up right away." She knew that Chad had probably consumed his weight in chocolate since last night. She didn't think he would starve.

"You're having garlic bread," the boy cried out, seeing the almost empty basket in the middle of the table.

"There's an untouched loaf in the oven," his mother assured him. "But you really have to clean up first."

"Okay!" Chad bounded from the room, flakes of mud flying up behind him. Susan restrained herself from further comment. Not in front of company, she decided.

The phone rang, and Susan got up to answer it. "The very second they get home, that thing starts," she muttered, smiling at Jed and pushing open the door to the kitchen.

"You don't think this is a police matter, do you?" she heard Amy ask as the door swung closed behind her.

Her daughter was on the other end of the line. "Chrissy, I'm so glad you called. You can answer a question for me."

"Sure, Mom. What do you need?"

"When you overheard Charles Grace talking on the phone

yesterday morning, did he say anything at all about recommending books? Or anything about explicit sexual passages? Or anything like that?''

"Gee, I don't think so." There was a silence while, presumably, the girl thought it over. "I think he said something about being insulted. Something melodramatic like 'How could you think I would do such a thing'—know what I mean?''

"Hmmm. I do." And it all fit together. "Why are you calling, hon?''

"I'm going to be late. Dorian and I are going to work on that report for American history class, but I helped her clean eggs off their porch first.''

"Halloween tricksters?''

"Yeah, and it was gross. They were bombed in the middle of the night, and by the time her parents discovered it this morning, all the eggs had hardened. We hosed it all down and then used long-handled scrub brushes to get it up. Egg yolk would make great glue, if you're ever desperate.''

"I'll remember that," Susan said, shuddering at the thought. "Be home before eleven.''

"I will. Bye.''

"Bye." Susan hung up the receiver and rather absentmindedly looked around the room. She should probably start some decaf brewing and scrounge around for dessert. There was coffee ice cream in the freezer, and she had once heard of a sauce that she wanted to try. . . . But first she had one more call to make. David was home, apparently alone and willing to talk. But he hadn't heard about this other problem with Charles Grace. "It's like I told you, I'm only on the board to worry about financial and business matters. He wouldn't necessarily bother me with something like that unless one of the offended ladies decides to sue—or he resigns. But I can't see either thing happening. That man loves his work. Who wouldn't? What other town would raise so much money for an elegant new library? And his book budget is astounding. Say, you don't think he's intentionally shocking those old ladies, do you?''

''It's probably just an accident. I know that the artwork on a book's cover frequently has little to do with what is in it. He could have handed out books with a picture of two women in crinoline sipping tea from porcelain cups and it could turn out to be the story of twin lesbian hookers—don't laugh. It is possible.''

''I prefer to think he's getting his kicks shocking little old ladies—it makes him seem less like a little old lady himself.'' David added a salutation, and they both hung up.

Susan had been stirring a pot while talking. She now put it on a back burner to keep warm and went to clean off the table.

The group around the table was no longer discussing Charles Grace. Rebecca was talking. As Susan cleared off the table, she realized that Rebecca was speaking of Jason.

''Jason had always wanted to live in a Victorian home. In the town where he grew up, the big white house on Main Street was the status symbol—except that in this day and age it's usually the local funeral parlor. I used to kid him about it when we were first dating. So I wasn't at all surprised when he fell in love with our house.''

''Everyone in town loves that house,'' Amy said. ''I think it reminds everyone of their childhood, don't you?'' she asked Rebecca.

''Frankly, it didn't turn out the way I thought it would. I was imagining something light and airy. My apartment in the city had just been done up in gray and puce, and I wasn't very happy with that—too dark and dreary even if it was very chic. So I was thinking of light prints and lots and lots of white wicker, and maybe some moiré-striped paper on the walls. But the decorator was so insistent on authentic, and Jason was so thrilled with the idea of antiques . . . well, you've seen it. I can't imagine how all those Victorians lived like that—so dark and ornate.'' She shuddered.

"So you're going to have it redone?" Susan asked, heading back to the kitchen with a tray full of dirty dishes.

"Oh no. I really don't care that much about where I live. Besides, *Architectural Digest* is doing a big spread on the house in their February issue. I'd look pretty stupid if I redecorated before the publication date."

Susan wasn't going to argue with that. She left the room as Amy began to reassure Rebecca that her home was wonderful, absolutely wonderful.

Chad was standing in front of the stove, trying to unwrap garlic bread without burning himself on the aluminum foil in which it had been heated. "Halloween is going to make you fat, you know," he said.

Susan pulled the loaf from his hands, removed the wrapping, and gave him a slice. "I thought I was being pretty good about not eating candy this year."

" 'Good'? Look at all those candy wrappers!" He pointed to a large pile of paper next to the stove. "How many Hershey's bars can one person eat?"

"I didn't eat them," she protested. "I melted them to make sauce for coffee ice cream. It's all I could think of for a quick dessert." She removed a half-dozen glass bowls from the cupboard. "Didn't I hear the phone ring while I was talking with Rebecca? Who called?"

"Kathleen. She asked if you were busy, so I told her that you were in the middle of dinner. She said to give her a call when you have a free moment—but that it's not important. Can I take the garlic bread up to my room?"

"No, you may not. I'll fix you a tray, and you may eat in your father's study if you don't want to stay out here. Just let me put out the coffee and dessert." She knew that her son would skip salad and milk if he got his own meal.

"Everyone at school is talking about Mrs. Armstrong staying here."

"What are they saying?" his mother asked, starting to scoop ice cream into the bowls.

"They're all really curious about her—whether she's glamorous, whether she sits around crying over her husband's death—things like that. I just tell the kids that I don't know, that she keeps pretty much to herself. One of the men who was here yesterday made a big deal about not helping rumors get started and stuff like that. Basically he wanted to make sure that Chrissy and I shut up.''

Susan didn't like people ordering around her children, but she tried to hide her anger from her son. ''We don't want to cause problems for Rebecca, but those men are guests, and they really don't have any right to tell you what to do, Chad.''

''I know.'' He stuck his finger in the almost empty ice-cream carton. ''They all think she did it, don't they?''

''What?''

''The network people think she killed her husband.''

''Why on earth would you say that?''

''Why else would they stay here with her?'' He licked off his finger. ''Look at it this way: If Mr. Armstrong had been killed in the middle of the street with lots and lots of witnesses to see who did it, would Mrs. Armstrong have gone to live in a strange home surrounded by people who work with her? It doesn't make much sense, does it?''

''No, it doesn't, does it?'' Susan agreed slowly.

''We were talking about it before practice today, and the only thing we could figure out is that she killed her husband and all these people are here to make sure that no one finds out.''

''Do you need some help out here?'' Jed joined his wife and son. ''I think that ice cream is beginning to melt,'' he added, looking at the tray of desserts.

''Would you take this out? I'm going to get Chad some dinner.''

''Sure.'' He looked at his wife. ''Anything wrong?''

''No. Chad just gave me something to think about, that's all—so I don't want him to starve,'' she added in a less serious voice.

''Then I'll take care of this.'' Jed took the full tray from the counter and left the room.

"Any other thoughts on the subject?" she asked her son as she prepared his dinner.

"I . . . I think I overheard something yesterday that might interest you—but I'm not sure. I was going to tell you last night, but then I thought that maybe I hadn't heard correctly, or maybe I was misinterpreting it, or maybe it wasn't significant. It was probably nothing."

Susan smiled. "Look, it's okay. I promise I won't make a big deal about whatever it is. But you really should tell me the whole story—then maybe we can figure out what is going on. Okay?"

"Okay, just as long as you don't hold me to it. I'm really not completely sure that I heard what I think I did," the boy insisted.

"Why don't you tell me the whole story. Who said what to whom and where it was said," Susan suggested.

"It was yesterday, but I said that, didn't I?" he began nervously.

Susan nodded yes.

"Well, I was trick-or-treating late, remember?"

She nodded again.

"But that snake got to be a real pain in the . . . pain. You know what I mean?"

She did.

"So I came home to drop him off, and I could see through the front window that there were all these people in the living room. So since I didn't want to disturb anybody, I came in through the back door. You know?"

Yes. She knew: He was afraid that if his mother and father spied him, they would tell him that it was late and he shouldn't go back out.

"But there was a man in the kitchen with that woman— the one who spent the night last night."

"Hilda Flambay."

"And I heard them talking."

"They didn't see you?"

"No, the window next to the back door was open a crack.

The house really smelled. Some chili had burned on one of the burners, and someone had probably left open the window to let out the stink. So I heard them while I was standing on the back steps.''

"And you could hear what they were saying to each other?''

"I heard what the woman said. I couldn't even tell you who the man was. I only saw his back, and one business suit looks just like another.''

"And what were they talking about?'' Susan asked patiently.

"Well, that's just it. They were talking and I heard them, but nothing really stood out—you know what I mean?—it was just sort of voices, and then the man said something like do you really think she did it.''

"And?''

"And the woman said yes very seriously, and they both stared at each other for a few minutes. Then he says that she could go to jail for something like that and that wouldn't be good for the show, that it wouldn't do to have a jailbird anchoring the morning news, and she says yes again. So they must have been talking about Mrs. Armstrong because she is the anchor of 'This Morning, Every Morning,' isn't she?''

"I don't see who else they could have been discussing,'' Susan agreed.

"Then the man says that it's a good thing she didn't hit you or anything . . .''

"Hit me?'' Susan was confused; were they talking about the murder or weren't they? The answer came to her as Chad explained.

"They were talking about stealing your purse. They were saying that Mrs. Armstrong stole your purse. I've thought about it, and that's exactly what they were talking about. Then I did something really stupid. I fell against the window and rattled it, and they both jumped like they were scared out of their wits, and I just dropped that damn snake and took off.''

"That's very, very interesting, Chad, and I think you ought to tell Brett."

"I thought of that, but when I saw that Mrs. Armstrong was at the dining room table, I thought I should wait."

"You're right. You need privacy. Why don't you go on into the study, and you can watch TV until I bring your dinner? I'll ask Brett to come in and talk with you as soon as I get a chance to see him alone."

"Okay. I have a test in biology tomorrow, though, so I'll just turn on the stereo."

"Fine." She smiled at her son. "Don't worry about telling Brett. . . ."

"I won't." He shrugged. "Brett's cool," he called over his shoulder, leaving the room.

"That he is." Kathleen agreed, opening the back door and sticking her head into the room. "Someone lose a friend here?" she asked, walking into the kitchen holding a very dirty, slightly damp stuffed snake in her hand.

"That was part of Chad's Halloween costume."

Kathleen looked the thing in its face. "I thought I recognized the poor guy. Chad and his friends came in and entertained Bananas last night. They made faces, danced around, and even gave him some candy corn to play with. He loved it!" She shook the snake. "I think this guy was looking a little better then."

"Trick-or-treating can be pretty rough," Susan commented as she finished fixing Chad's dinner.

"If that's for Chad, I can take it out to him." The women turned around as Brett came in from the dining room. "I've been wanting to talk with him for a few minutes, if you don't mind."

"No. Is something wrong?" Susan asked. "I mean," she added, "something new?"

"No. I just thought I'd like to chat with him, if that's okay. There were a lot of Halloween pranks pulled last night, and most of them were by kids in junior high school. Nothing serious, and I know that Chad is beyond all that now, but since I don't know any other kids in town, I was hoping that Chad might give me some clues to what's going on. I'm not asking him to squeal on his friends; I just hoped for some information—and then, when people call to make complaints, I can assure them that I'm investigating.''

"Actually, Chad has something else that he wants to talk with you about. He's in Jed's study. It's right behind the living room. You probably don't remember where it is?''

He picked up the tray. "I'll find it, don't worry. Hi, nice to see you again,'' he added, nodding to Kathleen as he headed out the door.

Kathleen smiled at his departing back and, pausing to hang the snake over a rack provided for dish towels, sat down at the kitchen table. "So what's for dessert?''

"Have some candy corn—it's in the dish over there on the counter,'' Susan said, removing the snake and tossing it down the basement stairs. "I'm not going to win a prize for being the perfect hostess. I used your idea about melting candy bars for ice-cream topping.''

"And everyone thought it was wonderful, right?''

"I don't know. I haven't made it back into the dining room since the main course.''

"They did. Everyone always does.''

"I can give you some coffee, though. Decaf. And you can tell me why you're here.''

"Bananas fell asleep early, and I was hoping you and I could talk about the murders on the way to the library.''

"The library?''

"You forgot, didn't you?''

"Forgot what?'' Susan started putting the dirty dishes in the dishwasher.

"We were going to go listen to that writer at the library tonight. You know, the woman who writes those travel books is speaking.''

"Oh, no! She wrote the book about the subways in London and that one about ferry trips around northern Europe and Scotland. I'd completely forgotten. I really wanted to hear her speak. I think being a travel writer would be the perfect life, and Jed is anxious to see the Orkney and the Shetland Islands, so I was thinking about starting to plan our vacation.''

''It doesn't start till eight,'' Kathleen glanced at her watch. ''We can still make it.''

''I . . .''

''Charles Grace will be there.''

They exchanged significant looks.

TEN

"AND IN CONCLUSION . . ."

The sigh of relief was almost universal. Members of the audience, gathered in the largest meeting room of the Hancock Public Library, swallowing yawns, surreptitiously stretching tired limbs, and, having tried not to look too bored for the last hour and seven minutes, disguised their feelings with loud applause.

"If Scotland has a tourist bureau, they should seriously think about hiring someone to silence that woman. No one who hears her will ever go there!"

Susan grinned at Kathleen. "I smell coffee. Where . . . ?"

"Back of the room. They always set up the refreshments there. Charles Grace will be nearby. He likes to stand at one end of the table collecting compliments on the program."

"You go to a lot of these evenings, don't you?"

"Ever since Bananas was born. Jerry's usually home in the evening to take care of him, and it is nice to get out regularly."

Susan remembered those days; it could be difficult living with a toddler. She should help out more.

As Kathleen had predicted, Charles Grace was stationed at the end of a long, bountiful table, but whatever compliments he was receiving weren't making him at all happy. He was scowling down at the woman standing before him.

Susan and Kathleen, who had been sitting together at the front of the audience, followed the crowd (for the speech had been very well attended) to the back of the room. There they poured decaf coffee from a large urn and selected slices of pumpkin and apple bread from a lavish display of food. By the time they made their way to Charles Grace, he was smiling benevolently upon his flock of library patrons.

"Interesting speech." Kathleen, being first in line, was first to offer her polite lie.

"She's quite a writer," Charles Grace insisted. "And very generous. She has donated copies of all her own work to us as well as many books that are sent to her—she reviews books for two or three major publications, you know."

"No, I didn't." Susan answered for Kathleen. "She lives in Hancock?"

"Yes. For quite a few years. We've been trying to fit her into our lecture schedule for a while, but, as you can imagine, it's been very difficult. She must travel so much, you know."

"Naturally, we would expect that of a travel writer," Kathleen answered. Susan was no longer paying attention. In fact, she surprised Kathleen by wandering away. She had seen Marion Marshall alone in a corner of the room and was curious to know why she was crying.

However, Marion didn't give her a chance to ask questions, but, forcing a smile onto her face, she started to speak. "She was a wonderful speaker, wasn't she? Charles is so pleased that she could be with us tonight."

Susan planted herself between Marion and the rest of the room before she answered. "So why are you so upset? Is there anything I can do?"

The smile melted. "No." A sniff. "It's just that Charles is so distressed, and I think he blames me."

"For what?"

Marion looked over Susan's shoulder before answering. "This is," she began slowly, "confidential library business."

"I won't run all over town talking about it," Susan promised.

"Of course, you might be able to help us find them," Marion said.

" 'Find them?' " Susan had been thinking about women upset to discover that their cozy read was being interrupted by an imaginary sex act. Who was "them"?

"Books. But not just any books," Marion continued the story. "Very, very expensive books: art books, medical and law books—some of these things cost well over one hundred dollars." She paused.

"You know . . ." Marion said the words slowly. Susan assumed that this idea was a new one. "You know, maybe that man stole them!"

"That man?"

"The homeless man. He's always hanging around. He annoys our patrons, pesters the librarians asking thousands of questions that he cannot possibly use the answers to, he drives Charles crazy by spending all day, every day, in the library since it opened. You know, if he's a murderer, he certainly wouldn't think there was anything wrong with stealing books. . . ."

"I don't think he's a murderer," Susan insisted quietly. "And I don't see why he would steal books."

"For resale!" Marion argued. "There is a fabulous market for some of the books we have on our shelves!"

"How would someone who is homeless find this market?" Susan tried to keep the irritation from her voice, but she did not appreciate every problem the town had being blamed on this one poor man, the one man least able to protect himself.

What Marion did might have been called a snort in anyone less feminine. "Just because he's homeless doesn't mean he's the stupidest man alive. He watches, he listens, he could have picked up that information, believe me."

"Then . . ."

"And if he isn't taking them, we need to find out who is. The library cannot possibly afford to buy these books twice, and Charles is very, very distressed over all this."

"Listen, I heard something else about Charles Grace—about something else that he's probably distressed over," Susan interrupted.

Was it her imagination or was Marion instantly on guard? "You're not talking about the murder this time, are you? Because I had a long talk with Charles this afternoon, and I am now convinced that he had nothing to do with that."

"No. I'm talking about complaints that he is recommending the wrong books to elderly ladies in town."

"What . . . ?" Marion's voice rose an octave, ending in something resembling a screech. "Wherever did you hear that ridiculous story?"

"It's not a ridiculous story—it's not a story. Someone is so serious about it that they've called the police to investigate."

"They have it in for him," Marion insisted, eyes flashing. "Charles is a very successful man, and many people are jealous of him. You shouldn't believe everything you hear."

"These are not idle rumors," Susan answered.

"Maybe it would be better if we spoke to Mr. Grace himself," Kathleen suggested, coming up behind the two women.

"Don't you think he has enough to worry about?" Marion asked. "So much is happening these days! Charles is under terrible pressure—"

"But maybe Susan could help," Kathleen interrupted. "Maybe if she could just speak to him for a few minutes."

"He is a very busy man," Marion explained.

"Just a few minutes," Susan pleaded.

"And think what a relief it would be for him if Susan can help solve just one or two of his problems," Kathleen added.

"Maybe I could arrange for you to have a minute or two." Marion sounded doubtful.

"Now that's an excellent idea," Kathleen said enthusiastically. "I have to hurry home to my family, but Susan . . ."

Susan was not so enthusiastic about returning to her houseguests. She was very anxious to find answers to some of her questions. "I can stay. I'll just find a neighbor to drive me home—or I can give Jed a call."

"Why don't you wait up in Charles's office? I'll make some excuse and bring him to you."

Well, at least Marion had cheered up, Susan thought, agreeing to the plan. "But I think I'll get some more coffee and cake," she insisted, really wanting a minute or two with Kathleen.

"Good idea." Marion positively bubbled. "When you're done, go on up. I'll make sure Charles talks to you just as soon as the last guest leaves."

"So what do you think?" Susan asked when Marion had skipped off on her errand.

"I think it's about time. This mystery started in this building; it's possible that there are a few answers around here, too."

"But do you think I should ask him about the books he recommended or just—"

"Ask him about anything and everything. Who knows what might lead where. . . . Are you really going to eat all that?"

Susan was filling a large plate with sweet breads, coffee cakes, muffins, and a large bunch of purple grapes. "I was worried about Chad at dinnertime and didn't eat very much. He's fine," she added, seeing the concerned look on her friend's face. "He just got home a little late."

"Oh. I wonder how I'll stand it when Bananas is going out on his own?"

"You have a long time before then," Susan assured her, picking up the last blueberry muffin. "Are you leaving?"

"Hmmm." She pulled a bulky green heather wool sweater over her head. "Call me after you've spoken with him. I'll be up late. Bananas is cutting his two-year molars. The doctor says he's never seen them come in so early, but the poor little guy is in a lot of pain."

"Don't worry. He'll be just fine once they break through. I'll call the moment I get home."

"Fabulous. Don't forget. I'll be waiting."

Susan and Kathleen walked together to the bottom of the stairway to Charles Grace's office. "Do you think he'd mind if I went up?" Susan asked, discovering that the door was unlocked. "Although I suppose I could always wait for him here . . ."

"Go on up. That's what Marion thought you should do, isn't it? We both know that she wouldn't do anything to upset her precious Charles. You can sit down comfortably and eat your snack. Who knows how long you might have to wait? Just be sure to call me. I'm dying to know what's going on with that man."

"Me, too." Susan said her good-byes and started up the stairs, balancing her full plate and taking care that coffee didn't slosh out of her cup.

She needn't have bothered. The light above the librarian's desk was turned on, and his heavy trench coat hung over the chair. Susan was so surprised to see the light, she spilled her snack. Luckily there was a roll of paper towels sitting under a bookshelf, and Susan hurried to sop up the mess. She didn't want her meeting to begin with an explanation of why she was crawling around on the floor.

She shouldn't have worried. There was plenty of time. The floor got mopped, the paper towels were replaced, and Susan was seated in the spare chair in less than ten minutes. She put her plate down on the corner of a file cabinet, selected a slice of pumpkin pecan bread, and started to eat. In the dim light, the room looked more interesting than it had the day before. The green-shaded light's reflection was repeated in the windows around the room. There were more books than Susan remembered. Books towered on tops of cabinets. Three large piles covered most of the surface on the desk. An even larger pile was tumbling over on the floor. Susan was afraid that her awkwardness had caused that one to unbalance, and she brushed the crumbs from her hands and began straightening it.

The books were new, and Susan couldn't resist peeking at

them. Apparently the ones placed on the floor had been cho-sen by size: they all looked like they were headed for the "oversize" shelf behind the fiction department. A fabulous book on Chagall sat on a world atlas, and a volume on nineteenth-century Russian folk art was sliding off a collec-tion of copies of all the baseball cards ever printed. The tapes had not yet been glued on the spines of these books, but it was obvious that their placement had nothing to do with either the Library of Congress or Mr. Dewey. Susan picked up a tome on Fabergé jewelry and continued to snack while slowly leafing through the pages. She never expected to fall asleep.

Susan awoke with a start, and the large book in her lap fell to the floor. Or had the sound of the book hitting caused her to wake up? She was disoriented, feeling that something was wrong or strange and not knowing what it was. The gentle hum from below had stopped, and she knew that she must be alone in the building. Glancing out the windows, she realized that there was no traffic on the roads. She looked at her watch. It was almost midnight. Well, once again Charles Grace had escaped talking with her. She was begin-ning to believe it wasn't accidental. There was one final muffin on the plate, and she picked it up and tasted it without thinking. Her family must be worried about her. She reached for the phone. It was dead. Or maybe it went through a switchboard that was turned off in the evening, she reminded herself. The thing to do was go downstairs and see if the phones there were working.

It was a good idea—if only someone hadn't locked the door at the bottom of the stairway. Susan just stared at the polished wood. Now what was she going to do? She walked slowly up the stairway, reminding herself that there was no reason to panic. The library opened in less than nine hours, and certainly the staff came to work earlier than that. Be-sides, her family would be missing her. They would come look for her. She sat down and looked out the windows. It was a long drop to the ground, and she certainly was in no position to try getting out that way. The windows didn't open, and if she broke one, she might freeze to death before anyone heard her. She wondered if someone would notice that the desk light was on before remembering that the bell tower was always lit up at night. She had always thought the sight most charming, not knowing it was something as prosaic as a desk light. Of course, if it was always on . . .

She reached over and turned the light off. Maybe someone would notice that!

Of course, now she was going to have to sit here in the dark. Her nap had left her wide-awake, and there was certainly a fair amount of reading material around. She turned the light back on and put out her hand for a book. She might as well get educated. Or maybe not, she reconsidered, spying a new mystery novel that she had been anxious to read.

Charles Grace's office must be very soundproof, she later decided. Or else she would have heard the car drive up and Brett Fortesque enter the library. She did hear the key turn in the lock, and, hurrying over to look down the stairway, Susan saw the door open, revealing the chief of police.

"Brett! Someone locked me in! I can't tell you how glad I am to see you. And why," she added a bit more soberly, "why are you pointing a gun at me?"

"I didn't know who you were. Didn't it ever occur to you to wonder who was on the other side of that door? Two men were murdered, and you were mugged, after all. . . ."

"I didn't think," Susan admitted slowly.

"Well, you were smart to turn the light on and off as a sign that you were up here," he consoled her.

Susan opened her mouth and then shut it again. Why admit it was a happy accident that he had spied her indecision? "I'd like to get home" was all she said.

"Good idea . . ."

"Did Jed call to tell you that I was missing?"

"Not that I know of—and I think I would have heard about it."

"That's funny. Kathleen should have been worried about me, too. I was going to call her after I got home."

"Maybe she just thought you were too tired."

"No, it was important. She should have known that I would call."

"Of course, you couldn't call from here."

"How did you know that?" Susan asked, surprised.

"The line was cut outside. I noticed it when I came in—it wasn't hard to see; the raw end is hanging down over the front door. Let me look around for a few minutes before I get you home," he suggested.

"Fine. You don't mind if I use the ladies' room while you look, do you?"

He chuckled. "Not at all. I have some questions to ask you, too. Like why you didn't yell that you were locked in while there were people still in the building?"

Susan hurried toward the rest rooms. "I fell asleep," she called back over her shoulder, thinking that she heard him chuckle again at her answer.

When Susan returned to the office, she discovered Brett standing in the middle of the small room, staring into the distance.

He turned as she reached the top of the steps. "Why were you up here?"

"I was waiting to speak with Charles Grace."

"This is his office?"

"Yes."

"I thought so. Why did you want to talk with him so late at night?"

"There was a speaker this evening—one of the library's regularly scheduled programs—and I thought it might be a good time to see him. That's why Kathleen and I left right after dinner."

"About the murder? You wanted to ask him questions about the murder?"

"And the dirty books and the stolen books."

"What stolen books?"

"Actually that just came up tonight," Susan said, and then

explained about her conversation with Marion a few hours ago.

"And you think all this is connected in some way?"

"I don't know what to think. I only know that a man was killed here yesterday, a homeless man who spends most of his days here confessed to the crime, and a group of senior citizens is upset because they see this place as a hotbed of pornography. The only thing going on here that seems natural is the stolen books—libraries always have problems with stolen books. Now someone locks me in the bell tower and cuts the phone wires! You think I'm getting overexcited by connecting all this to the library?"

"Not at all. I think speaking with Mr. Grace is an excellent idea—and it should be done immediately."

"Good. But I should let my family know I'm okay first."

Brett gave her a stern look. "I was planning on dropping you off at home before going to find Mr. Grace."

"Oh, Brett, you can't! After all, I was the one locked up here all this time."

"And that means you can ask him questions that I can't?"

"Brett, please. You asked me to help you solve these murders. Can't I at least . . ." She thought quickly. "Can't I sit in on you questioning someone—I know I'd learn a lot and . . ."

"Look, you can come with me. You can even ask questions. Just don't try to convince me that you're hanging on to my every word. I know you better than that."

Susan smiled, satisfied. "So let's find a phone, and I'll give Jed a call."

"Why don't we just stop at your house? It's on the way to Grace's house."

"You know where he lives!"

"Sure . . ."

"You think he's the murderer, and you've been having him watched!"

"I drove around late last night and checked out the addresses of everyone involved in the case. I'm new here, and

I didn't want to make a fool of myself by not knowing my way around, Susan.''

"Do you . . . ?"

"I've listened to you. I've listened to Chad. I've listened to about thirty people who were at the library on Halloween. And I still have no idea who the murderer is—unless we decide to accept John Doe's confession.''

"But . . ."

"I didn't say we were going to accept it; I just said that it was a possibility,'' Brett reminded her. "You sure have a lot of energy. I guess that nap you took helped.''

"You must be exhausted.''

"I've felt better,'' he admitted. "Let's head for your house, and you can make coffee while I spend some time on your phone.''

"Great.'' Susan grabbed her sweater off the chair. "You know,'' she added, looking at the coat underneath, "it's a little strange that Charles Grace didn't wear his coat home in this cold weather, isn't it?''

"Maybe that's the first thing we should ask him. Let's get going. I'm beginning to wonder exactly why no one in your family noticed that you were missing.''

Susan followed him down the stairs and out of the building, pausing only while he locked all the doors behind them. "Do you think it will take a long time for the phone lines to be reconnected?''

Brett opened the door to his patrol car for her while answering. "I'm going to call one of my men to look at it before there's any fixing done. After that, it depends on the phone company.'' He got in and started the car.

"They'll probably be able to make calls by Christmas, don't you think?'' Susan asked.

"If they're lucky.''

Brett used his two-way radio to check in with the station, sending orders for men to go to the library and photograph the phone line as well as check the grounds. "Not that I know what they're to look for—or what they might find—but

you never know,'' he added to Susan after he had finished
his business. ''Now we'll go to your house.''

''And get you that coffee,'' she suggested.

''I need it,'' he agreed, pulling into the drive.

The house was dark, and Susan wondered again at her
family's acceptance of her absence. Where did they think she
had been? She pulled keys from her purse and opened the
front door. Why had no one left the hall light on? Weren't
they expecting her to return before daylight? ''You don't mind
calling from the kitchen, do you? I can make the coffee there,
and then I'd like to go upstairs and let Jed know that I'm
home.''

''Why don't you go on up? I can make myself coffee while
I call. Go ahead,'' he urged when she didn't move. ''I'm not
completely helpless in the kitchen, you know.''

Susan left him and headed toward her bedroom. She had
noticed that the door to Jed's study was closed and assumed
that Hilda Flambay was still in residence. So Rebecca was
probably still here, too. She walked slowly up the stairs,
glancing into the living room. Luckily tomorrow was her
cleaning woman's regular day. She walked down the hall to
her bedroom. The light by Jed's side of the bed was on, and
the television in the corner was trying to sell sunglasses to
her sleeping husband.

She smiled and walked across the room to turn off the TV.
''Wha—?''

''Jed, it's only me.'' Susan hurried to his side. ''You fell
asleep watching TV. I was just turning it off. It's almost two
A.M.''

Jed was beginning to wake up. He rolled over on his side
and propped himself up on one elbow. ''I'm glad you're
home. I was worried about you. You must be exhausted.''

''I am, but Brett and I have something to do. . . .''

That woke him up. ''Susan, doesn't that man realize that
you have a family to care for and a life besides investigating
murders?''

''You know, Brett did rescue me tonight. If he hadn't seen

the light and checked out the tower, I might still be locked in the library.''

"What?" Jed rubbed his eyes and brushed his hair off his forehead.

"Why didn't you worry when I didn't come home?" Susan asked, irritated that he could be so casual about a missing wife, especially when the missing wife was his.

"Worry about you? Why should I worry about you? Kathleen called and said you and our illustrious new police chief were out investigating or something. Why should I worry? You had police protection, didn't you?"

"Kathleen called and said what? Wait a second," she added, lowering her voice. After all, her children were asleep right across the hall. "Why don't you tell me this story right from the beginning?"

"It isn't a story, and there really isn't much to tell. Kathleen called tonight and said that you were out with Brett Fortesque and would be home very late, so I should go ahead and go to sleep. I did plan on waiting up for you, but . . ."

"I don't understand. Didn't you ask her any questions? Weren't you curious about what I was doing?"

"Yes, I was curious. But I didn't talk to her. Hilda took the call and relayed the message. I . . ."

"Someone locked me in the library tower tonight and cut the phone lines."

"I really wanted to wait up for you and find out what— You were what?" Jed sat up and grabbed his wife. "Exactly what happened to you?"

"I'm okay. No one hurt me. I fell asleep, and someone locked me in the library tower. Look, Brett is making coffee downstairs. Do you mind if I go down and have a cup, and you can tell me what happened here and I'll tell you what happened there?"

"Sure. Let me get a robe. But should you be drinking coffee? Shouldn't you be getting some sleep?" he asked, getting up.

Susan handed him a large green terry-cloth robe. "We're

going to find Charles Grace. Then, I promise, I'll come home and go to sleep. I'm exhausted, but Brett thinks we should talk with him tonight. After all, I was going to meet him in his office when I got locked in. If he had been there like he was supposed to, none of this would have happened.''

''I think I'll have some coffee, too, and then maybe you'd better start from the beginning.''

They headed to the kitchen together.

''I didn't know which mugs you would want me to use, but these were in the sink, so I just washed them out,'' Brett explained, handing Susan a steaming cup.

''The place is kind of messy,'' Jed admitted. ''I tried to clean after dinner, but Rebecca was making tea late and Hilda . . .''

''Don't worry about it,'' Susan insisted, sitting down at the table and flicking some crumbs onto the floor. ''Brett, Jed says that Kathleen called tonight with some sort of story about you and me being out late investigating something. You didn't tell her anything like that, did you?''

''Of course not. I haven't spoken to her since I left here this evening, and I wouldn't have said anything like that anyway.'' He turned to Jed. ''What exactly did she say?''

''I'm not sure. Hilda—the woman from the network who is staying here with Rebecca—took the call. I was helping Chad with his algebra up in his room, and I didn't hear the phone ring. When I came downstairs, she said that Kathleen Gordon had called a few minutes ago with a message from Susan. . . .''

''What time was this?'' Brett asked.

''About eleven, I'd guess.''

''Chad was working on algebra until eleven o'clock?'' his mother asked.

''Yes. Seems that new teacher he has this year really has him worried.''

''She must,'' Susan agreed.

''Could we get on with this?'' Brett asked gently.

''Sorry. Well, by the time I got the message, I thought it

was a little late to call Kathleen back, although I did think the explanation was kind of brief.

"According to Hilda, Kathleen said that Susan had tried to call here, but the line was busy, so she had called there and asked Kathleen to get a message through. And apparently the only message was that you and Susan had one more thing to investigate together and then Susan would be home."

"That's all?"

"That's all," Jed insisted. "At least that's all I got. Hilda is asleep, but maybe we could wake her and check."

"Hilda is not asleep. Hilda has a very difficult time sleeping with this commotion going on." Hilda Flambay stood in the doorway. A scarlet kimono covered her nightgown. Curlers stuck out of her hair. Gigantic green glasses were perched crookedly on her nose. "Is that decaf?"

"No, but there is some instant Sanka around here somewhere."

"I'll just have some seltzer." She opened the refrigerator.

Well, she had told everyone to feel right at home, Susan reminded herself.

Brett had better things to worry about. "We were just talking about the call you got tonight. . . . The one from Kathleen Gordon. About Susan being out late." He prodded her memory.

"Oh, it wasn't all that big a deal." She shrugged. "Did I get the message wrong?"

"You certainly got something wrong. My wife has been—" Jed began angrily.

"I think Kathleen may have made a mistake. We were just wondering if you could remember exactly what she said," Susan interrupted. Hilda Flambay had no reason to know anything more.

"She said hello and that she had a message from you to Jed. . . ."

"I thought you said that she explained that Susan had been trying to get through, but the lines were busy so she had to call Kathleen's house," Jed reminded her.

"Oh, that's right." She smiled at Brett. "This has been a very tiring few days."

"I'm sure it has." He returned her smile.

Susan ground her teeth.

"Maybe if you explain right from the beginning," Brett suggested.

"Okay." In response to some female instinct, Hilda removed her curlers as she talked. "I picked up the phone. I was expecting a call from the city, so I assumed it was for me. But, needless to say, it wasn't. There was a woman on the other end of the line. She said she was Kathleen Gordon and could I please give a message to Jed. Well, naturally, I agreed. . . ."

"She didn't ask to speak to him?" Brett interrupted.

"No, she just wanted me to give him the message." Curlers out, she fluffed up her bangs. "So, anyway, I said I would, and I got a pen and paper and wrote it down. All she said was that Susan was doing some late-night investigating with Brett Fortesque and that she would be home very late and no one should worry about her. That's all. When you came downstairs, I relayed the message to you."

"You didn't call Kathleen back?" Brett asked Jed.

"Kathleen didn't explain that I had stayed at the library and she had gone home without me?" Susan was completely puzzled.

"No. I assumed the message was real," Jed explained. "Besides, it was late. Kathleen and Jerry need their sleep. That little boy of theirs is a real handful."

"There was nothing in the message about the library," Hilda insisted. "Nothing."

Susan and Brett looked at each other.

"It doesn't make sense to me," she said.

Brett reached for the phone. "What's Kathleen's number? I'm afraid we're going to have to wake her up."

"It's on one of the auto-dial buttons. Gordon," Susan elaborated.

Brett pressed the correct button. The phone was answered

on the first ring. "Hello? Kathleen? It's Brett Fortesque. I'm over at the Henshaws. Sorry to wake you up, but we have a problem here. . . . No, no. Everyone is fine. We're just checking about that phone call you made here tonight. . . . The one from Susan . . . She didn't? That's very interesting. I'm sorry we bothered you. . . . Yes, she's right here." He handed the receiver to Susan.

"Hi, Kath—Yes . . . Well, it's a long story, but I got locked in the library tower. . . . The phone cord was cut. . . . No, he never did, in fact. . . . Listen, give me a call early tomorrow, and I'll tell you the whole story, okay? Bye." She hung up and turned to Brett. "She got a call from someone who said they had a message from me. . . . She just passed it along."

"So it was all a hoax," Jed said. He put his hand on his wife's shoulder. "You might have been in serious danger, Sue."

"I don't think so. I fell asleep. Anyone could have snuck up behind me and hit me on the head or, I suppose, stuck another of those knives in me, but they didn't." She smiled at her husband. "I don't think you have to worry."

"I wonder if Kathleen can identify the voice," Brett said slowly.

"We should have asked. I'd love to know who locked me in that tower."

Hilda looked at Susan sharply. She had forgotten that this was the first time the network woman had heard the story.

Brett nodded. "It's likely to be the same person who called. He or she didn't want anyone to come looking for you."

"Is there any way to track this down? Can we find out who called Kathleen?" Jed asked.

"No. We can't track down calls after they're made," Brett answered. "We could get a court order for a tap on the line now, but I can't imagine that would do much good. We'll have to talk with Kathleen first thing tomorrow."

"What I don't understand is why someone wanted me

locked in the bell tower. What's going on tonight that I'm not supposed to be around for?" Susan asked.

"Excellent question," Brett said. "A really excellent question."

ELEVEN

"This is where he lives?" Susan peered out the window into the darkness.

"Yup. I haven't been inside, but this is the address. I double-checked last night. It's something, isn't it?" Brett opened his car door and got out. Susan followed suit.

They were standing in front of a gigantic stone home. Almost more a castle than a home, Susan thought. There was definitely a turret or two poking into the sky from the roof of the dark, dreary structure.

"Hancock must pay its librarians better than its policemen."

"I doubt it. Maybe . . ." She searched for an answer. "Maybe he inherited it."

"It does look a little like something one's elderly aunt might leave. Do you think it's full of cats?"

"Cats?" They walked up the crazy paved walk.

"You know—elderly ladies, cats. Don't mind me; it's late and I'm babbling. Well, maybe we'll get some answers now." He lifted the polished brass owl that served as a door knocker and dropped it with a bang. "I hope he hears this."

"I think the dead in the cemetery on the other side of town heard that." Susan wrapped her coat more closely around her neck and looked up as a light went on in one of the rooms on the second floor. "He must be—"

"What?"

A grumpy voice, apparently coming from the owl's beak, asked them what they wanted.

"I'm Police Chief Fortesque, Mr. Grace. I'm sorry to bother you. . . ."

"Press the button. Press the button," the owl barked.

"Wha . . . ?"

"I think it's some sort of intercom system. You have to press that button right under the owl to be heard. Maybe." She ended uncertainly.

Brett did as Susan suggested, and after Brett had identified himself a few times and apologized many more, Charles Grace agreed to see them. A loud buzzer sounded, the door unlocked, and they entered a huge, dark hallway.

"This place is a little strange, isn't it?" Susan had no idea why she was whispering.

"More than a little," Brett answered, staring. They were standing in a circular hallway at least two stories high. They could not see the walls, as some sort of screen had been installed from the floor to the ceiling, and tropical trees formed a lush hedge around them. As they waited, something moved near Susan's feet.

"It's alive. There's something alive in there!" She grabbed Brett's arm.

"Don't be silly. Of course there's something alive in there. What do you think a cage is supposed to hold?" The voice came from the middle of what appeared to be a banana tree.

"I . . ." Susan didn't know what to say.

"Mr. Grace? I'm afraid we can't see you," Brett called out to the sound.

At the sound of his shout, two things happened simultaneously. A racket of bird calls, squawks, and fluttering wings filled the air, and a light went on, illuminating the place where they stood.

"Why . . . We're in the middle of an aviary. . . ."

"Amazing!" was Brett's only comment.

"I've heard of this place," Susan said slowly. "This is Mrs. Grayson's house, isn't it?" She peered up into the jungle, where the voice had come from. "But she's on a trip or something, isn't she? I think someone was talking about it at the club in the beginning of the summer. . . ."

"Yes, this is Mrs. Grayson's home, and she has gone on a tour of the Amazon and other parts of South America for nineteen months. She asked me to house-sit for her, and I agreed." Charles Grace stood in front of them. Apparently there was a winding stairway that he had used to get from where he slept to the door between the walls and the aviary. The birds, dozens of them, chattered out the greeting that he apparently thought unnecessary. Charles looked around, annoyed. "Damn birds! They're going to drive me mad. Come in here, and we can talk."

A tunnel through the cage led to a heavy wood door, and they followed him into it. Susan looked up and noticed that the roof of the tunnel was solid metal instead of wire; they were in no danger of being baptized by the birds above. Charles opened the door and proceeded before them into a traditional wood-paneled library.

"This is the only room in the damn house that is cage-free. Here we can hear ourselves talk." He sat down in a large leather wing chair and motioned for them to do likewise.

"This is a fabulous house," Brett said, taking the seat closest to the other man. "Susan said something about it belonging to a Mrs. Grayson. . . ."

"Yes. The famous Mrs. Amelia Grayson. The last of the Victorian crazy ladies. This is her home, her family home, in fact; she grew up here, as she would tell you herself if she were present. Mr. Grayson moved in the night they were married. She couldn't, you see, be expected to leave her birds."

"But she is not here now?"

"No, all her life she has collected and bred tropical birds. Now she has gotten her long-awaited chance to see some of the animals she loves in the wild. Mr. Grayson died a few years ago, and once his affairs were in order, she hired a guide through a contact at the Audubon Society and left. After, that is, she found me to house-sit for her.'' He grimaced. ''I had been looking for a place to live. The two-year lease on the apartment I had been renting had expired, and I was desperate. The building was tacky, noisy, and totally without class. I found it very difficult to be comfortable there. But everything suitable was so . . . so expensive.''

''How did you find this?'' Brett asked.

''Good fortune. I was at the library helping some of our patrons, and Mrs. Grayson came up to me and introduced herself. She asked me to recommend something for her to read—to get ready for the trip she is now on.'' (Susan wondered if there were any juicy parts in guidebooks to the Amazon.) ''I, naturally, assisted her to the very best of my ability. It took a fair amount of research, and we spent a few hours together in interesting conversation. She happened to mention that she was looking for someone to stay in her house while she was away, and I happened to mention that I was looking for a new domicile. And . . .'' He paused to smile at his good fortune. ''Here I am.''

''You're taking care of the birds?''

''Heavens, no! Never! These things are dirty creatures. Always molting and dropping . . . uh, stuff.'' He glanced at Susan and seemed to be considering her delicate ears as he chose his last word. ''Taking care of these cages is a full-time job. They are built into the walls of most rooms in the house. There are over six hundred birds here and miles of aviaries. Two men come in each day and . . . uh, clean things and feed them. I am here in the evening and at night. It's quite enough, believe me.''

''Are you paid to be the house sitter, is it just a convenient place to stay, or is there another reason?'' Susan asked, looking around the room.

''You're looking at the reason.'' All three stared at the book-lined walls. ''This is one of the most extensive collections of original editions of natural-history books in the country. The librarian who has this behind him can have his choice of jobs.''

''She's giving you the books as some sort of payment for living here?'' Brett asked for clarification.

''She feels deeply obligated to me for making it possible for her to go on this trip. It has fulfilled a lifelong dream.''

''To you or to the Hancock Public Library?'' Susan needed a little clarification of her own.

''I will be acting as trustee of the collection.''

''Then it will go wherever you go,'' Brett said.

''Exactly.'' Charles looked sober at the prospect. ''It will be a huge responsibility, of course. We will have to look very carefully at the many places that will want to possess such a collection.''

''We?''

''When Mrs. Grayson returns, we are going to tour many libraries looking for just the right place.'' He paused and scowled at a tiny green feather in the middle of the Aubusson carpet. ''I dream of that day. It is the only way I can make it through this.

''This collection isn't just of interest to American libraries,'' he added, getting into his subject. ''There are libraries in Mexico, Central and South America, and even in Europe that would just love to possess these books— although, of course, they are all in English.''

''So you're going to have some trip,'' Susan suggested.

''Yes.'' He sat back and crossed his legs. ''I'm quite looking forward to it.

''But why,'' he added, apparently realizing that few people planned social visits for this time of the night, ''are you here?''

''Why didn't you meet me in your office tonight?'' Susan asked before Brett could say anything. ''Marion said that you were going to meet me there after the crowd from the speech had gone home.''

''Why . . . Marion did mention it to me, but I forgot. I certainly didn't think it was terribly important. I can't imagine that you think you should barge in on me in the middle of the night because I forgot our meeting. After all, I'm a working man, not a suburban housewife with nothing to do but lie in bed in the morning."

"That is not exactly why we're here," Brett assured him. Susan wondered if he had noticed her clutching the arms of her chair. "You see," Brett continued, "while Mrs. Henshaw was waiting for you, she was locked in your office."

"She didn't hear someone lock the door?" the librarian asked.

"I fell asleep," Susan admitted, refusing to be intimidated.

"And what hardship did this cause? I assume someone didn't know you were there and locked you in during the general evening security check. When you had finished your little nap, you called your good friend the chief of police, and he came and got you out—"

"It isn't quite that simple," Brett interrupted. "You see, whoever locked Mrs. Henshaw in did not want her to get free. The phone lines were cut."

That got his attention.

"The phone lines? All of them? Do you have any idea how that is going to inconvenience us? Not only do we need to be in contact with publishers, book jobbers, other libraries, but our modems will be useless. The lifeblood of our library is going to be inactive. This is dreadful, absolutely dreadful!"

Susan, who, if she had been asked to describe the lifeblood of libraries would have answered, simply, books, was amused by his distress—until she realized how little he had cared about hers.

"Who was supposed to be the last person out of the library tonight?" Brett asked.

"Marion Marshall." The answer came promptly.

"Does she always lock up?"

"No, the job alternates between the librarians—the same as the chore of opening up in the morning. There is a regular schedule. It is posted in the office—the office of the other members of the staff, not my office,'' Charles Grace answered.

''So you never lock up—or open up,'' Brett surmised.

''I do. In fact, I often work much longer hours than those I employ, but I am not on the regular schedule. I have my own keys and can come and go as necessary.''

''And you're the only person who can do that?''

''The only one of the librarians, yes . . .''

''Then how does the person whose job it is to open and close get the keys?'' Susan asked.

''Oh, well, both jobs are assigned by week. The keys are given out weekly.'' He shrugged as though it were obvious.

''Whoever has the keys could, of course, make copies of them while they were in their possession.''

''I suppose so,'' Charles Grace answered. ''Do you think there are duplicate sets of keys around?''

''Well, there could be.''

''I really don't think any of my staff would do such a thing,'' he protested.

''When does the cleaning get done? Vacuuming and scrubbing out the bathrooms and things like that?'' Susan asked.

''An excellent point!'' Charles Grace looked as if he finally understood the reason for Susan's existence. ''There is a cleaning crew that comes in two nights a week.''

''And who . . . ?''

''I don't have any contact with them, but I understand they are the same people who clean the rest of the municipal offices. They might have had copies of the keys made. You should check into that.''

''I will. What sort of routine is followed when the library is locked up for the night? Your office is locked, as well as the rest of the building?''

''Yes . . . Well actually, I usually lock my office myself.''

''Does anyone else have the key? Is it locked with a key?''

''Not usually. I have given it to one or two other people

on occasion. But there are a lot of personnel things kept in there that are confidential—such as salary information, things like that.''

''And are the other offices usually locked at night?''

''No. There's no reason. All someone has to do is break into the main part of the library to have access to a very expensive computer system, as well as millions of dollars' worth of books, tapes, records . . . you know.''

''I understand you are having a problem with the theft of expensive books,'' Susan said.

''Yes, but there is absolutely no evidence that anyone has broken into the building. These are books that someone is just walking off with, I'm afraid. It's very distressing.''

''But don't librarians usually have these problems?'' Brett asked.

''Yes, of course, but I'm afraid that one of the staff must be involved here. The books have been selected with a professional eye to what they are worth. If it had been something else, I would have contacted your department. As it is, I'm afraid this is going to be a personnel matter.'' Charles Grace grimaced. ''Just one of those things that executives have to deal with no matter how distasteful, I'm afraid.'' He looked at Brett. ''I'm sure you understand.''

Susan, the woman who was still lying on that chaise lounge eating those pastel bonbons, couldn't possibly have any knowledge of this. ''Who do you think is doing it?'' she asked bluntly.

''I really don't think I could comment on that.'' He looked down at her.

''I still don't understand how you forgot me tonight,'' Susan began.

''I . . . I'm sorry. It's been a long week, I just forgot.''

''Then why did you ask to meet me this afternoon and then cancel that appointment?'' she asked, pursuing her subject.

He paused a moment before answering. ''I . . . I thought that perhaps you could help us with solving the murder of the man in the library. But, of course, that dreadful man confessed, and there was no need for you to get involved, was there?''

''And why didn't you wear your coat home tonight? It is very cold,'' Susan continued.

''I . . . my coat? Whatever do you mean?''

''Your coat. The coat that was lying across your desk chair.'' Susan felt as if she had scored a point—just for a moment.

''I did wear my coat home. What sort of fool do you think I am? I wear a very expensive overcoat from Acquascutum, and I hang it up carefully in the closet in the workroom each and every day. I would certainly never fling it over a chair back. The coat you're referring to was found in the library after we closed yesterday. It is in my office awaiting its owner.'' He glared at her. ''Do you have any more questions? I'm sorry I forgot our meeting. I am very sorry that you got locked in the library. I am sorry the last few days ever happened. But I am totally exhausted now, and I need my sleep. Unless there are more pressing questions for you to ask me''—he carefully avoided looking at Susan—''I'm afraid I must ask you to leave.''

''I'll be coming over to the library first thing tomorrow morning. Maybe we could go into this more fully at that time,'' Brett suggested before Susan could continue her questioning.

''I have no problem with that.'' Charles Grace stood up, and his guests had no polite option but to do likewise. ''I am aware of my responsibilities in this terrible tragedy, but I know you'll understand that a librarian isn't trained to deal with this type of thing. I am finding it all very fatiguing.''

''Of course.''

''There is one thing I don't understand,'' Susan said as they returned to the main hall.

''Really?'' Charles didn't sound interested in enlightening her. He opened the front door. ''We really have to say good-bye very quickly. The birds, you know.'' He glanced over his shoulder malevolently. "The cold drafts are very bad for them."

"What I don't understand," Susan continued, preceding Brett through the door, "is why you keep recommending that people read books with pornographic passages."

The door slammed behind them.

Brett chuckled. "He certainly was anxious to protect those birds from the cold air. Good of him, considering how little he likes them."

"He has a very short fuse," Susan mused.

"But it is true that a lot has happened in his life in the last twenty-four hours. Things that, truly, a librarian isn't trained to deal with."

They got into the car together. "So far," Susan said, fastening her seat belt, "all we know about Charles Grace's idea of librarianship is giving out dirty books, complaining about management responsibilities, and gathering a collection that will get him a plush job somewhere else—along with free housing for nineteen months. You know, I've never liked that man, and the more I know, the less I like."

"That doesn't make him a murderer."

"I know. I don't see him that way, in fact. If he were going to murder someone, why do it in the library? Why connect himself? And why on earth would he kill Jason Armstrong? There doesn't seem to be any connection between the two of them."

"There doesn't seem to be a connection between Mr. Armstrong and anyone in town—except for his wife," Brett answered. "I have some people working on his background. They were busy all day. I should have an answer or two on my desk in the morning."

"Which you will share with me?" Susan asked.

"Fine. But . . ."

"I won't do anything wrong. I'm just listening to what people say. I'll certainly bring anything I learn to your attention."

"Immediately."

"Immediately," she assured him.

"There's still one thing I'm very worried about," Brett said, heading toward her house.

"What?"

"What happened tonight that it was so important to keep you away from?"

"Good question." They drove a few miles, the silence broken only by smothered yawns. "Although," Susan began slowly, "when you think about it, my house is the only logical answer."

"Your house?"

"That's where I would have been if I hadn't gotten locked in. I would have gone right home after speaking with Charles Grace—if I had spoken to Charles Grace and if I hadn't been trapped in the library. Am I making any sense, or has the lack of sleep finally gotten to me?"

"It's gotten to both of us, but I get your point." Brett drove the car up into her driveway. "Why don't you get some sleep. I'll be at my desk most of tomorrow morning if you want to hear what we've learned about Jason Armstrong—if there is anything to be learned about Jason Armstrong."

"I will," she agreed, getting out of the car. She closed the car door quietly (the bedroom she shared with Jed was at the front of the house) and, unlocking the door, slipped silently into her house.

She need not have bothered. Jed was sitting on the couch in the living room, his body turned so he could see into the hall. He stood up as soon as he saw her.

"Jed!" Susan was startled—and then worried. "What are you doing up? Has something happened?" She remembered what she and Brett had just been talking about.

"No." He smiled. "I was too worried about you to go to sleep. How did the meeting with Charles Grace go?"

"It was interesting, I guess. Do you think we could talk about it in the morning? I'm glad you waited up, but I'm completely exhausted."

"Of course. I just wasn't thinking. You go on, and I'll close up down here."

Susan was mounting the stairs before he stopped speaking. Her house was toasty warm but stuffy. Someone had been smoking. She'd have to remember to open windows in the morning. Her bedroom, however, smelled of fresh sheets, and she dropped her clothing on the floor as she walked toward the adjoining bathroom. The view in the mirror over the sink woke her up long enough to consider whether or not a shampoo could wait for another day. It could. She had barely enough strength to brush her teeth before she returned to the bedroom and fell across the bed, instantly asleep.

Sometime in the night, she was vaguely conscious of being gently tucked under a down quilt. And later, probably toward morning, she heard voices outside her bedroom door and the unmistakable smell of fresh coffee and burning sausage. But she was too tired to be hungry, and she rolled over and slept.

It was past noon when she finally became fully conscious, and the air in her room smelled more like pizza than sausage. Susan stretched and groaned. She was groggy from too much sleep and too little food. Pizza sounded good. She got up and headed for the bathroom.

Twenty minutes later, she was eating cold pepperoni pizza and drinking warmed-over coffee. Both were delicious. She leaned back in her chair and wondered where her cleaning woman was—the place was a mess. And where was everyone else? Empty pizza boxes gave testimony to the presence of other lunchers earlier in the day, but the house appeared empty.

The Henshaws left messages for other family members on a magnetic pad stuck to the refrigerator door. The height changed as the children grew, but the idea remained the same, and each was supposed to write down his or her whereabouts. She glanced over and found a few messages. She pulled them off and read as she munched.

Sue—

Brett Fortesque called at nine A.M. and said he would call back later.—Jed

Sue—

Mrs. what's her name (who cleans) called. She has the flu and will not be here today.—Jed

Sue—

Chad needed a ride to the soccer field. Back soon.—Jed

Sue—

I am going to drive Rebecca to the police station. Will be back soon. I love you.—Jed

Sue—

The network people are meeting with Brett at the police station. I will give Hilda a ride over there and return to do something about lunch.—Jed

Mom—

Mrs. Ellsworth called and said for you to call her as soon as you wake up.—Chrissy

Mom—

Over at Cindy's. Home for dinner.—Chrissy

Susan—

Chrissy called. Needs info about some college tour next week. Call her at Cindy's when you wake up.—Jed

S—

Rebecca and her entourage have gone to New York City for some sort of press conference. I have gone to pick up Chad at field. Chrissy called, and she is spending the night with Cindy. I'll be home soon.—Jed

Susan neatly piled up the papers she had read and smiled. It would do her husband good to play housewife for a while, she thought, realizing it must be Saturday.

The notes had raised some interesting questions—what press conference? What college tour? What did Brett want to talk with her about? She grabbed another slice of pizza in one hand and the phone with the other.

It took a few minutes to get through to Brett, and Susan was pouring another cup of coffee when she heard his voice. "Brett, it's Susan Henshaw. I just woke up and got the message that you called."

"I'm glad you got some sleep. It sounds like you're going to need it."

"Why? What's happened? I woke up, and the house was empty and . . ."

"So no one has told you what's going on?"

"There were a few cryptic messages from Jed—but nothing about the murders. Does this have something to do with the reason Rebecca's gone to New York for a press conference?"

"Bingo."

"Do you have time to explain?"

"Sure. I don't suppose you subscribe to some of our country's scandal sheets—or have time to peruse them in the checkout line at the grocery store—but this morning all of them ran the same story. (I take this as proof that it's not only the great minds that think alike.) The headlines were different, but the general idea is that Jason is not the first man Rebecca murdered."

"What?"

"You heard me."

"You do have more details than that," Susan suggested.

"As much as these rags ever give. I think it was the *National Smut* that said that Rebecca got her first job from a news director somewhere in the Midwest—who fell in love with her and subsequently died."

"How?"

"Heart attack—the story suggested that the exertion of keeping up with a younger woman was too much for him."

"Pretty tacky. Any evidence?"

"None that they gave. A different, even less distinguished paper has a front-page headline claiming that Rebecca loved the anchorman at the second station that employed her, they had an affair, he died, and she got his job."

"An interesting death benefit. How did he die?"

"Food poisoning."

"What?"

"Botulism from improperly canned beans. That station's annual promotion campaign was the presence of their on-air personalities in the judging at the county fair."

"And no one else died?"

"No. The weatherman got pretty sick, though."

"Anything else?" Susan was almost afraid to hear the answer.

"One more. Rebecca was hired by a very well liked producer—the creator of this morning show that she's on. He was said to have taken a personal interest in her career."

"And he's dead, too."

"Yup."

"Are you going to tell me how it happened, or was it something he ate again?"

"Good guess."

"You're kidding!"

"No. Evidently this producer was big on doing the in thing. And the in thing in the beginning of the eighties was food. Exotic food: vegetables in strange colors, game birds, new varieties of old standbys."

"I remember. What got to this man?"

"Wild mushrooms. There was to be a spread in the food section of the *New York Times* extolling the virtues of wild mushrooms and the famous people who love to gather and eat them."

"Gather the mushrooms or gather together with other famous people to eat them?"

"Both. Happily for the rest of the distinguished group (a cranky restaurant critic and his lawyer wife, a fashion designer and his live-in lover/model, a playwright, and one or two others I can't remember), the producer tasted his mushroom pie while he was preparing it and before it got to the table. Apparently he made a serious mistake in his gathering and died."

"Was Rebecca there?"

"No, she was new on the show and didn't go out much in the evening. But she had been with him when he was gathering earlier in the day."

"And she picked the poison mushroom?"

"There is absolutely no evidence that she did. But that's not what the paper implied."

"Did any of these accusations ever make it to the police in the places where they happened? Did anyone ever take any of this seriously?"

"I checked all that out this morning. This is all nothing but innuendo and scandal. Rebecca may have killed Jason, but there is no reason in the world to believe that she caused any of these other deaths. The heart attack was the logical way for a stressed-out, overweight man in his late fifties to die. She wasn't even at the food booth in the county fair; the women from the station judged the handwork contests. And from the description of the producer that I got from the men who investigated his death, he would do anything to stand out and be in the forefront. 'The man would have eaten toad shit if he thought it was chic' is the way it was put in the report of his death. It was never considered to be a suspicious death—just a stupid one. And Rebecca was never considered a murderer."

"Of course, now . . ."

"Now is a problem. If our homeless man changes his confession, she's a suspect. And, I think, the best one we have. No one else in town knew either Jason or Mitch Waterfield."

"Did you get the background report on Jason this morning?"

"Yes, and it's just what we expected—in fact, nothing that we didn't know. The man has had a very dull life—until becoming an overnight star at the network."

"Did he really? So how did he get the job?"

"Evidently Rebecca saw him while she was traveling around on some sort of publicity jaunt, and she pointed out his work to her producer, and he hired him—practically a story out of *A Star Is Born*."

"Too good to be true?"

"Apparently not. These things do happen in real life."

"I suppose so."

"Hey, I thought it was the cops who were supposed to be cynics."

Susan laughed and then turned around, hearing the door open behind her. "I have to go. Jed just came in." She turned and smiled at him. "Hi!"

"Hi." He kissed the top of her head as she hung up the phone. "How are you feeling?"

"Fine. How are you?"

"As fine as I can be right now. Susan, what would you say if I said that I think we could have a murderer living in our house?"

TWELVE

IT'S FREQUENTLY SAID THAT COUPLES MARRIED AS LONG as Susan and Jed were (nineteen years) stop listening to each other. But Jed had his wife's complete attention.

"Who? Rebecca?" Susan guessed.

"No, Hilda," he surprised her by answering.

"Did she kill Jason and Mitch Waterfield? Why would she do something like that? Jed, what do you know?"

"I know she would be perfectly happy to kill anyone who got between her and what she wanted," he answered, pouring himself a cup of coffee. "You wouldn't believe the way she's been acting since last night."

"But you don't really know that she killed someone." Susan was disappointed.

"No, but I wouldn't put it past her."

"So what has been going on?" she asked, sighing.

"A lot. To begin with, the public relations department got copies of three scandal sheets that are running front-page stories on Rebecca."

"I know about that. Brett told me. He says that there is no question that they're fiction."

"Then you can imagine their reaction."

"What exactly happened?"

"It was right after you and Kathleen left. Brett got a call first—I don't know what that was about—and he took off a few minutes later. Then two calls came in for Hilda. I had answered the phone, and the voice on the other end of the line was frantic. Turned out to be Hilda's secretary. He . . .''

''He?''

''Men can be secretaries, you know.'' (Susan had the grace to blush at her chauvinism.) ''He was calling about these so-called news stories. The early reports on these newspapers had come out, and the entire public affairs department was frantic. Phone calls and faxes must have filled every satellite between here and New York.''

''We don't have a fax machine.''

''They installed two in the study yesterday morning.''

Susan decided she would think about holes in walls and things like that later. ''So that was the evening? Calls and faxes?''

''As the evening went on, the mood became hysterical. Hilda screamed into the phone, sent faxes that were just short of obscene, and thundered that she was going to kill everyone involved in these stories. Rebecca's mood progressed from very sad to very mad. I went in and out of the living room delivering coffee and helping take messages and things like that.'' (Now they'd turned her husband into a gofer.) ''Around eleven o'clock last night, everyone had agreed that the best thing to do was to hold a press conference today. Rebecca was exhausted and went to bed, leaving Hilda to set up everything.''

''Which she did,'' Susan finished for him while he rummaged in the refrigerator.

''Yes. You know,'' he added, ''someone needs to go to the grocery store. We're completely out of juice.''

''Maybe you could pick up a few copies of those scandal sheets at the same time.'' She grinned.

''Maybe *we* could?'' Jed emphasized. ''Chad is spending the afternoon hanging out at Bobby's house, and Chrissy isn't going to be home until late, and we could use some time to catch up. Don't you think so?''

''Why not? I'd like to do some normal things, in fact.''

"Great." He looked around the room. "Unless you think I should stay here and clean up?"

"I'll tell you a little secret about housework—you don't have to worry—it's always there waiting for you." The phone rang, and she reached for it.

"Don't. The answering machine will pick it up." Her husband stopped her. "Chad and Chrissy are fine. It probably isn't even for us."

Susan looked at the ringing machine and hesitated. "You're sure?"

"We could have left fifteen minutes ago, and we wouldn't even know it was ringing."

She took a deep breath. "Okay, let's get out of here." She put on a heavy loden coat and opened the door to the garage. Her husband followed.

"My car or yours?"

"Mine. Groceries fit into my trunk better. Besides, you don't want your car to smell like food, do you?"

He laughed and opened the door to the driver's seat for her.

"Did anything else happen last night?" Susan asked, backing the car into the street.

"I think I told you everything. Certainly nothing happened here that was as exciting as being locked in the library."

"That's what I'm wondering about. Brett has the idea that I was locked in the library to keep me away from something—presumably something that happened at home."

"I told you everything, I think."

"Did anyone leave the house? Rebecca or Hilda?"

"Both of them—not together, though. Rebecca went out for a walk late in the evening—right before she went to bed. She was gone for quite a while. I wondered if she had gone back to her house, in fact."

"She drove?"

"She didn't say she did, but she could have. Her car was

parked in the street. I didn't watch to make sure she was on foot, and I don't think anyone else did.''

''And Hilda?''

''Hilda went out late, too. She took off for a pack of cigarettes.''

''She did drive.''

''I assume so.''

''How long was she gone?''

''Probably fifteen minutes or so. I didn't pay that much attention, to be honest.''

''So either of them could have driven over to the library and back.''

''Sure.'' He looked intently at his wife. ''You think Hilda or Rebecca locked you in the office?''

''I have no idea. But I'd like to know if it's a possibility. And it sounds like it is.''

''But how would they have gotten out of the building? They wouldn't have had a key or anything.''

''True, but they might not have needed one. I've been thinking about it,'' she added, swerving around a large pile of leaves that had been raked into the street. ''Someone could have locked the door to the office by reaching inside and turning the latch and then just left the building with everyone else. Marion Marshall locked up. If she had found Charles Grace's office locked, she would have assumed that he had done it and just gone on to lock up the building.''

''You didn't hear anyone lock the door?''

''No, but I think I fell asleep almost at once. I've been pretty tired these days. In fact''—she sneezed—''I have a horrible feeling that I'm catching something. My throat is awfully sore.''

''You should be at home in bed with a glass of orange juice, not out running around trying to solve murders.''

''I was hoping for a hot toddy,'' she kidded him, turning into the parking lot in front of the store. ''But that will have to wait. Did Amy Ellsworth tell you what she wanted when she called this morning?''

"No, she said it was urgent, but you know how she is . . . although maybe I should have taken her more seriously?"

"Don't worry about it. You're right, she is like that. I get sick of calling her back over something she calls urgent and then finding out that it's nothing." She switched off the engine and turned to her husband. "Well, here we are. I hope you can remember what it is that we're out of."

"I . . ." He followed her through the lot and to the building.

"You know, though," she began, grabbing a cart. "Maybe Amy saw the person who locked me in."

"Does she even know you were in the office?"

"I guess not. That was a foolish idea." She stopped to pick out some apples. "Jed, I just don't understand. Why was I locked in? There was no reason for me to be kept away from anything that happened last night. Why couldn't whoever locked me in just have let me go home to bed?"

"Do you think it could have been done to scare you? You know, make you have second thoughts about being involved in the investigation?"

"Why would it scare me? I admit I was shocked for a minute or two, especially when I realized the phone wasn't working, but I thought they must turn the phones off at night. The only thing that concerned me was that you might wonder where I was, but I didn't get frightened. Why would I? The worst that was going to happen was that I was going to spend the night in Charles Grace's office."

Jed was examining a display of autumn pears. "I guess the person who locked you in doesn't know you very well— thinks you get hysterical easily or something."

"Someone who doesn't know me well doesn't exactly eliminate anyone in this situation, does it?"

"Have you talked to Kathleen? You did say you were going to call her about that phone call last night."

"That's a good idea."

"It is, and you can do it right now."

The Henshaws turned to discover that Kathleen Gordon was standing right behind them.

"Does everyone in town go shopping on Saturday afternoon?" Susan asked, laughing.

"It's the best time for me to get out of the house. Jerry is taking care of Bananas for the day—and putting some last-minute touches on his costume."

"His costume? Oh, no. The Ellsworths' costume party! It's tonight, isn't it?"

"It certainly is. Didn't Amy call you this morning to remind you that it was going to go on as planned?"

"She probably did. I got a message from her, but I didn't bother to call back."

"She also wanted to remind Rebecca about the party . . ."

"What?" Susan shrieked so loudly that some of the shoppers nearby turned and stared.

"And invite whoever else is staying at your house. She called me and asked if I thought it was appropriate."

"I hope you told her no. After all, Rebecca's husband just died. To say nothing of her being suspected of murder. She certainly wouldn't go to a costume party."

"That's what I said. But you know Amy. She said that she wanted to ask my opinion, but really she wanted to tell me hers. I'd bet that call to your house was to issue invitations."

"Well, my houseguests have gone to the city to take part in some sort of press conference about the murders, so we don't have to worry about that." She moved her cart closer to a bin packed with tiny round acorn squash.

"You were going to ask me about the phone call last night," Kathleen reminded her, filling a bag with chestnuts.

"That's right." She weighed one squash in each hand. "There's too much to think about these days," she sighed, and tossed both into her cart. "What time did this person call and what did she . . ."

"He."

"He? Then it wasn't a voice claiming to be me."

"I'll tell you all about it. Mind if we do this at the butcher's counter?"

"No." They moved in that direction and continued to talk. Susan noticed that her husband had disappeared. "So what happened?"

"Well, I got the call almost as soon as I got home from the library. I'm not completely sure of the time, but I think it was around eleven or eleven-thirty. I was ready for bed, but Bananas was teething, and so I was trying to get him to sleep and not paying much attention, if you want to know the truth.

"Well, a man called up and said that he was from the police department. He was very brief. He explained that you were with Chief Fortesque, and that your home phone was constantly busy and they didn't have a lot of time, so Brett had requested that I call Jed and tell him that Susan was just fine but that she was going to be with him for a while. He didn't really leave any time for me to ask questions; he just hung up."

"How long did it take you to get through to Jed?"

"Oh, I did that right away. I thought I must have been lucky and caught the line free between calls. Of course, now that we know the person who called was lying . . . I know the next question you're going to ask. The call could have come from a woman disguising her voice. There was a lot of background noise on the other end of the line—and a lot of noise coming from Bananas in my lap—I really can't be sure of everything. You know," she added, peering at a tray of tiny pheasants, "I used to get so mad at witnesses who couldn't remember things. Now I've become one of them."

"Now you have a life besides a profession—and life can be very distracting," Susan said as her husband appeared at her side, a large bottle sticking out of the bag in his hand. "What is that?"

He pulled out a magnum of Mumm's. "Champagne. I thought we could use a prop to go along with our costumes tonight."

"What are you going as?"

"We're wearing something old. And that's the only hint you're going to get," Susan answered. "Do you really think we should go?"

"Definitely," her husband answered. "Chad and Chrissy are busy with other things. Our houseguests will probably stay and eat in the city—and, if not, they are more than capable of fending for themselves for one evening—and you need a break."

"True," Kathleen said. "Besides, Amy just happened to mention to me that Charles Grace was invited."

"What's he going as? The birdman of Hancock?"

"What?"

"It's a long story, and you're going to finally get waited on," Susan said, nodding to the butcher who was approaching them. "I saw Mr. Grace in the middle of last night. I'll tell you about it if we get a moment together at the party." She pushed her cart off down the aisle. "What did we come here for?" she asked her husband, looking into its almost full interior.

"Juice," he reminded her.

She turned toward the correct aisle. "And we should pick up a frozen pizza. Chad is bound to get hungry if we leave him alone."

"We'd better pick up a few in case he isn't alone," Jed said.

They did their shopping, miraculously chose the shortest checkout line, and arrived home before four.

"What time do you think we'll hear about the press conference?" Susan asked as they carried their groceries into the house.

"I think it was scheduled for about now, but I don't suppose there will be anything on TV about it until the local news this evening."

"What about CNN?"

"I suppose it's worth a try." Jed turned on the small TV that sat on the end of the kitchen counter. "There aren't any other major stories right now—and no other scandals for them to turn their attention to.''

The anchorwoman said something about Pittsburgh, and Susan headed back to the car for the last bag. When she returned to the house, Jed was sitting on a stool, eyes on the television.

''Is it on?'' She dumped the bag on the counter.

''No. I'll help put those away. But I think it may be coming up. They said something about a murder in Connecticut. . . . Wait! That's it. She said Hancock, Connecticut.''

''Turn up the volume. I can listen while I work.''

''. . . The anchorwoman, married for only a few months, has decided to give the press a chance to ask questions. The network issued this statement this afternoon: 'Rebecca Armstrong, devastated by the death of her husband, has been attacked by various disreputable papers that have tried to increase their circulation by printing stories that are untrue and libelous. She is going to hold a press conference this afternoon, despite her desire for privacy at this trying time, because she feels that it is important for the true story to be told.' . . . Here she comes now.''

The picture changed to a close-up shot of Rebecca sitting in a chair similar to the one she used each morning when interviewing guests on her show. She was wearing a navy suit with a gray blouse. She looked appropriately subdued. As the camera zoomed in on her face, she bent her lips into a gentle half smile and rustled the papers she held in her lap.

''I was going to read straight from this prepared statement—and I will—but first I want to say something. I went to my office this afternoon for the first time since my husband was killed. The room is filled with flowers, letters, and cards from viewers who felt it important to express their sympathy for me in this terrible situation. I can't tell you how much that touched me and how much I appreciated it. Thank you all.'' She wiped a tear from her eye, looked down at the script she held, and took a deep breath.

''Thank you all for coming. As you all know, Jason Armstrong, my husband, was killed on Halloween. He was stabbed on the porch of our new home in Connecticut. A homeless man well known in the area has confessed to the murder—as well as to another that happened earlier in the day.

"Naturally I am devastated by this. Jason and I have had a very public courtship on 'This Morning, Every Morning,' and our marriage was well known. We had expected to continue to do the work we loved, as well as raise a family and, eventually, live a more private life, away from publicity—with a chance to sleep late in the morning." The tiny sad smile reappeared for a moment. "None of this is to be.

"And now, I find that I am the subject of numerous attacks in various so-called newspapers on sale around the country. My lawyers and the lawyers at the network will be filing suit against these scandal sheets, their editors, and their owners. I have long believed in a free press and in journalistic freedom. But freedom without responsibility is a travesty, and I do not intend to allow it to destroy either the memory of Jason, the memory of our marriage, or my career.

"There are also rumors about the other man who died the same day as Jason. Mitchell Waterfield was employed by this network for many years. We knew each other in a professional capacity, and no other. I would like very much to publicly express my sadness over his death to his family and his many friends. I am ready to answer some questions, but my lawyers"—the camera panned back to include three solemn-looking men standing nearby—"are advising me to be careful and not jeopardize our case in any way. I'm sure you understand." She looked straight into the camera as she said this.

"Ms. Armstrong. Rebecca," a woman's voice called out from somewhere in the room. "First we want you to know that, as your friends and colleagues, we all sympathize with you and feel that it is terrible that you should find yourself in this situation. . . ."

"But we all have our jobs to do," Rebecca interrupted, the half smile reappearing on her face.

"Uh, yes." The camera had found the speaker, a woman reporter well known in New York City for her incisive reporting and irritating mannerisms. "Are you saying that there is no truth to the stories that hit the newsstands today—the stories about men in your past?"

"It is true that people I have known have died. But that is true for all of us. Never were any of those deaths related to me—nor did I ever have more than professional relationships with any of the men mentioned." She nodded curtly to another reporter in the audience.

"Are you convinced, Ms. Armstrong, that the man who confessed is the man who killed your husband?"

"I see no reason not to believe that, if the police are convinced of his guilt. One of the hazards of being in the public eye is that sometimes people who are unbalanced develop a hatred for us—there are many famous cases of this in the past, of course. Although he caused me a great loss, I feel sorry for this man. I hope he will get proper psychiatric care if that is what he needs."

"That sounds pretty artificial to me," Susan muttered. "I know I'd hate anyone who killed you."

"Thank you," Jed said. "I promise to hate anyone who kills you, too."

Susan punched him gently in the stomach, and they both returned to the television.

"Have you met the man who confessed?" a gentleman in the rear of the room asked.

"No, the police haven't asked me to do so. I'm following the direction of Brett Fortesque, Chief of the Hancock, Connecticut, police department. I do whatever he asks me to do."

"Do you plan to return to 'This Morning, Every Morning'?" The question came from a woman on a different network who was often mentioned in articles as a replacement for Rebecca if she became pregnant and retired from the business, or if her ratings dropped.

"I am approaching the future one day at a time," Rebecca answered. "A private funeral—family only—will be held for my husband on Monday morning. There will be a public memorial service sometime next week. The time and place will be announced when that information is available. I plan on returning to my professional family here at the network as soon as I feel that I can fulfill my obligations to the wonderful people with whom I work and to the viewers." She sighed deeply, and one of the men she had identified as a lawyer walked up and put his arm around her shoulder.

"Ms. Armstrong has had a very difficult few days. I think just one or two more questions," he suggested.

"How long have you lived in Connecticut? And will you stay there now that your husband is dead?"

"Jason and I moved to Connecticut less than a month ago. We enjoyed fixing up our new home, meeting new neighbors, finding our place in the community. I'm afraid I can't plan for the future right now. I think I'll just let things settle down a bit before making any big decisions."

"Maybe just one more question?"

"Of course."

"There are rumors that you and your late husband weren't getting along, that there might have been a divorce in your future if the murder hadn't . . ."

"Any rumors, innuendos, or statements that my marriage to Jason wasn't perfectly happy are lies. We were perfectly happy until my husband was killed." Rebecca stood up, and Hilda rushed forward.

"It's possible that Ms. Armstrong could answer questions all day, but this has been a terrible time for her, and I'm sure you understand her need for privacy. Now there will be refreshments in the room down the hall, and the public relations department will handle all questions from here on out."

Hilda hurried Rebecca, clutching a damp handkerchief of Italian linen in her hand, from the room, and the interview was over. Cameras swerved around the milling crowd, and Jed reached to turn off the set.

"Nothing new there," he commented. "It will be interesting to see which sound bites they use on the news shows. I'll bet the beginning where she thanks all her fans for their support. That was a well-staged news conference."

"They didn't ask her very difficult questions, did they?"

"Just another example of an industry taking care of its own," Jed said.

"You think that's it?"

"I'm sure that's it. Even journalists aren't fond of seeing their own dirty linen hanging on the line."

"No, I suppose not," Susan agreed, and sneezed. "You know, I need to shower and do something with my hair if we're going to be in costume tonight."

"I should check to see if everything is in place. I haven't worn my tux since that dinner at the Waldorf last spring. I hope I had the shirt cleaned."

"So what did the press conference accomplish?" Susan asked, following her husband from the room.

"Well, she alerted everyone that she would sue if untrue stories about her were printed. And it looks like the network is supporting her completely. In terms of empowerment, it did a good job. I think that was the whole point."

"I suppose so," Susan agreed reluctantly. "But don't you think it's sort of much ado about nothing?"

"No, I think it's much ado about at least a couple of million dollars' worth of revenue to the network—maybe more. Where are you going?"

"The attic," she answered, turning at the top of the stairs. "My costume is up there, remember? It's been in storage for the last nineteen years. I hope it doesn't smell musty." She opened the door at the end of the hall and headed up the uncarpeted stairs.

They went their separate ways. Jed peeked into the bathroom half an hour later and told his wife that Brett had called.

"Should I call him back?" Susan asked from under a mountain of mousse and hot curlers.

"No. He said he was just checking in to see if you had any new thoughts about the murder. I told him that we were going to be at Amy's party tonight. He knew about it—evidently she issued him a last-minute invitation this morning. He says that if he has to talk to you, he'll appear. You'll know him; he'll be the police officer."

Susan chuckled. "You know what I forgot? To pick up my bouquet. I ordered it a few weeks ago at Festoons and Flowers," she mentioned the florist in downtown Hancock, "and I was supposed to pick it up this morning."

"It was delivered a few minutes ago. They called, and when I said that we had forgotten and I'd be right down, they explained that their truck was going to pass nearby on the way to make a delivery to the Presbyterian church, and it would be dropped off."

"How does it look?"

"Beautiful. Did you have an orchid bouquet when we got married?"

"Daisies. Remember, we were into simple things then?"

"And cheap things?"

"Think of it as a prop—like that expensive champagne you bought this afternoon."

"We can drink that champagne."

"Orchids are beautiful, but I can't think of any other way to defend them."

"Well, maybe every woman deserves a dozen orchids at least once in her life. How long will it take you to get ready?"

"Another hour. Want a snack?"

"No, I'm fine. I'll call the kids and write a message for Rebecca and Hilda."

"Well, I'm going to need your help zipping up that dress. Thank heavens it was too loose when we got married, or I'd never make it now."

"I'll be back up in a while."

Susan spent another half hour finishing her hair and put-

ting on makeup. Jed reappeared and helped her into her padding and then into the dress she had worn when she married
him.

"Thank goodness we're only going next door. I would
hate to have to sit down in this."

"You did drive to the church when we got married."

"I was twenty pounds thinner then."

"You look about forty pounds heavier. How did you make
that thing?"

"A cut-up pillowcase and lots of polyester batting.
Ready?"

"Sure am. I was watching out the window, and people
have been arriving for the last fifteen minutes."

They headed off to the party, picking up her bridal bouquet
and his champagne as they passed through the kitchen.

"We'll probably get the award for the cutest couple," Jed
suggested as they knocked on their neighbors' door.

"In this costume, I think of us as a threesome," Susan
said as the door opened and their hostess greeted them.

THIRTEEN

"A PREGNANT BRIDE? A PREGNANT BRIDE! AND JED'S THE groom! I don't believe it!''

Susan's costume was a success, even though the padding needed a lot of pulling and tugging to keep it nearer her waistline than her knees. She wandered through the party, greeting friends and neighbors, exchanging stories of Halloween and cabbage night mischief, admitting that she did have a famous houseguest, but no, she knew nothing, nothing at all about the murders. She was looking for Charles Grace.

"Amy!" Susan spied her hostess, busy passing around a tray of bacon-wrapped sea scallops. "Wonderful party. And I love your costume." Actually she didn't. Amy was masquerading as Elizabeth Taylor dressed as Cleopatra. Except that Amy had neither the impressive chest nor the beautiful violet eyes. Susan took an orange paper napkin and some food before continuing. "I was talking to Kathleen, and she said that you had invited Charles Grace. That was so nice of you." She hoped Amy would pick up the cue.

She did. "Yes. I wanted him to feel like part of the community. But I never thought he would choose that particular date."

"Who . . . " Susan began.

"Marion somebody—that librarian who's always mooning over him. Can you believe it? He's always acting like he would do anything to be free of her for one night."

"He brought Marion Marshall?"

"That's her name. Yes. He really should have mentioned to her that this was a costume party. She's wearing a tailored navy suit and mid-height heels. Although maybe she has a very acute sense of humor, and she came as a dowdy librarian."

"Do you know where they are?" Susan decided to ignore the comment.

"The last time I saw Charles, he was at the bar in the dining room. I have no idea where Marion is—probably staring up at him with adoring eyes."

Susan hurried off without waiting to hear more. She found the librarian standing beneath an enormous plastic spiderweb that covered the ceiling of the Ellsworths' dining room. He was again wearing his giant caterpillar costume, although he carried the tail over his left arm after a few guests had tripped on it. He had a glass of scotch in the other hand.

"Hi! Guess you can't wear that at home. I mean, the birds might think you were food or something."

He responded to her cheery greeting as though she were the worm and he the bird. "Mrs. Henshaw. I didn't know you would be here—I thought your houseguests and your work with Hancock's police chief would keep you busy."

"It's been an unusual week," she agreed, ignoring his look. "You know, I was wondering if you might have locked me in your office last night—accidentally, I mean."

"I told you, Mrs. Henshaw. I had nothing to do with the locking up last night. Marion was in charge of it. I was very busy speaking with people after the presentation; I certainly didn't have time to lock up, and it wasn't my job to do so. And"—he lowered his voice and pulled her over to a corner of the room—"I would appreciate it if you wouldn't spread rumors about me. I was very upset about your visit to my home late last night. I can assure you, you can look into my life very carefully, and you will find that it is circumspect. I have dedicated it to taking care of the patron—and I do not include pushing pornography in that category."

Susan forced herself to respond. "I'm sorry about that. But we do have to follow up any leads—no matter how unlikely." She took a deep breath and plunged in again. "I understand you brought Marion Marshall to the party tonight."

"Yes. I'm afraid this is my last kind gesture toward her. She has become a terrible pest. She overheard Mrs. Ellsworth extend an invitation to the party tonight. She actually went home, changed, and appeared on my doorstep about five minutes before I was about to leave. She asked me for a ride over here—I had no idea she was presenting herself as my date. I assumed she had been invited on her own. This is very presumptuous of her. Monday morning I'm afraid I'm going to have to give her two weeks' notice."

This is the way he treated people who were in love with him? He should be wearing a snake costume, not maligning innocent little caterpillars. "You probably shouldn't be telling me about personnel matters, should you?" she muttered, and, seeing Marion through the entrance of the room, she turned and left.

But when she got to the hall, Marion had disappeared. She looked at the costumed guests and spied Kathleen, dressed in a pair of rosy silk harem pants, a yellow-embroidered halter top, and dozens of glittering necklaces. She had red silk slippers on her feet.

"Wow. You look fabulous!"

"Thanks, but the top is just a scarf, and I'm about to do a topless act. Do you have any idea where there's a bedroom I can slip into and pin up this thing?"

"Upstairs. Follow me," Susan suggested. "I've been up a few times already. My padding insists on following the laws of gravity."

They hurried to the master bedroom. The king-size bed was covered with coats, but there was a seating area in front of a large bay window. Susan plopped down on one of the chintz-covered chairs as Kathleen tugged at her top.

"I'm going to have to take this off and start fresh. I think

I'll use the bathroom as soon as it's free. I really don't want someone to come in to pick up their coat and find me doing a striptease.''

''Do you need any help?''

''No, I can manage. How about you?'' she asked as Susan pulled up her long skirt and was yanking at the padding.

''I'm fine. Go ahead. I'm going to see if I can find someone with safety pins.''

''I have safety pins. I always carry them. You never know when they'll come in handy.'' Marion Marshall stood in the open doorway to the bathroom. ''I have them in my purse.'' She pulled the large brown leather bag off her shoulder and began to scrounge around its spacious interior.

''I'll just use the bathroom and tie this,'' Kathleen said, edging past the other woman.

''You don't need a pin?'' Marion looked surprised.

''No, I'm the person who needs the pin. My baby keeps falling off,'' Susan said.

Marion looked a little startled at this description, but she pulled a pink-flowered satin bag from her purse and, unzipping it, offered its contents to Susan.

''Wow. Where did you get that?'' Susan asked, looking down at an array of safety pins from one-eighth of an inch to almost three inches long, lined up in order of size.

''Oh, I've collected them over the years. It's amazing how often someone needs one. Go ahead. It looks like you could use more than one.''

''Thanks.'' Susan selected two large pins and got to work.

''Have you considered pinning them to the dress itself? Or maybe that would damage it?''

''I hadn't thought of that, and it's a good idea. I'm not too worried about hurting the dress. It was fashionable to wear cotton when I got married, so this is pretty tough. I don't think I'll ever wear it again—unless we go to another costume party sometime.''

''This is the dress you got married in?'' Marion moved

back with respect. ''You should cherish it. What if your daughter wants to wear it someday?''

''Chrissy has her own very definite taste. I can't imagine her wanting to wear this—besides that, she's three inches taller than I am.''

''If you're sure . . .''

''I'm sure.'' Susan stabbed a large pin through the dress's lining to confirm her opinion.

''Then why don't you let me help?'' Susan found herself, long skirt over her head, being firmly pinned into both dress and padding. Well, it was a step on the road to intimacy. And she did have to ask Marion some pretty personal questions— starting now.

''Why were you so anxious to come to this party?'' she asked, and held her breath, hoping she hadn't insulted the other woman.

''I guess Charles is telling everyone that I barged in, isn't he?'' Marion's voice was colder than Susan had heard it before.

''Well . . .'' Susan began.

''You don't have to lie. I know what's happening. You should have heard him talking to Mrs. Ellsworth when we got here. He almost accused me of gate-crashing. I was terribly embarrassed. And mad,'' she added almost to herself. ''He's been acting terribly toward me ever since the murder. I know how upset he must be, but that doesn't excuse his behavior, does it?''

''No, I don't think so,'' Susan agreed, her voice muffled by the layers of cotton and lace that still covered her head.

''That's what I think, at least,'' Marion went on as though she hadn't heard.

''Why were you so anxious to come to this party?'' Susan repeated.

''I wanted to talk to you. I wanted to apologize for locking you in the office last night.''

''You . . . !''

"I didn't know you were there, of course. I mean, why would I want to lock you in?"

"But the phone line. I can see that you could have locked me in accidentally—Charles did say it was your night to lock up—but I don't understand why you would cut the phone line."

"I didn't! I would never have done anything like that! It must have been an accident—maybe a tree branch fell on the line outside or something."

Susan didn't think it was worth arguing. Brett said the line had been cut, and he would know a cut line from one that had accidentally broken, so Marion either hadn't cut the line, or for some reason had decided to cut it and was lying about it now.

"Charles seems to think that you think that he locked you in, but of course he wouldn't. The last thing in the world that Charles wanted is for you to be locked in his office overnight—believe me!"

"I do. . . ."

But Marion was going on. "Charles is so upset about all of this—he hated that homeless man being around the library so much—and then the murder and everything—he's terribly upset. And because of Jason Armstrong being famous, these murders are getting a lot more attention than they would usually. I think everything is going wrong for him these days. It's all so tragic, don't you think?"

"Yes. Of course. But it's been difficult for you, too. You seem to have been so fond of Charles Grace. . . ."

"I was in love with him." Marion insisted on correcting her. "But those feelings have died completely. I guess I never really accepted how badly he was treating me. I just couldn't see it. And, once I realized it, I . . . I stopped loving him. Just like that. I thought I'd never do it, but I did." Her voice had gotten quieter and quieter, and Susan, still blinded by her costume, wondered if the other woman was crying.

"Marion," she said softly through the material. "I really think you're doing the right thing. Marion?"

"You might be interested in knowing that you're talking to yourself."

Susan heard Kathleen's voice clearly. She pulled down her skirt and looked around. They were alone in the room. Marion had gone, taking her purse and the rest of her safety pins with her. Susan was more than a little bewildered. "She left?"

"Apparently so. What were you talking about? I just saw her go through the door—she was almost running."

"I guess she needed to be alone. She's had her eyes opened about Charles Grace in the last twenty-four hours," she added, and proceeded to tell her friend about their conversation.

"Do you think she did it?"

Susan was surprised. "Of course. Why would she admit to doing something like that if she hadn't?"

"Because she's protecting the person who did?"

"Who?" Susan looked intently at Kathleen. "You think she's still protecting Charles Grace, and he's the one who did it."

"I think it's possible. She could be lying about this great change of feeling for him, couldn't she?"

"I suppose it is possible . . ." Susan began slowly.

"Suppose she didn't know that he cut the phone line—so she didn't know to admit to it as well. That would make sense. After all, I don't think we can believe that a different person did the cutting. The only logical reason to cut the wire was so that you couldn't call for help. And the person who trapped you there is the person who wanted you to stay there until morning. Right?"

"Probably. But there might be other explanations."

"Such as?"

"Maybe you're right and Charles Grace locked me in— and suppose Marion saw him, and she realized that I could call out from the office and that he would be caught right away, so she cut the phone line . . . it doesn't make any sense, does it?"

"No, but maybe it doesn't make any difference right now," Kathleen surprised her by saying. "A lot of people might be the person who locked you in. Unless someone else confesses or we find that they were seen by someone, we will probably be forced to believe Marion. Maybe, right now, we should concentrate on why it was done."

"Why I was locked in."

"Exactly."

"That's what Brett says. I've thought and I've thought, and I can't imagine why I was locked in. Nothing happened while I was at the library that there would be any reason to keep me away from."

"You're sure?"

"At my house, Rebecca and everyone heard about the lies that were being printed in grocery store papers about her and they were planning to give a press conference, but apparently no one knows where Rebecca was that night . . . or Hilda either. I don't know what Marion Marshall and Charles Grace were doing, but it doesn't look like they were involved in anything unusual. No one got mugged that night, no one else got killed. The man who confessed to the murders is in jail, so there's nothing there. I just don't see it. I've been looking and looking for the last three days, and I have no answers. I don't even have any questions that make any sense. . . . Nothing is working here." She flopped down on the bed, only to realize she was sitting on a very expensive fur coat. "Damn!" She hopped up. "I'm so frustrated!"

"So let's go downstairs and party," Kathleen suggested. "After all, this is the first chance Jerry and I have had to go out together at night for a few weeks. I love Bananas, but being forced to be with him all the time is making me crazy. I'm forever looking for stimulation. In fact, I'm beginning to realize just why middle-of-the-day talk programs are so popular on TV and radio."

"I know what you mean. I remember when the kids were little—" Susan stopped and stared at her friend with her mouth open.

"Are you okay?"

"I just had a wonderful thought. I know what's going on here."

"You know who killed Mitch Waterfield and Jason Armstrong?"

"No, but I think I know how to find out," Susan said, and explained what she was thinking to her friend.

Kathleen thought about it before agreeing. "You're probably right. What are you going to do now?"

"I don't know."

The door opened and a couple of bandits, guns slung over their shoulders and stockings covering their faces, walked in holding hands and laughing.

"Come on out in the hall," Kathleen urged Susan after greeting the mayor and his wife. "I have an idea. Why don't you call Brett," she suggested after they were alone again.

"Brett . . . That's a great idea! You know, I think I'll do it right now."

"You'll need his private number."

"You have his private number?"

"Don't make a big deal about it, Susan. Brett and I are old friends. And the next person who intimates that we're any more than that is going to be the next murder victim!"

Susan laughed. "I'll remember that. I'm going to call immediately. It would be great to figure this out right away, wouldn't it?"

"A miracle." But Kathleen spoke too late. Susan had already headed off to find a phone—and her husband.

She quickly explained to Jed what was happening, found a phone in the kitchen that no one was using, and called the number Kathleen had given her. Fortunately Brett answered. She explained her idea while munching from a large brandy snifter filled with candy corn. "You could meet me there," she suggested.

"No." Brett's voice was solemn. "I will pick you up at the Ellsworth house and take you there. And," he added before she could interrupt, "I will come to the door and get you. Do not leave that house and stand on the curb. Do not let anyone know that you are leaving. Don't even think about talking with Rebecca or anyone from the network or anyone connected with the library. In fact, why don't you just go stand by the table where food is being served, eat, make polite party conversation, and I will come find you. All right?''

"No." Susan lowered her voice as someone peeked in the kitchen door.

"What?"

"Sorry. Someone came in the door, and I didn't want them to hear us. See—I am being careful."

"Who was it?"

"I couldn't see. Anyway, as I was saying, I have to tell Jed that I'm leaving, and I should say good-bye to the Ellsworths. And if you come barging in here, everyone is going to wonder what is going on. That might alert whoever it is that we don't want to alert, won't it?''

"Okay. How about this . . . What was that noise? Did someone else come in?"

"I just choked on a piece of candy. It's nothing."

"Candy?" He sighed loudly. "Okay. Listen: You can tell Jed, but don't say anything to anyone else. He can do the social good-byes for you at the appropriate time. And I won't come in. Why don't you get Kathleen and spend some time talking about that little boy of hers near the front door—with your coat on a nearby chair. I'll just stick my head in when I get there. Okay?''

"Fine. Anything else?"

"No. I'll be there as soon as possible. You get ready."

Susan hung up and went off to find her coat and her friend.

"You wait by the door," Kathleen urged her. "Who knows how long it will take Brett to get here. I'll get your coat and purse."

"It's my green loden coat. We were only coming from next door, so I didn't wear anything else. I'll wait downstairs."

"Remember not to look like you're expecting anything.

Brett is obviously worried about your safety, and he may have good reason to be.''

"I'll be careful," Susan assured her, heading for the front door and thinking that she would be happier if she knew who or what she was supposed to look out for. Luckily she ran into Jed on her way. She explained briefly what was going on.

"You'll be safe, won't you?" he asked anxiously.

"I'll be with the chief of police. What more can you wish for?" she whispered as some guests passed by.

"I could wish this whole thing was over and our house-guests were gone and you were home in bed. That's what I could wish," he insisted. "That's what I do wish."

"If I'm right, if we find what we're looking for, then this will all be over soon and . . . Here's Kathleen."

"I'll leave you, then. I'll stay here an hour more and then head home. You'll call?"

"I'll call." She squeezed his hand as he left. "He's worried about me," she explained to Kathleen.

"Of course he is." She threw a green coat across the end of the banister and leaned against the wall. "The more I think about this, the more I think you're right."

"What other explanation could there be?"

The front door opened and Brett's head appeared. "Ready?"

"Ready." She and Kathleen exchanged looks.

"Take care of her," Kathleen ordered the policeman.

"I won't let her out of my sight."

"I don't see why everyone thinks something is going to happen to me. Everyone who is involved in this is either here or in New York City. I think I'm pretty safe."

"You think you're the only one who can change location? I think we'll be careful."

"At least if someone tried to kill me, we would know that we were on the right track."

"I think we are, don't you?" Brett opened the door to his police car for her.

"Definitely. You have the keys?"

He patted his pocket. "Right here. We'll be there in a few minutes. Can you roll that thing up or something?"

"This *thing* is the dress I got married in," Susan answered, laughing.

Brett looked startled. "I . . ."

"Chrissy was born three years after we got married—you may as well ask, everyone else has. And I'm not going to worry about the dress. After all, I've already gotten more use out of it than most women do from their wedding dresses. But I wish I hadn't let Marion pin me into the padding. I'd be more comfortable without it." She peered out the window. "Are we almost there?"

"Sure are. Where do you plan to start?"

"I have no idea. I supposed if I'd actually been locked in all night, I would have had at least four or five hours—but I do hope it doesn't take that long."

"I hope not," Brett agreed as he drove up to the front of the library and parked illegally. "One of the perks of being chief of police," he added.

Susan got out of the car, and they walked up the well-lit sidewalk to the building. "It looks kind of spooky at night, doesn't it? Very Halloween-like with the light in the tower and the moon in the background."

"Let's not give our imaginations anything extra to play with." Brett unlocked the door and reached inside to turn on the overhead lights. The entire building lit up at once. "We're looking for facts," he reminded her.

She followed him in. "And wouldn't it be nice if we knew which ones?"

"I can't argue with that." He used another key, opened the door to Charles Grace's office, and followed her up the stairs. "We're not doing badly, you know. It was good thinking to realize that if you weren't locked in so you wouldn't see something last night, you were locked in because you were supposed to find something here."

"Kathleen was talking about needing stimulation when she was cooped up in the house with Bananas, and it occurred to me that I was supposed to spend some time here looking around . . . that I was supposed to find something. But what?'' Susan looked around the office. The abandoned coat was on the back of a different chair, there were possibly a few more papers on the desk, and a pile of art books that she hadn't noticed before sat atop a filing cabinet. Otherwise the room looked as she remembered it. ''Should we start on one side and go around?''

''It's probably as good a way as any other,'' Brett agreed. ''Why don't we start with the desk?''

''I'll take the top and you take the drawers?''

''Fine with me.''

They searched for over an hour and found nothing. ''I wish I'd grabbed some refreshments and stuck them in my pocket. I'm getting hungry,'' Susan said, sitting back in a chair. ''All that's left is the file cabinets. I sure hope we find something there. If I was wrong about this, I'll start to scream.''

''Don't do that. . . .'' He turned and stared at her. ''What are you doing?''

''I can't stand leaning over this padding one more second. I'm going to get rid of it. Just look over in the other direction for a few minutes, if you don't mind.'' She struggled to unpin the wad of fabric and stuffing.

''Let me help.'' Brett reached over and unhooked the last pin, and the lump fell to the floor.

''Thanks. That feels better, and now I have something to sit on.'' She plopped down on the pillow. ''I'll start with the bottom drawer and work my way up. You can . . .''

''Work my way down. Watch your head.'' He opened the top drawer and pulled out the first file.

Susan grabbed the last one. And found what they were looking for.

''Except that there isn't really a motive for murder here, is there?'' Susan said, picking up the relevant sheets of paper.

''No. There's some pretty fancy financial dealing, that's

for sure. An accountant could probably explain this better, but it looks like what we have here is two sets of books."

"These are all the records on remodeling this building . . . fund-raising . . . designs . . . insurance. I hate to admit this, but Jed has always taken care of this stuff in our family. I can't make head or tail of it—except that it doesn't match these figures." She motioned to a pile of papers in her lap. "And these papers seem to be the ones that were shown to the public and the city council." She looked up at Brett. "Was he keeping money for himself?"

"Looks like it." Brett shuffled through the papers. "And it looks as though he was going to have a nice little nest egg when he got through. Although I have to admit that I probably don't know a lot more about this than you do."

"This is all very interesting, but I don't understand what it might have to do with the murders. The man killed here . . ."

"Mitchell Waterfield," Brett reminded her.

"Mr. Waterfield was a public relations person from New York City, and Jason had no connection with the remodeling of the library." She tossed the papers onto the floor.

"It looks like we found a crime, just not the right one," Brett said.

Susan got up, ripping the hem of her dress as she did so. "I don't get it. Maybe this is what we were supposed to see."

"It certainly isn't something Charles Grace would want made public."

"Who else?"

"I . . . I have no idea. We just keep going around in circles, don't we?

"We just keep going around this library," Brett suggested. "Unless you can think of something to do up here, let's go downstairs and look at the place where Mr. Waterfield was found. Maybe that will be an inspiration."

"It's worth a try." Susan looked around the room one more time. "And to think I was so fascinated with this place only a few days ago."

"It is a nice library," Brett said, as she followed him back to the main floor.

"It's a fabulous library. There are a lot of people in town who have worked very hard—without pay—to make it special. They are going to be very angry when they hear that Charles Grace has been embezzling funds for his own use. In fact, there are still a lot of things left to be done, and they probably won't be completed when word about this gets out. It's kind of a shame, really." Susan stopped talking as they approached the corner where she had discovered the body.

"I didn't mean for this to upset you."

"It doesn't, really. I didn't know this man—or Jason Armstrong, for that matter—so there isn't any sense of personal loss. It bothers me, though, that the person who killed them has gotten away with it."

"I know what you mean," Brett agreed. "Sometimes when a case is going like this, I imagine the satisfaction the guilty person must feel watching us work and struggle and still not discover his identity. It makes me sick to think of it."

Susan nodded. "I hadn't really thought of it like that, but I see what you mean." She looked around the well-appointed room that she loved to visit and, for the first time, it seemed unfriendly, almost threatening. Who had been sitting on those bright couches? Who had been thumbing through the extensive collection of magazines? Who knew the answer to this terrible puzzle and was amused by their impotent struggle? She looked at the floor where the body had lain and then back up at the bell tower.

"Brett!" Susan grabbed his arm. "I know."

"You know who did it?"

"I know what we were supposed to find in the office. And I think I know who did it—and why!"

FOURTEEN

"I CAN'T BELIEVE THAT WE'RE GOING TO WAKE UP Charles Grace for the second night in a row!" Susan giggled. Since discovering the identity of the murderer, she had been feeling a little light-headed.

"You did this last night?" Hilda Flambay spoke up. She didn't sound any happier than Susan expected Charles Grace would be.

"It doesn't matter, Hilda. All that matters is that we find out who killed Jason," Rebecca reminded her.

Susan thought that Rebecca didn't sound as though she particularly meant what she was saying. Well, it had been a long day for all of them, but it was almost over. She leaned her head against Jed's shoulder.

"Are you all right?"

"I will be soon." She smiled up at him.

"You're looking forward to this?" He whispered the question.

"In a way. I think these are particularly nasty murders. I'll be glad when the murderer is behind bars."

"You seem almost happy about it." Marion Marshall, standing between Brett Fortesque and Amy Ellsworth, sounded accusing.

"I . . ."

Susan didn't get a chance to finish her thought. Charles Grace opened the door, the bewilderment on his face changing to anger when he realized that there were seven people standing there. "What is this, may I ask?"

"We're here to tell you what has been going on in your library," Brett said, taking the first step across the threshold. "I assume you'll be interested."

"Of course, but . . ."

"Then maybe we can all go to your study?" Brett suggested, not waiting for an answer but heading in that direction regardless.

Susan followed the group, more to watch their reactions to the extraordinary house than for any other reason. She did glance over her shoulder and see Kathleen, two policemen, and one other person that she hoped she recognized as the door swung shut behind her. "I don't think it really matters where anyone sits," she heard Brett say as she reached the library. "We won't be here that long."

Charles Grace flopped down on a small Chippendale chair that creaked out a protest, which he ignored. "So what do you have to say that could not possibly wait until Monday morning?"

"We know who killed Mitchell Waterfield and Jason Armstrong." Susan made the announcement from the doorway.

"Shouldn't the police be telling us this?" Even in these circumstances, Hilda managed to bat an eyelash or two in Brett's direction.

"Susan put the pieces together and made the discovery. I think it's up to her to tell about it—if you want to," Brett added.

"I guess so." Susan looked around the room, trying to figure out just where to begin.

"Maybe you have time to waste at this hour of the night . . ." Charles Grace began in an irritated voice, and then Susan knew just where to start.

"We can begin with the new library building," she interrupted loudly. "And how you embezzled funds that were meant for the building. You don't have to bother to deny it. We found the second set of books in your office.

"You know," she continued, becoming confident, "I run with Linda Scott, and we were talking together on the day of the murders and she said something interesting—that she had no idea why you had asked David Pratt to be on the library board. She said something about there being a lot of gung ho accountants and businessmen in town who would do a better job, but you knew that, didn't you? In fact, you were counting on how casual he was, weren't you? You thought that would keep you from getting caught stealing from the library. By the time there was a major audit, you were to be long gone—you and your money and this collection of books." She waved her arm around the room. "Maybe even to some South American country where you would be safe from prosecution?"

"I didn't know you were investigating the library's finances—I thought you were looking for a murderer," Charles Grace replied.

She liked him less and less. So little, in fact, that this was almost going to be fun. "But you are a murderer, Mr. Grace, aren't you?"

It didn't stop him for a moment. "You may be able to accuse me of misuse of public funds, but you're not going to be able to pin a murder rap on me. There's no way to connect me with either man who was killed, and, besides, someone else has confessed to the murders already. Or are you forgetting that?"

"I'm forgetting nothing, absolutely nothing." Susan was angry and worked for a minute to control her emotions. "Everyone has been very impressed with the job you did building the new library, but things have been changing lately, haven't they? You've been becoming less and less liked here in town, haven't you? There were a number of elderly people who had been shocked by books that you personally had recommended to them."

"I don't know much about fiction—"

"But some of your fellow librarians do. You could have suggested that they offer to help. I think you might have enjoyed shocking these elderly ladies—just as you apparently enjoyed taking advantage of the woman whose house you're living in.''

''That is not a crime,'' he reminded her smugly.

Susan chose to ignore him. ''True. And I should have been looking more closely at things that weren't criminal. Like the power of a television personality to raise lots and lots of money for charity.'' She smiled at Rebecca. ''The very first time I saw Rebecca and Jason in person, they were being approached to do fund-raising for someone's pet project. In fact, it happened to them so often that when I spoke with Rebecca initially, she assumed that I was going to ask her to help out with my own charity. Her response was very tactful—she recommended that I speak to someone in the public relations department at the network. She didn't have to refuse; someone else would refuse for her.''

''We get so many requests,'' Rebecca said, vaguely apologetic.

''You're very popular, very important, and always wanted,'' Susan agreed. ''The exact opposite of the poor homeless man who confessed to two crimes that he didn't do and has been sitting in our local holding cell for the last two days.

''I was bothered by his confession right away because of what he said to me after the first body was found. He said that he was going to be blamed for the death—that he would be blamed just because he was the only person around who didn't belong.

''I felt bad for him. I've heard people's comments about how dirty he is—how he smells. He probably heard those comments, too. Because Marion said he was always around, always listening to people talking. So it's likely that he knew what was going on. Maybe he even knew what Mitch Waterfield, a consulting public relations person, was doing at the Hancock Public Library in the first place.

''I thought,'' Susan continued, turning to Rebecca, ''that you must be the murderer. You were the only person who was connected both with Mr. Waterfield and with Jason, and then it occurred to me that I was looking at this from the wrong direction. Logically you were the only person who would kill Mr. Waterfield—you knew that, and I think that's why you've been so concerned about those silly made-up stories from your past. A person as famous as Rebecca Armstrong is always being written about in those trashy weeklies, so there was no real reason for you to get so upset. Except, of course, that there was a true connection between you and the man who was murdered—and no one else in town had a previous personal relationship with Mitch Waterfield—''

"It was merely a professional connection . . ." Hilda began in an indignant voice.

"If you'll just wait until I finish!" Susan insisted. The woman was the perfect pest. "What I'm trying to explain is that Rebecca was the logical person to kill Mitch Waterfield—only she didn't."

"I'm glad you believe that," Rebecca spoke up. "Mitch didn't come to Hancock to see me—just like I said at the press conference. But I don't know who else he might have been in town for."

"But there is someone who does," Susan announced, opening the door.

The homeless man, a policeman on each side of him, followed Rebecca into the room.

Susan smiled at the man. He didn't smile back. "When Marion Marshall was talking about this man, she mentioned that she didn't feel comfortable around him because he just sat around the library and listened in on what everyone says. And you heard something that connected Mr. Grace with Mr. Waterfield, didn't you?" Susan asked the man, praying silently that he would answer.

"I know that the dead man came to see that tall, skinny, ugly guy sitting over there on the morning that he was killed, if that's what you're talking about, lady." He waved his arm at Charles Grace. "And I'd suppose that he killed him after they had that fight in that bell-tower office he's got."

"This man is ridiculous. Mitchell Waterfield wasn't ever in my office that morning. I told you"—he looked at Brett—"I told everyone that I had no idea who he was."

"Then why"—Susan crossed her fingers hoping he would answer—"was Mitch Waterfield's coat in your office?"

"I . . ." Charles Grace got up, and, at a signal from Brett, the two policemen moved away from the homeless man and took positions in front of the door. Charles Grace looked at them angrily and then turned back to Susan. He waited a few minutes, apparently considering his options before answering. Then, as everyone in the room watched, he gave up. "That was the only mistake I made, you know. And this wasn't an easy murder to carry out on the spur of the moment. That was the only mistake I made," he repeated.

To Susan's ears it sounded almost as though he was bragging.

But Rebecca had something more important on her mind. "But Jason . . . Why did you kill Jason?"

"She's so smart, ask her." He pointed at Susan.

"Because you were banking on everyone thinking that Rebecca killed Mitch Waterfield—or at least everyone would assume that he came to town to see her. But Jason knew differently, didn't he? Jason was the person in the marriage who kept track of that type of thing—Rebecca also told me that. If Mitch had come to town to see you, Jason would have known. I don't know how Charles Grace found out. . . ."

"I called the Armstrong house as soon as the police left the library, if you must know. Jason answered, and I pretended to be from Waterfield's office, trying to reach him. Jason (I recognized his voice from television) said that neither he nor his wife had heard from Mitch in months. He was very definite. I knew then that I had to get rid of Jason. Then everyone would think that Rebecca was the only person Mitchell Waterfield knew in Hancock, the only person who might have had a reason to kill him. I said that there had been some sort of confusion, and Mr. Waterfield was on his way to the Armstrong house. Jason promised to meet him there.

"He was on the front porch. I introduced myself—no one ever suspects a librarian—and checked to see that no one was around—pulled out the knife I had brought, and killed him. I was back at the library in less than half an hour."

Rebecca was in tears, and Susan was madder than she had ever been in her life. How could Charles Grace talk so calmly about killing two men—just to save himself. But the tale continued.

"I bought that stupid set of knives from some school kid, thinking that I would fit into Hancock if I supported the local charities—but it turned out to be a pretty good investment, didn't it? Luckily I hadn't even bothered to take them home; they were still in the bottom drawer of my desk."

"But why did you kill Mitchell Waterfield?" Marion cried out. There were tears running down her cheeks. "I knew that you did it, but I couldn't understand why."

"Because he knew too much. I had been taking money from the library fund for a while, and I knew that the crunch was coming—I had to have some way to pay it back. Then I heard that the Armstrongs were coming to town. Well, it's like Mrs. Henshaw says, everyone loves celebrities, and I figured that if I could get them to do something for the library—some sort of benefit or fund-raiser or something . . . I had to think of some way to raise a lot of money, don't you see? I needed so much money that some of it could be used to pay back what I had taken without anyone noticing." He looked around the group. "Look, I was desperate. I had even started to take our most valuable books home late at night and sell them to a dealer that I know in the city. He gave me only about half of what they were worth, but I thought if I could pay back some of the money, the losses wouldn't be discovered quite so soon."

"Dave mentioned that there was going to be an audit coming up—he seemed to think that it made his job easier. That he didn't have to worry, since someone else would do it," Susan explained.

"I had to do something soon," the librarian said. "So anyway, I was going through some of the financial magazines that we subscribe to one night in my office, and I stumbled on an article about Mitchell Waterfield and his public relations firm. The author mentioned that Mitchell was close friends with Rebecca Armstrong. I thought that if I hired him, he might talk the Armstrongs into doing fund-raising for the library. And he could probably get us publicity on 'This Morning, Every Morning.' "

"That isn't the way things work in television." Rebecca sniffed.

"Are you telling me that it isn't who you know? Ha! I've been watching people who know the right people get ahead all my life!" He glared at her.

"So you set up an appointment with Mitchell Waterfield?" Brett asked, not terribly interested in Charles Grace's view of the world.

"Yes. But I had a feeling that he wasn't going to do as I asked before I met him. He called early in the morning, and when I asked if I should invite Jason or Rebecca to the meeting, he was almost insulting. He said that he had traveled to Hancock because he understood that I was interested in hiring him for public relations, not as the Armstrongs' agent. I was more than a little offended, I can tell you. And I let him know it."

"That's the argument Chrissy heard on the phone between you and someone on the other end of the line," Susan said.

"Probably. But there are a lot of people who don't seem to see things my way these days—it may have been someone else," Charles admitted.

"But Mitchell guessed that I was desperate to raise money, and he made some sort of comment about it. I had to kill him. I couldn't let him leave and risk that he would tell anyone about the books at the library. There was nothing else I could do. After we talked, I suggested that he might want to look around. Luckily he agreed. The party in the children's room was just coming to an end, and there were dozens of children running around acting as though no one had ever taught them to behave." Charles Grace paused, apparently remembering the event. "I waited until Mitch Waterfield went behind the stacks, and then I followed him there and killed him. One thing about that damn caterpillar costume: it was easy to hide the knife."

"You don't understand other people—it's one of the ways that you make things so difficult for yourself," Marion cried out.

"You knew that he killed Mitch Waterfield, didn't you?" Susan asked. "Why were you in the office pretending to cry?"

"I never was much of an actress," Marion admitted. "I was worried that the office would be searched and something would be found that might incriminate Charles. I knew that there was something hidden in the office. . . ."

"Because it was soundproofed—at Charles's expense," Susan suggested.

Marion nodded at Susan. "He had to be hiding something. The library is quiet—noise wouldn't bother him working there. And there were no personnel secrets. We're a small place; we don't hide things from each other. I thought if I was in the office, no one would search it—I wanted to protect Charles. But no one ever searched the office."

"Except for you," Susan said. "The day of the murder, the office was immaculate, and a day later, it was a mess. Someone had searched it."

"I didn't do that," Marion said, "and I was astonished when it happened. I had worried about the police finding out something that would incriminate Charles, but I don't have any idea why anyone else would be looking for anything in that place. Later in the afternoon, I went up to say something to Charles, and he was dressed to leave the building in his overcoat, and I noticed the other coat on the chair for the first time. And I realized that it must be Mr. Waterfield's coat. I couldn't bring myself to say anything to anyone. But I thought if you spent some time in the office, you would realize what the coat meant.''

"I should have known," Susan said. "Mitchell Waterfield was lying on the floor in a business suit. He had left his coat in the office, and no one connected it with him.''

"Until now," Brett added quietly.

"Until now," Susan agreed. She stood. "I wonder who's going to take care of all these birds from now on.''

"I told you. I don't take care of the birds—there are people who do that type of thing. I merely live in the house.'' Charles Grace pulled himself up to his full height.

"Not for long." Brett stood up and nodded. One of his men put handcuffs on Charles Grace.

"I think you're going to be occupying my temporary home for a while," the homeless man said. "Don't worry. I kept the bed warm for ya.''

Charles Grace merely shuddered as he was led from the room.

FIFTEEN

"They're leaving."

"I had no idea that extra phone lines were strung up outside the house."

"They're leaving."

"Who broke the microwave?"

"They're leaving."

"Someone spilled something black on the rug in the living room . . ."

"They're leaving."

"And on the couch and on the coffee table . . ."

"They're leaving."

"And on your new CD player."

"Don't you want to say good-bye?" Jed turned from the window and looked at his wife sitting on their stained couch. "My CD player? My new CD player?"

"Don't you want to say good-bye?" She mimicked him but smiled.

Jed looked back out the window. "I don't think we're going to get a chance for fond farewells. They're driving away."

"Don't worry about it. They left this envelope on the table in the hall. There's a note inside and . . ." She shook the contents of the envelope onto her lap. "Something else." They both looked at the shiny trinkets: large disks with the initials of Rebecca's network embossed on them. "They're freebies from the network, aren't they?'' Susan asked, handing her husband one of the twin key chains.

''They're nice,'' he said.

''The key chain Rebecca uses comes from Tiffany's,'' his wife said slowly. ''I recognized it from their Christmas catalog.''

''After all, she didn't have to give us anything,'' Jed reminded her.

''True.''

''And this has been a difficult week for Rebecca.''

''It hasn't exactly been easy for me—or you—or the rest of the family.''

''Susan?'' he asked when his wife didn't respond.

She sighed loudly. ''Look, I don't want to sound selfish, and I certainly didn't get involved in this whole situation looking for some sort of material reward. But the woman could have at least left a nice hostess gift, don't you think?''

''Well . . .''

''After all, she moved into my house with her own entourage; she made a mess of more than one room; she asked me to go with her to identify her husband's body at the morgue, for God's sake. . . .''

''She . . .''

''And, damn it, she mugged me!''

''She what?''

''She stole my purse.''

Jed gave her a look of disbelief. ''Charles Grace,'' he said slowly. ''I thought that was Charles Grace.''

''No, Chad overheard Hilda Flambay and one of the network men talking about it. She definitely did it.''

''But why? And why was she even staying here?''

''I'm not so sure about that, but I can guess. I think she was hoping that by being here, she would learn more about the investigation. I know Charles Grace tried to use me as a conduit from the police department—he told me so when I met him at the library yesterday—and I think Rebecca was trying to do the same thing.''

"Right away? From the very beginning of all this?"

"Yes. Practically the first thing she said to me when we met in the library that morning was that she had heard that I had been involved in murder investigations. And one of the first things that impressed me about her was how well she relates to her fans—her public. She picks up on people almost immediately. Someone probably told her about my background, and, instead of just offering a few polite comments to me, she tried to use my experience for her own benefit. There had to be a reason that Rebecca refused to go back to New York City despite the fact that everyone from the network wanted her to go. I think she moved in here so that she could find out what was going on and then possibly try to manipulate the investigation as well. She was desperate. When she asked me to go help her identify her husband's body, she sat in Brett's office and told me how scared she was—and she had good reason to be. She really was the only person in town who was connected with both murdered men. And her fame wasn't going to protect her from prosecution for very long.

"But, for Rebecca, her fame was a handicap when it came to finding out what was going on," Susan continued. "She could impose on us because we were polite—and maybe just a little awed by her celebrity status—but she couldn't run around without being noticed. . . ."

"Except on Halloween!"

"Exactly! She's so tall that I thought at first the person in costume was a man, but then she reminded me of her height when she explained why she could see Mitch Waterfield over the crowd that had gathered around him. And, of course, in costume and on Halloween, she could run around town and even back to her own house without anyone suspecting her true identity."

"Of course," Jed said slowly. "She even admitted that she hadn't been lying down after she had insisted on being left alone in our guest room. I just assumed that she wanted to spend some time alone coming to terms with her husband's death,'' Jed added. ''But what reason did she have for mugging you?''

''I'm not sure. I think she grabbed my purse out of desperation—maybe she just didn't know what to do when she found herself standing so close to me on her own porch.''

''And what about your library card?''

''The library card shows what a fabulous opportunist Rebecca was. I'm not sure what happened, but I think she probably got worried that something in that office might connect her and Mitch Waterfield—that was before she was forced to admit that she knew him—so she . . .''

''She's the one who searched it—who made such a mess!''

''Yes. And to make doubly sure that she wouldn't be suspected, she left my card behind. Rebecca Armstrong made the most of every break in her career to reach her position at the network. She did the same thing in this case. Only this time it almost got the wrong person convicted of murder.''

''Funny how that office has popped up so frequently in this investigation.''

''Hmmm. It's a great office—interesting architecture, wonderful ambience, fabulous view of the town. It would be nice if the next person who worked there was worthy of it.''

''Hi! Looks like your houseguests have gone home!'' Amy Ellsworth appeared in the room's doorway. ''I knocked on the back door, but you didn't seem to hear me, so I just walked right in. I hope you don't mind . . . ?''

''Of course not.'' Jed stood up, and Amy perched herself on the arm of the chair he had occupied.

''You were talking about the murder,'' Amy began in a more hesitant voice than the Henshaws were accustomed to.

''Yes, we were.'' Jed glanced at his wife.

''Did you come over for a reason?'' Susan asked.

Amy took a deep breath. ''A confession. I came over to make a confession. . . . Well, they say confession is good for the soul, don't they?'' she asked rhetorically.

''So what do you want to confess to?'' Susan asked, hoping this was going to be short but doubting it.

"Oh, Susan, I feel so stupid. You've worked so hard putting together all the pieces of the story and figuring out exactly what happened . . ."

"And?" Jed prompted when Amy's dramatic pause continued longer than necessary.

"And I was helping Charles Grace. I was helping a murderer! Can you ever forgive me?"

"I suppose so, but I sure don't understand what happened. Did you know that Charles Grace was the killer?" Susan asked.

Amy physically recoiled at the thought. "Of course not!" she cried. "I would have turned him in immediately if I had had any idea! What sort of person do you think I am?"

"Why don't you tell us what happened," Jed suggested before his wife could answer that question. After all, they did have to live next door to the Ellsworths.

"I was fooled—completely fooled. I have to admit that." The Henshaws sat quietly, both hoping she would continue. "You must understand, Charles came to me a few weeks ago. He trus—he told me that he had come to trust me (we worked together on the library board, remember) and that I was the only person in town who could help him. I suppose I should have suspected something," she added in a rare moment of self-awareness.

"Anyway, Charles said he suspected that someone on his staff was, as he put it, out to get him."

"In what way?"

"Well, he said that someone was stealing from the library. I didn't understand, and I asked what he meant. He explained that money was being stolen, money from the funds that were meant to finish the library. He . . . he led me to believe that Marion Marshall was the thief."

"What?"

"I know, horrible, isn't it?"

"It certainly is. He used her feelings for him—she cared about him, and he, in turn, manipulated her. I shouldn't be surprised by that, though. Not after watching him sit in his office and complain about her while consuming the food that she had spent hours making especially for him.''

"Well, I don't know about that. He didn't exactly say that she had done it. He just said he thought she might be stealing. And, to give credit where credit is due, apparently he thought better of it. He called me about a week later and said that he had made a mistake, that there wasn't any money missing, and that I should disregard anything he had said about his staff members. So I guess his better self prevailed after all.''

"Or else he figured out another way to avoid being convicted of embezzlement,'' Jed suggested.

"He probably saw that article about Mitch Waterfield,'' Susan agreed.

".'Whatever happened, I . . .'' Amy hesitated, "I didn't tell anyone about it. You have to understand—he said that talking about it could damage Marion's reputation, and I certainly didn't want to do that to an innocent person.''

"That's understandable,'' Jed insisted.

"But that's not all,'' Amy continued, not surprising Susan one bit. "You see, when Charles explained about the missing money and his suspicions about Marion, he also said that he was having some other problems with her.''

"Did this have anything to do with pornography or maybe stolen books?''

"I suppose so. He just said that there were other problems. He said that it was hurting the library, hurting all the patrons. He made me think that I wasn't helping him, I was helping the community! And then he asked me to do just one last thing. . . . You have to understand that I really felt I was doing the town of Hancock a favor, not just Charles Grace!''

"By doing what?'' Jed asked.

"By keeping track of what I was doing,'' Susan explained to her husband. "That's right, isn't it?'' She turned to Amy. "You've been hanging around ever since Mitchell Waterfield was found dead. You've stood in my bushes, peeked in my windows, snooped around my family, followed me to the Armstrong home. : . .''

''You were suspicious of my reasons for being there, weren't you? I thought so at the time, but I didn't understand why. Rebecca had shown me the list of things she wanted—she even explained about where to find the tea—so how did you know that she hadn't really asked me to get anything for her?''

''I wouldn't have thought anything about it if you hadn't said that Rebecca wanted you to pick up a white negligee. I had gotten her a nightgown the day before, and there were two others listed on the list she gave me. Either Rebecca was planning on spending a long time at my house, or you were lying. And then, there wasn't really anyone outside, was there?''

''No . . .''

''You knew I was spooked, and you said you had heard something, and my imagination took it from there.''

''Yes. Charles had asked me to talk to him before the board meeting that afternoon—to tell him what was going on. I was anxious not to be late. And then he called your house and asked to see you, and it didn't make any difference after all. I guess we had gotten our messages crossed up.'' She shrugged.

''It's been a long three days,'' Susan said.

''It sure has. I'd better get home. We're going out to dinner tonight. I never cook for at least a week after giving a party. I'm too exhausted.''

''A small point,'' Jed insisted. ''How did you know Rebecca would have a white negligee?''

''She's a new bride. All brides have white negligees,'' his wife explained.

''Rebecca's wardrobe contained a large pile of them,'' Amy agreed. ''I'd better run now. Don't bother to see me out.''

''Were you going to bother to see her out?'' Jed asked as he heard their back door slam shut.

''Not a chance,'' Susan informed him.

''So what does the note say?''

"Wha—Oh, I'd forgotten!" She unfolded the note that had accompanied the key chains.

"Are you going to read it out loud or is it a secret?"

She folded it back up and stuffed it in her pocket. "I never read other people's mail. It's not for us—it's for Brett—thanking him for all his help." She ran her finger down a large brown splotch on her favorite needlepoint pillow. Then she looked up and smiled at her husband. "So I peeked. Maybe I shouldn't have bothered investigating those murders."

"I think there's probably one homeless man who wouldn't agree with you."

"I'll never get any thanks from him either. . . ."

Jed sat down and slid his arm around her shoulder. "Then you can get some thanks from me: Thanks for being my perfect wife and the perfect mother of my children." He kissed the top of her head. "Hey, where are you going?" he cried as she slipped from his grasp.

"To the kitchen. I'm starving. Want to join me? I'm going to steal a candy bar or two from Chad's trick-or-treat loot."

Jed stood up. "Lead the way. It's a crime I can ignore."

ABOUT THE AUTHOR

Valerie Wolzien lives in Tenafly, New Jersey. She is also the author of *Murder at the PTA Luncheon*, *The Fortieth Birthday Body*, *We Wish You a Merry Murder*, and *An Old Faithful Murder*.

The
Mysterious
Mind
of
Valerie
Wolzien...